THE MEASURE
OF A MAN

Marco Malvaldi

THE MEASURE
OF A MAN

*Translated from the Italian
by Howard Curtis and Katherine Gregor*

Europa
editions

Europa Editions
214 West 29th Street
New York, N.Y. 10001
www.europaeditions.com
info@europaeditions.com

Library of Congress Cataloging in Publication Data is available
ISBN 978-1-60945-551-4

Malvaldi, Marco
The Measure of a Man

Book design and cover illustration by Emanuele Ragnisco
www.mekkanografici.com
.

Cover illustration: Collage of following images:
© RMN /Archivi Alinari, Florence (f. 88v, MS B, Institut de France, *left side/right*;
f. 80r MS B, Institut de France, *center/left*)
© Biblioteca Nacional de España ("Study for fusing the horse for the 'Equestrian
Monument to Francesco Sforza,' MS II f.157r, *bottom*)
© Bridgeman Images ("A rider on a rearing horse," Fitzwilliam Museum,
Cambridge, *center/left*).
© Fine Art Images/Archivi Alinari, Florence (Leonardo da Vinci, "Self-portrait",
Biblioteca Reale, Torino, *top/left*)
© Royal Collection Trust © HM Queen Elizabeth II, 2019 /Bridgeman Images
("Study of hands," RL 12558, *center/right*; "The muscles of the shoulder," RL 19003v,
bottom/right; "Profile drawing of a young man," RL 12557, *top/center*)

Prepress by Grafica Punto Print – Rome

Printed in the USA

CONTENTS

To Giovanna Baldini,
Luisa Sacerdote,
Marcella Binchi,
Lia Marianelli

To all public school teachers

THE MEASURE
OF A MAN

Dramatis Personae

THE WORKSHOP

LEONARDO DI SER PIERO DA VINCI:
painter, sculptor, architect, court engineer, much prone to daydreaming. In other words, a bit of a genius.

GIAN GIACOMO CAPROTTI,
also known as SALAÌ: general factotum in Leonardo's workshop and his favorite apprentice, a thief and a liar, stubborn and greedy. But he also has a few faults.

MARCO D'OGGIONO, ZANINO DA FERRARA, GIULIO THE GERMAN:
other apprentices of the da Vinci genius.

RAMBALDO CHITI:
Leonardo's ex-apprentice and, unfortunately for him, ex-many other things too.

CATERINA:
Leonardo's loving mother, who conceived him with the notary Ser Piero da Vinci when they were both young and inexperienced. A woman who lavishes far too much care on our protagonist, and is also far too outspoken.

THE COURT

LUDOVICO IL MORO:

Duke of Bari and Lord of Milan, one meter ninety of Machiavellian substance, the illegitimate son of Francesco Sforza. He cannot decide which is better, to command or to fuck, but loves doing both.

FRANCESCO SFORZA:

dead as a doornail for more than twenty-seven years, but still the omnipresent father of Ludovico il Moro. There is a gargantuan bronze horse to be erected in his honor.

GIACOMO TROTTI:

ambassador, eyes and ears of the Duke of Ferrara, Ercole I d'Este. Not so young anymore, a skilled interpreter of court life. A bit of a snitch, perhaps, but that's what they pay him for.

BEATRICE D'ESTE:

daughter of the Duke of Ferrara and wife of Ludovico il Moro, large in body and dowry, naïve but not so naïve that she doesn't notice the many petticoats rustling down the corridors of the castle.

ERCOLE MASSIMILIANO:

baby son and heir of Moro and Beatrice. He is two years old but already a nobleman.

TEODORA:

little Ercole Massimiliano's nurse.

MAXIMILIAN I:

Viennese, Holy Roman Emperor. He is not in the palace but might as well be.

BIANCA MARIA SFORZA:
niece of Ludovico il Moro, betrothed to Maximilian I. The wedding is set for next Christmas.

LUCREZIA CRIVELLI:
Ludovico il Moro's official mistress. She will be portrayed by Leonardo in the painting known as *La Belle Ferronnière*. But better not tell anyone.

GALEAZZO SANSEVERINO:
Count of Caiazzo and Voghera, trusted son-in-law of Ludovico il Moro, a man of action who commands respect. Of the three Galeazzos in the novel, he is the most important.

BIANCA GIOVANNA SFORZA:
his wife, illegitimate daughter of Ludovico il Moro.

AMBROGIO VARESE DA ROSATE:
court astrologer, all clad in crimson. An expert on the movements of the stars and a diligent producer of horoscopes. He likes to say that what matters most in predictions is to foresee an event or a date, but never the two at once.

PIETROBONO DA FERRARA:
direct rival of Varese da Rosate.

BERGONZIO BOTTA:
tax collector to the Duke of Milan.

YOUNG MARQUESS STANGA:
overseer of the court treasury, official paymaster, unofficial pain in the pocket.

BERNARDINO DA CORTE:
lord of the manor.

REMIGIO TREVANOTTI:
servant.

ASCANIO MARIA SFORZA VISCONTI:
cardinal, brother of Ludovico il Moro. There were no conflict of interest laws back then.

GIAN GALEAZZO MARIA SFORZA:
legitimate Duke of Milan, being the son of Ludovico's older brother, Galeazzo Maria, who was assassinated a few years earlier. After trying to rule in his place by fair means and throwing the Festa del Paradiso in honor of his wedding, assigning the spectacular décor to none other than Leonardo, Uncle Ludovico kindly locked him up in the Castle of Vigevano.

ISABELLA OF ARAGON:
his wife. You never see her around, and so much the better.

BONA OF SAVOY:
wife of Galeazzo Maria and mother of Gian Galeazzo Maria Sforza, as well as regent of the Duchy of Milan until Ludovico locks her up in the castle tower that will be named after her.

CICCO SIMONETTA:
her trusted advisor, a talented statesman who pays with his head (and not in the metaphorical sense) for his loyalty to Bona.

CATROZZO:
court dwarf of some repute, a polyglot. As scurrilous as befits a past master of laughter and jests.

PALAZZO CARMAGNOLA

CECILIA GALLERANI:
a woman of great education and refinement, saved from life as a nun by Ludovico, who makes her his mistress when she is very young. More recently, after discovering he had gotten her pregnant, Ludovico himself made sure to give her in marriage to Count Carminati de Brambilla, known as Bergamini. She is the *Lady with the Ermine* we can all admire in Krakow.

CESARE SFORZA VISCONTI:
illegitimate son of Ludovico il Moro and Cecilia. He is not very old—only two, in fact—but already owns some sizeable property: when he was born, his father decided to give him Palazzo Carmagnola—the building where the Piccolo Teatro di Milano is currently based.

TERSILLA:
cheerful and talkative companion of Cecilia Gallerani.

CORSO:
servant of Cecilia Gallerani.

THE FRENCH

HIS MOST CHRISTIAN MAJESTY CHARLES VIII:
king of France. Weak in body and intellect, he talks a great deal about war, about invading Italy and taking Naples, even though he himself has never been in a battle. His motto could be *Let us arm ourselves and you go to war.*

LOUIS DE VALOIS:
Duke of Orléans, his cousin, future leader in the campaign to conquer the kingdom of Naples, he harbors secret claims

on the Duchy of Milan (as descendant of Valentina Visconti, his grandmother).

PHILIPPE, DUKE OF COMMYNES:
French envoy to Italy, in cahoots with the Duke of Orléans.

ROBINOT AND MATTENET:
the ugly and the handsome. The Duke of Commynes's sinister but clumsy henchmen, they are on a secret mission to Milan.

PERRON DE BASCHE:
originally from Orvieto, later ambassador of His Most Christian Majesty Charles VIII and the Duke of Orléans.

CARLO BARBIANO DI BELGIOIOSO:
Ludovico il Moro's ambassador to the French court.

JOSQUIN DES PREZ:
singer at the service of Ludovico il Moro, a musical genius in body and counterpoint.

THE MERCHANTS

ACCERRITO PORTINARI:
corpulent representative of the Medici Bank, a glutton for steaks and lucre.

BENCIO SERRISTORI:
Messer Accerrito's associate, an indefatigable worker but not during official holidays.

ANTONIO MISSAGLIA:
prestigious armorer, a true artist in iron, and Leonardo's friend.

GIOVANNI BARRACCIO:
wool trader.

CLEMENTE VULZIO, CANDIDO BERTONE, RICCETTO NANNIPIERI AND ADEMARO COSTANTE:
wool, silk, needle, and alum merchants who enjoy credit at the Medici Bank.

THE CLERICS

FRANCESCO SANSONE DA BRESCIA:
General of the Franciscan Order.

GIULIANO DA MUGGIA:
Franciscan preacher.

DIODATO DA SIENA:
prior of the Jesuates (the now defunct congregation of the apostolic clerics of Saint Jerome), tenacious shepherd of his flock.

GIOACCHINO DA BRENNO:
Jesuate friar and intransigent preacher, stirrer-up of crowds and disturber of the peace.

ELIGIO DA VARRAMISTA:
Jesuate and expert graphologist, well-versed as he is in promissory notes and letters of credit, being a former banker converted to the faith on the road to Milan.

GIULIANO DELLA ROVERE:
cardinal who has not yet come to terms with the election of his rival, Borgia, as Pope Alexander VI.

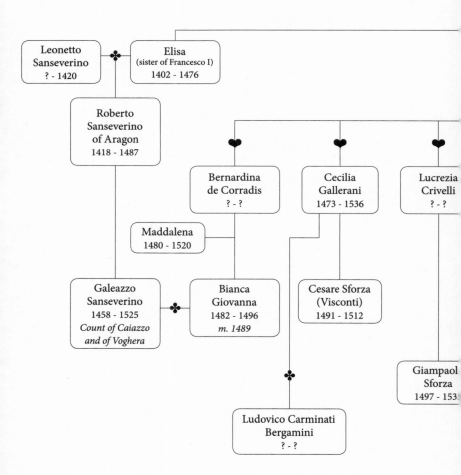

Leonetto
Sanseverino
? - 1420

Elisa
(sister of Francesco I)
1402 - 1476

Roberto
Sanseverino
of Aragon
1418 - 1487

Bernardina
de Corradis
? - ?

Cecilia
Gallerani
1473 - 1536

Lucrezia
Crivelli
? - ?

Maddalena
1480 - 1520

Galeazzo
Sanseverino
1458 - 1525
*Count of Caiazzo
and of Voghera*

Bianca
Giovanna
1482 - 1496
m. 1489

Cesare Sforza
(Visconti)
1491 - 1512

Giampaol
Sforza
1497 - 153

Ludovico Carminati
Bergamini
? - ?

♣ *marriage*

♥ *lovers*

The Sforza
Dukes of Milan

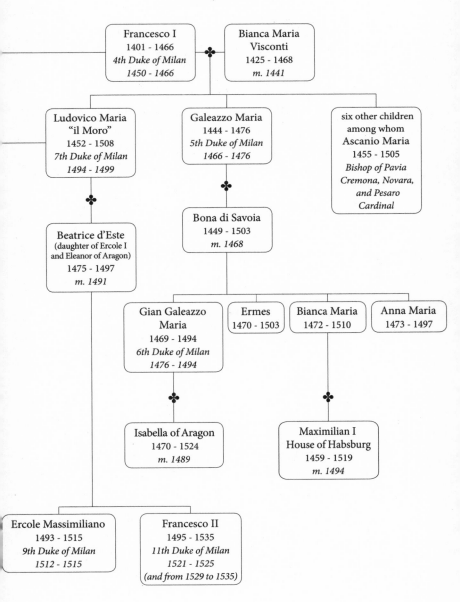

Francesco I
1401 - 1466
4th Duke of Milan
1450 - 1466

Bianca Maria Visconti
1425 - 1468
m. 1441

Ludovico Maria "il Moro"
1452 - 1508
7th Duke of Milan
1494 - 1499

Galeazzo Maria
1444 - 1476
5th Duke of Milan
1466 - 1476

six other children among whom Ascanio Maria
1455 - 1505
Bishop of Pavia Cremona, Novara, and Pesaro Cardinal

Beatrice d'Este
(daughter of Ercole I and Eleanor of Aragon)
1475 - 1497
m. 1491

Bona di Savoia
1449 - 1503
m. 1468

Gian Galeazzo Maria
1469 - 1494
6th Duke of Milan
1476 - 1494

Ermes
1470 - 1503

Bianca Maria
1472 - 1510

Anna Maria
1473 - 1497

Isabella of Aragon
1470 - 1524
m. 1489

Maximilian I House of Habsburg
1459 - 1519
m. 1494

Ercole Massimiliano
1493 - 1515
9th Duke of Milan
1512 - 1515

Francesco II
1495 - 1535
11th Duke of Milan
1521 - 1525
(and from 1529 to 1535)

Talent hits a target no one else can hit;
Genius hits a target no one else can see.
—ARTHUR SCHOPENHAUER

PROLOGUE

The man paused for a moment before going in.

No use glancing around to see if anyone had followed him. The entrance to the castle was situated in one of Milan's old districts, on a dark, damp street that could be reached only via other dark, damp streets, so if anybody had tailed him he would have shaken them off a long time ago, in spite of the garish pink cloth garment he wore.

To tell the truth, he sometimes feared he would get lost himself. Once before, he had been unable to find his way through the web of alleys around the castle. Partly his fault, of course, he had never had a strong sense of direction. And partly the fault of this city, which had expanded so badly, without a plan, without a shape, without a vision. This city had to be rethought from top to bottom, reorganized in a different way. A radically different way. A way never seen before. For example, as a city on several levels. From the bottom to the top, from the water to the sky. A city the opposite of a house, where the poor lived up in the air and the gentry down on the ground, like in the Roman *insulae* described in Vitruvius's book. Francesco di Giorgio had been right to translate it from Latin, it had truly been worth it. That book had been a good purchase. It had cost him an arm and a leg, but had made him think of so many—

The man in pink snapped out of his reverie, becoming aware that he had gotten lost, even if only in his own thoughts. This happened often and was by far the best part of his day.

But now was not the time to indulge in daydreams. Now he had things to do.

Slowly, but not calmly, the man knocked at the front door. Almost immediately, a creaking sound informed him that someone was opening the door, and in the pitch black of the street the tiny entrance hall looked almost bright.

Just two words.

"Come in."

And so the man stepped in, leaving the darkness behind him.

BEGINNING

The first thing you noticed on entering the Council Room was the lack of light. Even though it was not yet mid-October, Milan was already chilly, and even before the castle filled with the masters on their return from Vigevano, the servants had already covered the windows with sheets of white canvas soaked in turpentine to make them as transparent as possible, letting in very little light from the outside but at the same time shielding from view everything that took place inside the room. To those living in the castle, this was the Room of the Chevrons because of the red and white decorations that went by that name, but for everybody else, in other words the majority of Milan's residents, this was the Council Room: the room where the Secret Council would usually assemble. Six individuals, the most powerful individuals in Milan, plus their master, the most powerful of them all.

"Show the next one in, my lord."

Bernardino da Corte, the castellan, nodded, pulled the heavy timber door toward him, and announced, "His Excellency, the General of the Franciscan Order, Francesco Sansone da Brescia."

Tuesdays and Fridays were days reserved for audiences. Days on which Ludovico Sforza, il Moro, Duke of Bari but nonetheless Lord of Milan, would grant an audience to anyone requesting one in order to resolve a problem. Any kind of problem and any kind of citizen of Milan—which meant anybody who paid the taxes levied by il Moro, except for those who did not pay them by kind exemption of il Moro himself. Any Milanese who paid taxes had the right to be heard, partly because his tax bill was generally pretty steep.

But the head of the Franciscan order was not a citizen of Milan, nor was he just any citizen. Technically speaking, he did not have the right to usurp even a minute of the precious time il Moro reserved for his subjects, listening to the pleas of the wretched instead of imposing his will on unruly ambassadors, fiery steeds, or compliant servant girls. On the other hand, common sense would deem it foolish to deny an audience to the General of the Order, who presented himself as an ordinary citizen.

And Ludovico il Moro, Duke of Bari and Lord of Milan, was not in the least foolish.

"What an honor," il Moro said, sitting on his high-backed seat. "The General of the Franciscan Order requests an audience like any citizen. To what do we owe such a modest visit?"

"I am a humble Franciscan, Your Lordship," Francesco Sansone replied, "unaccustomed to honors or frills. Besides, the question I wish to submit to Your Lordship's sagacity requires so little time that requesting a private audience would have been arrogant."

Welcome to the Renaissance, where every sentence is calibrated and adorned like a jewel, every single word weighed on miniature scales and then displayed, not to show off its beauty but to suggest how powerful its wearer is. Where the meaning of every speech must be interpreted on the basis of who is delivering it, who is listening to it, who is or isn't present in the room, which names are mentioned and, above all, which names are not even uttered.

In effect, in welcoming the friar, Ludovico il Moro had addressed him not by his name but by his title, appreciating the fact that he was calling on him as a humble citizen; which meant that the friar as head of the Franciscans mattered not a fig either to him or to the Council. To which the friar had responded that he could have used different, more official, more solemn and implacable means to secure il Moro's attention, and had called him Your Lordship and not Duke, thereby reminding him that for most of Italy, Ludovico was merely a usurper.

"I am glad of that, Father," il Moro replied. "Do tell us. The Council and I are ready to listen."

"Your Lordship . . . Forgive me, I do not see His Eminence the Bishop of Como. I hope he is not unwell."

"Not unwell at all, Father. We have recently reduced the number of councilors, since forty-two people were really too many to perform this function, particularly in virtue of the fact that the cases requiring an audience have decreased significantly over the past year."

Of course, the friar could have remarked that, if forty-two had been too many, perhaps six was far too few—not to mention the fact that there was no cleric among the six, which could hardly have been a coincidence. Father Sansone cleared his throat again.

"Your Lordship, I am here at the request of my Order so that you may reconsider the case of Friar Giuliano da Muggia, who continues to preach against the rules of his Order and the content of the Holy Scriptures."

"I would be unable to do so, father," il Moro replied, his eyes drifting to each member of the Council in turn.

"So the Lord of Milan would be unable to silence a poor Franciscan?"

There is certainly no need for a skilled interpreter to convey the meaning of the Franciscan's heavily allusive question, the use of the conditional mode in particular. And if the reader has grasped it, it certainly did not escape any member of the Council. Or Ludovico il Moro, for that matter.

"Friar Giuliano was arrested and tried sixteen months ago,

on your own initiative. Not being the prior of a religious order, I ordered that the trial be reviewed and authorized His Excellency Archbishop Arcimboldo to preside. You know perfectly well the outcome of the trial."

Father Sansone took a deep breath.

The farcical trial of Giuliano da Muggia had been a genuine masterpiece on il Moro's part. All the witnesses—laymen, as it happened, and, as it happened, members of Ludovico's court—had enthusiastically praised the monk's sermons and downplayed, or else pretended not to remember, his jibes against the Church of Rome. Which were, in fact, the least of it.

Friar Giuliano did not limit himself to saying that the Roman Curia was corrupt, worldly, decadent and repulsive; plenty of people were already saying that, including that Dominican with the whiny voice, Girolamo Savonarola, who had gained fame as a notable bringer of bad luck after prophesying the death of Lorenzo de' Medici and other calamities that promptly took place.

No, Friar Giuliano maintained that the Church of the Lombard capital could be independent from the Church of Rome. Like Savonarola, whose aim was to obtain independence for the monasteries; only, this fellow wanted to persuade Milan to split from Rome. Milan, the city that was conspicuously becoming the wealthiest province in the whole Italian peninsula, the place that attracted the greatest artists, that sent the nearby University of Pavia the best physicians and most distinguished mathematicians, and paid them handsomely.

This, in the opinion of Father Sansone and an influential colleague of his who sat on the throne of Rome, must not be allowed to happen. It was why he had attempted to bridle Friar Giuliano. Some things are better not said out loud, and to have a Franciscan calling, in a booming voice, for the Ambrosian Church to split from Rome by any means possible—barring bulldozers: they didn't exist back then—was really not an ideal situation, when it came down to it.

But the trial prepared by Sansone had been hijacked by il Moro with typical Renaissance skill. Court poets had composed verses that had been recited throughout the city; everywhere, in the streets around Broletto and along the Navigli, you could hear Bellincioni's sonnet *Oh Most Christian Milan* and a sestet by a certain Giacomo Alfieri, who was very famous at the time but is justly forgotten nowadays, both giving thanks to Heaven for sending Friar Giuliano to Milan. Both dreadful, but effective. Il Moro had curried favor with the city, even more than with the Court, squeezing the Curia in a pincer movement between his own conscious will and the people's bovine one.

"I know very well that Friar Giuliano was charitably acquitted," Father Sansone said after another very deep breath. "Friar Giuliano is a worthy man and his sermons are inspired by his deep fervor. Deep fervor and a deep love of his flock. Friar Giuliano is a man who knows how to talk to people, because he tells people what they want to hear."

In this way, the cleric was sneakily reminding Ludovico that the people's favor ebbs and flows, and at this particular moment the people were not at all on the side of il Moro.

The salt tax and other recent levies had not been welcomed by the people, and Ludovico's popularity was not as sky-high as it had once been. If opinion polls had existed then, Tuesday morning Council sessions would probably have begun with a prior meeting to analyze il Moro's approval ratings and steer his intercessions accordingly. But, back in those days, statistics were a long way in the future, the average man hadn't been discovered yet, and the will of the people could be expressed only through cheers or rebellion.

"And Friar Giuliano, being a highly intelligent man," Father Sansone went on, "cannot easily be silenced. Whenever he preaches in San Francesco Grande, he fills the church.

People come from far and wide to hear him and they leave inspired. Perhaps it might be appropriate to—"

What might have been appropriate, though, Father Sansone was unable to say, because it was at this moment that Ludovico stood up from his seat.

Had we been in the vicinity of Lodi, Ludovico il Moro would have been about four lengths of cloth and one hand's breadth tall; if, however, we had wished to measure him in city units, il Moro would have been a little under three lengths of Milan cloth. In the metric system, the Lord of Milan was one meter ninety, which, when added to his icy glare and long, severe black brocade garment, meant that whenever Ludovico il Moro stood up, he was truly scary.

Having stood up, Ludovico slowly went up to Father Sansone and gently took him by the elbow.

"Come, excellent Father," he said in a pleasant voice, but like someone who knows he commands respect. "I want to show you something."

And, still holding him by the elbow, he led the austere but terrified cleric across the entire room, until they came to a splendid fresco of a map of the city.

"You see, excellent Father, Milan is a wheel." Il Moro's hand traced a large circle on the map, showing the walls protecting the city, then jabbed his finger into the middle of the fresco, which corresponded to the Cathedral. "Milan is a wheel and its church is its hub. A solid, sturdy, straight hub. But do you know what will happen if this church remains immobile?"

Il Moro's finger began to trace ever smaller circles until they became a narrow spiral around the Cathedral and stopped.

"The wheel can turn and turn and turn, but those who live inside it"—il Moro opened his hands wide—"won't get anywhere." Then he placed his right hand in a friendly yet heavy manner on the Franciscan's shoulder. "Do you understand, excellent Father?"

* * *

"Yes, yes, I understand, Ambassador. I beg you, do not torment yourself over this. We've seen worse, I can assure you."

"I cannot but apologize for the pitiful state in which you see me, but . . . "

Giacomo Trotti, ambassador of Ercole I d'Este, Duke of Ferrara, at the Court of the Sforzas, was usually one of the most distinguished and reliable people in the whole of Milan. But reliability and distinction are often helped by having an appropriate external aspect, and when someone pours the contents of a chamber pot over you, these qualities are greatly compromised. Unfortunately, on his way to Palazzo Carmagnola for the customary Tuesday music gathering in Cecilia Gallerani's salon, the elderly ambassador had been targeted by a boorish fellow who had emptied the pot out the window without a second thought and without the usual "coming dooown!!" which even the less polite would yell to the street so that you could dodge involuntary potfuls of shit.

"Come now, Ambassador, have no worries." Cecilia Gallerani made a sign to one of the ladies in waiting at the far end of the room, who approached with an exaggeratedly graceful step. "Take Ambassador Trotti to the West Room and help him. We certainly shan't start without you, Ambassador."

"I don't know how to thank you, Countess."

"By changing quickly and rejoining us so that we may enjoy your company," Cecilia Gallerani answered, smiling. "Tersilla, I'm counting on you."

Still smiling, she disappeared through a door to instruct the musicians to wait a little longer. For a moment, the eyes of Giacomo Trotti, Ambassador of Ferrara, lingered on the door through which Cecilia Gallerani had withdrawn. As always, he drew an automatic comparison with the one who was theoretically his protégée and his fellow-countrywoman. A comparison that, as always, proved harsh.

On the one hand, the slender, ethereal Cecilia Gallerani, still as beautiful as the portrait Messer Leonardo had painted of her years earlier, both peaceful and stern, partly turned away as though not to miss the imagined arrival of her lover, the aforementioned Ludovico il Moro, whom she awaits while stroking the ermine in her lap. On the other hand, that podgy, annoying brat who answered, alas, to the name of Beatrice d'Este, and was the beloved second child of his master Ercole. A girl who, for all her gentle manner, had a coarse heart, and whom, in his silent monologues, the Ambassador had nick-named Ugly Beatie—a moniker he barely dared think, let alone say out loud. Everybody else adored her: her father, her sister, her mother, and many others whose number clearly did not include Ambassador Giacomo Trotti.

"Come, your Excellency," young Tersilla said to Trotti, showing him the way with a motion of the hand but under-standably keeping her distance. "Have no fear, I'm sure we'll find you some clothes that fit you."

Beatrice, adored by so many, including, until recently, il Moro, who had fallen genuinely and passionately in love with her after she had ensnared him using one of the most tried and tested methods that women of every nation and rank had been using for thousands of years: not letting him have it even though the two of them had been married for months.

"Here we are," Tersilla said, walking into a room and head-ing confidently for a chest of drawers from which protruded a strange wooden object that looked like a rudder. "This is where the Count's clothes are kept. Madonna Cecilia's hus-band is not as tall as you, but I'm sure we'll easily find what we need."

Nevertheless, il Moro indulged his urges. Trotti had noticed that, during formal lunches—in other words, every day or near enough—il Moro would often vanish from the banquet and return an hour or so later with a smug smile on his face. It had taken only a few days to discover that, funnily enough, a few minutes before Ludovico would leave the table, Cecilia Gallerani would arrive at Torre della Rocchetta, always at the same time. And thus, while his unruly wifey enjoyed roasted meats, Ludovico *il Moro* would satisfy his appetite for fresh meat.

"Take this," Tersilla said, extracting from the drawer a brocade garment that would have been tight on a man half the size of Trotti, who wasn't exactly a giant. "I think this will fit you like a glove."

Subsequently, Cecilia Gallerani had become pregnant. So Ludovico, who, as he had once told Trotti, "found pregnant women repulsive," had quite simply stopped seeing her. At the same time, he began with increasing frequency to visit his young wife in her apartments at night, descending the steep steps between the two floors in nothing but a thin silk shirt, which he would, however, almost immediately remove. These, too, were things Trotti had learned straight from the lips of il Moro, who would describe his intercourse in ample detail.

We should not be too surprised by this lack of modesty in private affairs; during the Renaissance, sex between a husband and wife was definitely not viewed as a private affair if one of them was a reigning prince or an heir to the throne. If you could ask Trotti, he might also tell you about when Alfonso d'Este consummated his wedding night with Anna Sforza, in Ferrara, in the presence of Francesco Gonzaga, the Aragonese ambassador Simonotto da Belpietro, and four or five courtiers who first undressed Alfonso, then put him into bed with his young bride; but Alfonso had no interest in consummating his marriage and kept getting out of bed, perhaps intimidated by the large number of people in his bedroom or perhaps, not being experienced in the ways of the world, was convinced that the pussy would bite him. So the task fell to Gonzaga to do something about it, to send the noble scion back under the blankets, literally with a thrashing, and tell him not to dare come out of there before he'd accomplished something.

"And here are the legs," Tersilla said, taking from the drawer a long pair of multi-colored tights in the French style.

It was quite unsightly. Even Trotti, who paid little attention to fashion, wouldn't have been caught dead walking next to someone wearing that thing, and today he had to put it on himself.

Besides, if something was repulsive then it was repulsive.

And so, when Beatrice, after all these nocturnal visits from il Moro, also got pregnant, Trotti had immediately started to worry. He was sure that while his wife's belly was rising like dough, the Lord of Milan would refuse to touch her, even with a gloved pinky, and would seek to satisfy his urges elsewhere. And why not once again with Cecilia Gallerani, still the most beautiful woman in Milan, to whom il Moro was still bound, as many people said, by genuine, lasting affection? Cecilia, who, compared with Beatrice, was like a diamond next to a slice of salami?

Trotti looked with sadness at the clothes he had been randomly allocated. In Ferrara, he would have shut himself away at home rather than don such things. But Milan was not Ferrara.

In Milan, men rode on mules, while women, wealthy women, moved about in carts—carts that looked like a cross between an altarpiece and a Sicilian buggy, gilded and garish, drawn by two or four mares, and were a pedestrian's nightmare. Strange as it may seem, Milan already had a traffic problem back in the late 15th century.

Giacomo Trotti knew that, by order of il Moro, few carts were permitted to enter the Castello Sforzesco at any time of the day or night. Among them was the one belonging to Cecilia Gallerani, although she had not been in the castle for some time. Not that this necessarily meant anything. Il Moro could easily leave the castle on business and go to his mistress's house, since at the time her husband was staying in San Giovanni in Croce, near Cremona.

That was why Giacomo Trotti, ambassador to Ercole, Duke of Ferrara, was there today. To take a good look at Cecilia Gallerani and see if her forehead was adorned with a new jewel, or if she was sporting a dress of embossed brocade, the kind embroidered with gold thread, such as only il Moro could have given her, as was the custom, as a love token. That such gifts could not have come from her husband was, in fact, the one thing you could be sure of. Count Ludovico Carminati Bergamini, whom il Moro had arranged for Cecilia to marry when he sent her away from the Castello Sforzesco, was one of the stingiest men not just in the whole of Milan but in the whole of the Holy Roman Empire.

"Thank you, my lady Tersilla," Trotti said in a ruefully polite tone. "Do you require any help closing the chest?"

"Thank you, Your Excellency, but I am capable of doing it myself. Just as I opened it. Using this, you see?"

And, with a wink, she showed him the strange contraption made of wood and iron set between the chest and its lid, topped by a kind of rudder.

"It was Messer Leonardo who invented it and gave it to my lady as a gift," Tersilla said, as proudly as if she had manufactured it herself. "It's a lever device. You turn the rudder like this and the lid goes up and down, so you don't need muscles for it. It's a wonderful object. You've no idea how much time it saves us. Messer Leonardo is a genius, don't you think?"

"Without a doubt," Giacomo Trotti replied, able to say what he really thought for the first time during his day as a diplomat. "I don't suppose anything is impossible for Messer Leonardo da Vinci."

* * *

"But that's impossible!"

The man in pink closed the chest with an irritable gesture. Behind him, looking pensive, a woman of fifty or so with olive skin was holding her hands on her hips and looking at him.

"Perhaps you left it in the workshop upstairs, in the high room."

"Impossible! I remember very well, I put it here less than a month ago."

"Oh, well, if it's only been a month . . ."

The man in pink shook his head and looked at the chest as though it was his fault. Then he looked up at the woman. He had an odd kind of face, more masculine than handsome, with long blond hair in which there nested, however, many gray strands, unlike his beard, which was almost free of them. His usually soft eyes squinted with an annoyance only parents can provoke.

"Spare me the sarcasm, Caterina. These are important plans and I don't just carry them around as if they were of no consequence.."

"Could Salaì have taken them? You yourself say he'd steal anything that wasn't nailed to the floor."

Getting a sudden inspiration—something that often happened to him—the man turned and went into the adjoining room, still talking. "Giacomo knows perfectly well he mustn't touch my plans or I'll whip him and leave him without supper." He continued addressing the woman while rifling through papers on the large table. "Speaking of supper, a whole capon may be too much for three people, Caterina. I'd ask you to use some restraint this evening. We have beans and turnips, I think that should be enough."

"For you, yes. Except that eating a bit of meat would do

you a lot of good. You've grown much thinner since I arrived. You must have lost ten pounds in three months."

"Three months and it feels like ten years," the man said, still searching. "Besides the fact that I don't eat the flesh of dead animals—never have, never will—what's making me thinner is this blasted equestrian statue. That and being unable to find those damned plans—where the devil have they gone?"

"Plans don't just walk away, son."

"Whereas mothers don't do it often enough, Caterina, Mother. So why don't you just get off my back, stop breaking my balls, and let me search in peace?"

"You never used to be so vulgar when you were young. Or so stingy."

"How would you know? You weren't around. As for being stingy, they're making me like that. I haven't seen a payment in two months. Excuse me." He waved his mother aside, headed for the henhouse, and started rummaging in the cages.

"I didn't use them to clean the henhouse," Caterina said patiently.

"I wouldn't be surprised if you did," the man replied, getting back on his feet and adjusting his belt. "As if it never . . . Hold on a minute, I just thought of something."

His right hand still on his belt, he raised his left hand to the collar of his pink outfit, tugged on it, and pulled out a notebook crammed with folded sheets, some large and some small. He placed it on the table, opened it very carefully, and took out two sheets of yellow parchment containing drawings of horses with sentences and other objects around them. Almost immediately, he put a hand to his face and rolled his eyes.

"So you had them on you?" Caterina said, snickering.

"I must have put them there two days ago, before I went to the castle," he replied, looking at his mother as though trying to work out if she was angry. "Forgive me, Caterina."

"You could actually call me *mamma* sometimes."

"Sorry, *mamma*. I lose so many things, there are times—"

He was interrupted by the rapping of powerful knuckles on the door.

Caterina turned, but he nimbly got in ahead of her and went to open. Not that he was ashamed of his mother, oh, no. Well, maybe just a little. It depended who the visitor was. It could only be one person at this time of the morning.

The man in pink opened the door and there in front of him was a slightly shorter, much older figure, dressed in black brocade, his head uncovered, his hat already in his hand as a sign of deference. A manservant, one of the important ones, but a manservant nonetheless.

"Messer Leonardo da Vinci?" the elderly man inquired.

"At your service," he replied.

TWO

"Oh, Messer Leonardo, what a pleasure to see you."
Standing almost in the center of the large courtyard known as the Piazzale delle Armi, Ludovico il Moro beckoned to Leonardo to come forward. Beside him, ultra-thin and fierce-looking, the Duchy's tax collector, the Most Excellent Cavaliere Bergonzio Botta, with a large ledger under his arm, as always.

"I am Your Lordship's servant," Leonardo replied warily. You never quite knew the reason Ludovico summoned you. It could be enthusiasm, like the day after the Festa del Paradiso, when the Lord of Milan had showered Leonardo with praise and accolades in front of the whole court, or it could be the exact opposite.

"Come, come forward," Ludovico said, smiling serenely. "Signor tax collector, I think the chamberlain is calling you."

Which wasn't even a particularly Renaissance way of asking the tax collector to get lost because the Lord of Milan wanted to have a private chat with Leonardo. After a bow from which he began straightening up while already walking backwards, Bergonzio Botta turned and walked off in the direction of Santo Spirito. Ludovico was silent for a moment, glancing around without letting his eyes come to rest on Leonardo, then slowly set off for the wide south entrance and beckoned Leonardo to follow him.

"Your Lordship seems particularly cheerful this morning," Leonardo ventured to say, trying to assess the mood of the man who paid his salary.

"I am, Master Leonardo, I am," Ludovico replied, still smiling, still walking. "And do you know why?"

"I hope Your Lordship will be kind enough to share the reason for his happiness."

"It's no secret," il Moro replied. "Not anymore. Emperor Maximilian is going to do us the honor of marrying our beloved niece, Bianca Maria, on the occasion of Christmas. The House of Sforza will be united with the Emperor, Master Leonardo."

Now here's the thing. Ludovico had spent months trying to palm off Bianca Maria Sforza as a bride to Maximilian, Emperor of the Holy Roman Empire, flattering him with constant overtures of friendship and above all with an awesome dowry. In court circles the figure of four hundred thousand ducats was being mentioned, in other words, more than half the annual income of the entire Duchy. This is rather as though the current Italian Minister of Finance had promised his daughter in marriage to the President of the United States, and offered half the peninsula's tax revenue—amounting to billions—as a dowry.

"We shall leave with the wedding party in early November. And it certainly won't be difficult to organize the bride's departure, or to assemble our loved ones, our darlings, our retinue here in the castle. As a matter of fact, it will be very easy. And do you know why?"

Ouch! Ouch!

Ludovico il Moro had been educated to a particularly high standard even for a nobleman of the time, but without any particular emphasis on Greek philosophy. Even so, he seemed to have assimilated without any difficulty the techniques of Socratic dialogue, the purpose of which was to get your interlocutor to spit out the desired answer simply by cornering him. When il Moro starts giving you these little kisses on the neck, these hints, they would say at court, be careful: he's about to lift up your robe from behind.

"No, Your Lordship."

"Because we have this splendid courtyard at our disposal," Ludovico said, his sweeping gesture indicating the Piazzale delle Armi with the castle all around. "This large, spacious, splendid courtyard, and, right in front . . ." Now at the door, Ludovico indicated with his open hand the wide expanse in front of the drawbridge. "Right in front, you see, there's an even larger square, perfectly leveled, clear, without any embell-ishments. In other words, Messer Leonardo, completely empty."

And il Moro's gaze traveled from the square and came to rest on Leonardo. His mouth was still smiling. Not his eyes.

Four years had elapsed since the day Ludovico had offi-cially entrusted him with the task Leonardo had boasted he could bring off better than anyone else. And ten years since he had sworn he could do it.

Ten years earlier, Leonardo had appeared before Ludovico il Moro with a long letter in which he claimed he could engi-neer bombards, dig underground rivers and moats, build unas-sailable castles. Only at the bottom of said letter did he men-tion that he could also paint a little. This was remarkable, since da Vinci had been called to Milan in his capacity as a musician, player of a *lira da braccio* of his own invention. But one sen-tence in particular had struck Ludovico il Moro.

I will create a bronze horse that will stand in immortal fame and in eternal honor of the happy memory of His Lordship your father and of the illustrious house of Sforza.

This promise had led to a court appointment, thanks to which Leonardo had obtained lodgings, the two-story studio in Corte Vecchia, next to the Cathedral, where he worked, and—theoretically—a substantial salary. Over the years, though, that same promise had come to seem like boasting, according to some people. And these people included il Moro.

"It's been three years, Master Leonardo, since you assured

me you were once again dedicating yourself heart and soul to your study for the monument in memory of my father," Il Moro went on, still looking at Leonardo. "You have repeatedly assured me that work on this monument was already under way, so much so that I expressly had this large area in front of the castle—where we are now standing—cleared and leveled."

"I am delighted to inform Your Lordship that the clay model of the horse is almost ready and can be exhibited on this very square at the end of next week."

"The clay model?" Ludovico raised an eyebrow. "Really?"

"An actual-size clay model, Your Lordship. Seven meters, taller and more imposing by far than any other equestrian monument. In faith, the model will be exhibited here in less than ten days."

"Oh, this is excellent news. Splendid. Marvelous. Now tell me, do you intend to pay homage to my father with a terracotta monument or do you plan to go further and give him a nice bronze coat? We're not in your sun-kissed Tuscany here, Master Leonardo. Our winter nights in Milan are freezing, you know. I wouldn't want my father to catch cold without an appropriate metal cloak."

Ludovico il Moro was no fool and knew only too well that glazing an object over seven meters high in molten bronze was not easy. By that we don't mean that he knew what technical and engineering difficulties were involved, but simply that he was aware how hard it was to make bronze objects that would be both light and sturdy. Specifically, what Ludovico il Moro mainly had in mind were cannons. Cannons the French army could produce and he couldn't.

"Initially, Your Lordship, I thought of casting the molten metal into the mold with the horse lying on its back and its legs up in the air. This would have gotten around the problem of water bubbles turning into air because of the intense heat, escaping while cooling, and spewing all over the surface of the bronze, because—"

"It sounds like an excellent idea. If I understand correctly, the steam from the water would escape through the hooves. Why not do that?"

"Your Lordship has understood perfectly well. Unfortunately, your beautiful city is not cold and humid only above the ground, Your Lordship, but also beneath it."

"What do you mean?"

"That if we dig a hole large enough to be filled with the shape of our horse, we will hit the water table that runs under Milan, Your Lordship. Flesh and blood horses can swim, but water could cause serious harm to a horse made of bronze."

Il Moro looked at Leonardo for a moment with eyes like ice. Then, an instant later, his mouth tightened and, one second after that, the Lord of Milan allowed himself a smile.

"I hold you in high esteem, Leonardo, you know that," Il Moro said, turning to look at the square. "I have the highest esteem for you as an engineer, a painter, a master of uniforms and costumes, and, last but not least, I have great respect for your wit."

"Your Lordship is too kind."

"I'm beginning to think so," Ludovico said curtly. "If I were not too kind, I would have thrown you out on the street by now." As he said this, he looked up at an arch in the castle, through which a blond young man was walking. Even at a distance, he looked like a strapping, well-built youth, the kind that, rumor had it, appealed to Master Leonardo. "Ah, here comes Count Galeazzo. Tell me, how is that other business going?"

These last words of Ludovico's had been uttered casually, and at much lower volume.

Leonardo, in answering, also spoke softly. "All is as you wished."

"Good, good," Ludovico said, resuming his usual tone. "So you say ten days. I'll take that as a promise."

* * *

"My humblest respects to Your Lordship."

"Greetings, Galeazzo. How is my beloved Bianca?"

"As beautiful as a phoenix. She is almost a woman now," Galeazzo Sanseverino said, squeezing his father-in-law's fore-arm in the ancient gesture that meant *I have no weapon in my hand, for now.*

Not that this gesture was necessary between the two of them. Back in the times of the war between Milan and Venice, Galeazzo Sanseverino had taken il Moro's side against his own father Roberto, and that's not the kind of thing you forget. Ludovico trusted Galeazzo so much that he had given his eld-est illegitimate daughter, Bianca Giovanna, in marriage to him when she had just turned eleven. His mention of "almost a woman" did not refer to Galeazzo being a pedophile. Back then, eleven was considered old enough for many things, including bearing children, if nature allowed.

"You, on the other hand, look worried, Ludovico," Galeazzo said, addressing his father-in-law by his first name as he always did when there was nobody else present.

"As usual, Galeazzo."

"You weren't before you met with Master Leonardo."

Ludovico looked at his son-in-law, who held his gaze with candor.

Galeazzo Sanseverino was one of those people who seemed to have inherited everything from their parents, except their name. He certainly was handsome, anybody could see that. Strong and brave, too, unlike Ludovico, as all the Milanese who had attended the great tournament held to celebrate Ludovico's wedding to Beatrice d'Este had been able to observe. On that occasion, Galeazzo had unseated, skewered, or defamed all his opponents, breaking twelve opposing lances out of twelve with an ease than can only be described as disarming.

True, Galeazzo was also clever and rather cultured, all you had to do to realize that was talk to him for a while. But above all, Galeazzo Sanseverino had exceptional diplomatic skills: that was something only il Moro and few others knew. The kind of son-in-law every father dreams of for his own daughter, provided that father is living in the late 15th century, apart from one tiny snag: the one thing he had not inherited from his parents—their name. Galeazzo was the son of a mercenary, and some problems of birth are hard to remedy.

There could not have been two other men in Milan who understood each other better than Galeazzo and Ludovico. Both were fighting to earn titles they had not had by birth but were certain they had earned by ability.

"You're right, dear Galeazzo. I'm afraid I'll never see that accursed equestrian statue. Moreover, Master Leonardo has stopped making any reference to my father. He only ever mentions 'the horse.' It seems almost secondary that it should be carrying Francesco Sforza on its back."

"If you're worried about the rider, let me reassure you. Do you remember how Master Leonardo put me in the saddle?"

"I'm still amazed at the way you managed to stay in the saddle," Ludovico said, smiling. "With that winged serpent sticking out from behind your helmet . . ."

Galeazzo smiled. His entrance at the joust, in armor made of gold scales, had been one of the most triumphant and absurd moments in his life. And that helmet that turned into a winged reptile, its tail uncurling from the back of the crown and forming a large spiral in the air before touching the horse's rump, probably weighed a hundred pounds alone.

"Actually, the serpent's paws rested on my steed's rear end.

So it was the horse itself that held my head up. Everything in perfect balance. Leonardo is an expert at that kind of thing."

"Perhaps," Ludovico said, looking doubtful. "All right, we shan't worry about the rider. But as far as the horse is concerned—"

"He spent months in my stables, studying my Sicilian thoroughbred. He measured every bit of it."

"*Every* bit of it?" Ludovico said, snickering. "If I know Master Leonardo, I imagine he must have taken great pleasure in lingering over some of the bits in particular."

"Ludovico," Galeazzo replied, in earnest, "Leonardo knows what he's doing."

"Yes, but the problem is that he won't do anything he doesn't know how to do," Ludovico said, his face turning as dark as his nickname. "I'm not worried about his being able to sculpt a beautiful horse, but I doubt he can cast one. I heard he's spoken to the greatest experts in that art, like Sangallo and the engineer Francesco di Giorgio, and that both have expressed doubts. We're going to need the skills of the French. That's right, the French. No one is better than they at the art of casting."

"And that's all they're best at," Galeazzo replied circumspectly, sensing that il Moro's thoughts were taking an entirely different direction.

"But it's more than enough, Galeazzo," was il Moro's curt response.

The two men fell silent, as though a glass wall had suddenly dropped down between them—an entirely hypothetical description, since such panes of glass could not be manufactured back then, or else why the hell would they have needed to plug their windows with cloths dipped in turpentine? But, although separated by silence, they were both thinking the same thing.

It's no use having valiant knights like Galeazzo Sanseverino, or ones drunk enough to throw themselves into the breach with total recklessness, if what you have arrayed in front of you is a battery of cannons capable of shredding them like confetti. Bearing in mind that il Moro didn't even have valiant knights like the aforementioned.

In the Italy of city-states, that terrible jigsaw puzzle of towns, castles, and fortresses that spent their time waging war against one another, city dwellers and peasants would seldom take part in battles, and when they did they generally played the parts of victims. No city had a regular army composed of patriots ready to give their lives for the blessed land of their birth. War was entrusted entirely to companies of mercenaries and their captains; people like the Englishman John Hawkwood, known as Giovanni Acuto, one of the undisputed champions at fighting on behalf of a third party. Now, he did have an equestrian monument worthy of his feats, and a seven-meter-high one at that. (Although it should be pointed out that the work known as *Equestrian Monument to Giovanni Acuto* was in fact a fresco painted by Paolo Uccello in the church of Santa Maria del Fiore, and was only in 2-D.)

Whenever this English warrior was greeted with the words "Peace be with you," he would reply, "I hope not. I'd be out of a job." This wasn't cynicism on his part but simple professionalism. These companies and captains for whom war was a way of life had no wish to die in battle; since they were soldiers by trade, not heroes, battles and wars between city states were generally resolved with little more than skirmishes. Most of the violence was reserved for the residents of conquered towns, who were robbed, slaughtered, and raped without the slightest chance to fight back. Obviously, after decades spent playing silly games and taking it out on the defenseless, the troops who swept across Italy had grown soft and, in the absence of stimuli and fierce adversaries, adjusted their level increasingly downwards.

Totally unlike the French army, which, first and foremost, was made up of Frenchmen. No Dalmatian or Dutch mercenaries, in fact no mercenaries of any kind, but sturdy bunches made up of coarse compatriots of His Most Christian Majesty Charles VIII, whose language and intentions they shared. Secondly, whereas in Italy captains of fortune had grown refined and their sons had in some cases become lords or diplomats, in France the social elevator was out of order at the time and French soldiers were still soldiers—people trained to kill somebody else's subjects whenever they came face to face with them, and not stuff it in the rear end of their own ruler.

"We need to find out more about the intentions of the French," il Moro said after a long pause. "We've been waiting for too long now."

* * *

"Of course I've been waiting for too long!" the little man in stockings and nightdress said. "Where's my breakfast?"

"I'll see to it right away, Your Majesty," the Duke of Commynes immediately replied, heading for the door.

"You'd better, Duke," His Majesty said, kicking away his blankets and, in the process, a half-naked woman who looked like a prostitute. "Get dressed and clear out. We've got important stuff to discuss here."

"Sire, what the fuck . . ." the woman replied, thus revealing that she also had the manners of a prostitute, which was in fact her profession.

"Good girl. As long as you stick to that, my dear, you're a wonder." His Most Christian Majesty Charles VIII started getting off the bed, not without some difficulty since the mattress was some eighty centimeters up from the floor and his stretched-out legs were barely sixty centimeters long. "But since right now we need to discuss war, politics, and other things you wouldn't understand, put your clothes on and get out. Or else go just as you are, it's not like you're the kind that feels embarrassment. And while you're at it, find out what happened to my breakfast."

And with a spastic little hop, His Majesty landed on the floor.

His Most Christian Majesty Charles VIII's first problem was that his majesty was only in his name. It was certainly not in his physical appearance, the other duke present—Louis de Valois, his cousin and Duke of Orléans—thought as he watched that improbable collection of bones and hair attempt to don a woolen caparison. Short and hunchbacked, with a horrendous nose and tufts of unruly beard that were his only evident sign of masculinity, Charles VIII looked more like a badly-assembled stool than a king.

"So, gentlemen, now we can talk," His Majesty said as soon as he had managed to get the caparison on without smothering himself—the most perilous enterprise he had undertaken in his entire life. "Why that disgruntled face, Duke? You look as if you've swallowed a toad."

"Sire," the Duke of Orléans said after a little cough, "I do not think it advisable to mention so openly in front of just anybody that we're talking about war. After all, your guest from last night is a streetwalker, and frequents all kinds of people."

Even you, the Duke thought but didn't say.

"Yes, Duke, you're right, but the venture on which I'm about to embark is so glorious that I can't wait to start." With a bovine leap, His Majesty seized a halberd lying next to the bed and pointed it at an imaginary enemy. "Think about it, Duke. An order from me and our army will cross the Alps like Hannibal and enter Italy. All the Italian kingdoms will let us pass through their dominions with a nice little bow. Venice, Milan, and Florence are ready to cheer the liberator of Naples and assist us as we march into the fiefdoms of Alfonso of

Aragon. We're about to invade the kingdom of Naples without a fight."

Which is the only way you could manage it, the Duke of Orléans thought.

His Most Christian Majesty Charles VIII's second problem was the fact that he was a cretin—something the reader will no doubt have already gathered without any help. Weak in body and intellect, as Venetian ambassador Contarini had described him, the King of France not only had never taken part in a single military action in his life, he had no idea what war was. His only sources of information were the books and poems of chivalry that spoke of champions, conquests, glory, horns blown by dying knights, and from these books he had drawn the inspiration to be a great knight himself, one destined for glorious feats. To anyone with an ounce of military experience, like the Duke of Orléans, it was obvious that in a real war situation, be it at the project stage or in actual battle, His Most Christian Majesty would be the opposing side's best ally.

But Charles VIII, who had no experience, had convinced himself, on the basis of his reading, that in order to subjugate Italy to his will all he had to do was make up his mind and set off; something that still occurs to some of us nowadays, the difference being that instead of poems we have convinced ourselves that all it takes is the Internet.

"Or rather," the King went on, unaware of the Duke's thoughts, "we would be about to invade Italy if we had already left. What are we waiting for, Archbishop?"

Bishop Briçonnet of Saint-Malo raised his eyebrows and wondered where he should start. "The main problem at the moment, Your Majesty, is the cannons. They're heavy, which is a good thing in battle, but a bad thing when the army needs to be on the move. We don't yet have suitable means of transport or men to cross the Alps."

"Alright, then, let's build some," the King replied, giving proof of a genuine ability to rule.

"We have commissioned their construction from Master Duplessis. It would cost at least thirty thousand ducats."

"And don't we have thirty thousand miserable ducats? Let's ask our ally Ludovico to loan us the sum. He promised us extensive assistance, both territorial and financial. Come on, send for Ambassador Belgioioso. Ah, it's about time. Duke, whatever happened to my breakfast?"

"Your Majesty's breakfast is served," the Duke of Commynes said, entering the room followed by liveried servants carrying platters heaped with bread, roast meats, and carafes. "I hope Your Majesty did not find the waiting irksome."

"Not at all, Duke, not at all. I was just in the process of summoning Ambassador Belgioioso to ask him to have his lord send us an appropriate sum of money. We need thirty thousand ducats. A trifle for Ludovico il Moro. There won't be any problems, will there, Commynes?"

"I sincerely hope not, Your Majesty. But it might be dangerous to take it as read. Il Moro's financial situation may not be as thriving as it appears." The Duke of Commynes also coughed. "From my estimation, Sire, the Duchy of Milan may yield about five hundred thousand ducats a year. But il Moro takes much more than that through taxes. About seven hundred thousand, according to my calculations."

At this point, Commynes no doubt meant to explain to Charles VIII that such fiscal pressure was perhaps not a sign of healthy coffers in the Duchy and that such a situation could not go on much longer. But His Most Christian Majesty decided that he had heard enough and that there was no point in listening further.

"Very well. If he gets it, good for him. And good for us. I'll immediately give the order to Belgioioso to put our request forward. Bishop, if you'd be so kind, pass me that tray."

* * *

"Duke, a word . . ."

"Yes, Duke."

The Duke of Commynes, having caught up with his Orléans counterpart in the long corridor, put a gloved hand on his shoulder. A familiar gesture he would never have allowed himself before the King, but which in their current location—the royal stables—was more than understandable.

"I need to speak with you on a matter of the highest importance."

"Go ahead, Duke. We're safe here."

"I have a concern, Duke. A niggling thought that's been keeping me awake these past few nights, ever since Ambassador Belgioioso returned."

"Has the Ambassador perhaps told you there are problems? I understood everything was ready."

"No problem, no," Commynes replied. "The Ambassador confirmed the existence of a league in our favor and once again reiterated that we can pass through the territory of the Duchy of Milan without fearing any kind of danger to our army. Just today I received a letter from our envoy in Italy, Messer Perron de Basche, confirming that intention."

"So no problem, then."

"No problem. But that is precisely the problem. Why would il Moro leave us free to pass through his territory? We have the better army, we could overthrow him at any time."

"But that is not our intention. Our objectives coincide with il Moro's. We both want to get the Aragons out of Naples."

"His Majesty wants to get the Aragons out of Naples so that he can take their place," Commynes continued, pensively. "But His Majesty will certainly not lead the troops. You will lead them, Duke, and that's something il Moro is taking for granted."

The Duke (of Orléans) turned to the Duke (from that other place).

It was no secret that Louis de Valois, Duke of Orléans, had laid claims on the Duchy of Milan by virtue of his lineage, being the grandson of Valentina Visconti, who was directly related to the true dukes whose title had been swiped by the Sforzas. If the Duke—of Orléans (sorry for specifying but they're all dukes here, it's a real mess)—had been free to make his own decision, he would undoubtedly have marched on Milan at the head of an army to liberate the city from the usurper and install himself in his place; the Duchy of Milan was extremely wealthy and prosperous and would have tempted anybody.

But the Duke of Orléans was not at liberty to do whatever he liked, he had to obey the King. His King. In other words, that spidery little idiot we mentioned earlier, who couldn't have conquered a latrine, let alone a duchy.

So why did il Moro not fear this possibility?

"Il Moro has every reason to fear our armed presence on his soil, and yet he clearly doesn't," Commynes said, voicing the Duke's thoughts (one of the dukes, you work out which one). "I fear his confidence derives neither from diplomacy nor from finance."

"From what, then?"

"There's a brilliant man in Ludovico's service named Leonardo. Leonardo di Ser Piero da Vinci."

"I've often heard his name mentioned. Apparently, he's an excellent painter."

In actual fact, the Duke of Orléans knew perfectly well who Leonardo was. He had even met him. But it is always essential for a diplomat to appear a little more ignorant than he really is.

"You've heard of him, but I've seen his creations. He's not only a painter, he's also an engineer and an inventor of instruments of war. Two years ago, I saw Galeazzo Sanseverino in a joust, and he was wearing a suit of gold armor of which, trust me, the helmet alone must have weighed more than the man inside it. And yet he moved as lightly as a feather. Several people told me there was a complex system of winches and pulleys to magnify the rider's strength. And someone who was employed in his workshop told me of bombards that move like tortoises, and other similar inventions."

"What are you afraid of, Duke?"

The Duke of Commynes looked his fellow nobleman straight in the eye. "They say Messer Leonardo has succeeded in getting a suit of armor to fight without a knight inside it, providing the impetus with large springs inside the chest that trigger various mechanisms. I don't know if that's true. I don't know if it's true that he's designing other weapons, even more terrible ones, but I can't rule it out. If you'd seen Sanseverino in action, you'd understand. He didn't move like a man, there was something supernatural about him. It would be extremely dangerous to go to war through the territory of an enemy about whose weapons we know nothing."

As Commynes spoke, the Duke of Orléans's mind started spinning like a water wheel on a river in flood.

True, it would be dangerous not to know about the enemy's weapons. But it would be extremely gratifying to have access to those very weapons. And while stealing a weapon was dangerous and difficult, stealing a plan was much less so.

And Messer Leonardo did not build. Messer Leonardo planned. He calculated, measured, and, above all, drew with a clarity and precision never before seen. The Duke had seen the Florentine master's drawings with his own eyes and been dazzled by them. To build a contraption based on these drawings would be much easier than stealing one already made. One of these drawings, or all of them.

That Leonardo had a secret notebook, nobody doubted. Every mathematician and engineer at the time had one, it was their safe conduct and their fortune. If they ever divulged what they had discovered after years of study, they would no longer be the only ones capable of doing what they were doing. That's the problem with scientific knowledge: everybody can make a profit from it once they've understood it.

"You're right. We must find out more. What does the Duke of Commynes suggest?"

"Two of my most loyal men, Robinot and Mattenet, are in Perron de Basche's retinue and travelling up through Italy with him," Commynes replied. "We could instruct them to gather information."

"I would encourage you to do so. And, Duke . . ."

"Go on."

"To avoid compromising this venture's happy outcome, it would be best if only you and I know of our intentions."

"I shall have to tell Perron de Basche. Otherwise, he'll be suspicious."

"Very well, tell him. But just him and no one else."

THREE

"T ruly delicious. Whatever anybody says, to get the real taste of meat just throw it on the fire."

Accerrito Portinari's right hand came to rest on the table, palm facing down at first, then facing up, miming a steak, to which his hand actually bore more than a slight resemblance.

"One side for a minute, then the other for a minute, and there you have it. Not the way these Milanese barbarians do it, letting it simmer for a couple of hours. They torture it as though trying to make it confess some sin or other. Whereas we Florentines know that nature does things properly and that it's a shame to ruin them."

Accerrito Portinari put his knife down next to his now emptied plate and looked at Leonardo with a big smile on his smug, fat face.

"I agree," Leonardo replied, also smiling and also putting his spoon down next to his own plate, which was half full now and which, unlike Portinari's, contained only vegetables. "I'm glad you enjoyed Caterina's cooking. Would you like a little radicchio?"

"No, thank you, I don't eat landscape. Wine and meat is all a man needs. Wine and meat, that's eating, the rest is just to please the physician. Now, Messer Leonardo, in what way can I please you?"

Accerrito Portinari looked at Leonardo, his porcine eyes glistening in his lard-like face.

Being fat was a status symbol in the late 1400s: it meant you could eat more than required every day and that only a few of the calories ingurgitated were converted into manual work. As a matter of fact, in all his life, Accerrito Portinari had never had to strain a muscle to earn a living. First as the brother of Pigello, the representative of the Medici Bank in Milan, then as his successor, once Pigello had passed on to a better life.

"By doing your job, Messer Accerrito," Leonardo replied with a half-smile.

Accerrito's own smile grew broad and affable. "Do you have money you'd like to invest? That's good news indeed. You've approached the right man. The Medici Bank is here for you, in the form of my humble person."

This mention of the Medici Bank reassured Leonardo. After his brother Pigello's death, Accerrito had had quite a few solvency issues. So much so that at one point, Lorenzo de' Medici had decided to close the Milan branch, and the prestigious building in Porta Comasina, with its sculpted portal and its frescoes by Foppa, had even been put up for auction. But then Accerrito's luck had changed. He had found new investors, among them a certain Giovanni Portinari, with whom he had nothing in common except for the surname—and whom Leonardo also knew—and had resumed his former activities just as his brother had done. He made loans, invested, exchanged letters of credit, and there were many things to indicate that he was doing rather well.

"Not wishing to boast," Accerrito went on, "we are now among the most sought-after bankers in Milan. We're always at your disposal, Messer Leonardo. It all depends on how soon you want your money back. If it's after six months, I could return it to you with a ten percent increase. If, however, you could wait a year, we could agree on twelve percent."

"And what if I wanted it right away?"

"Right away?"

"I have no intention of entrusting money to you, Messer Accerrito, but of asking you for a loan."

"Ah."

Leonardo's skill at studying and evaluating human expressions was probably unparalleled in the world, but you certainly didn't need his genius to grasp his dinner guest's attitude. Even someone like, well, perhaps not Botticelli, but definitely a pupil of his, a Marco d'Oggiono or someone like that, would have perceived that Accerrito Portinari's face was that of a genuinely disappointed man. It should be said that of all the aforementioned, Leonardo would have been the only one capable of painting that expression accurately, but for the moment that was of no consequence.

"I've been told that you lend money with interest, even large sums," Leonardo said, trying to remind Portinari of the essence of his work.

"That's true, Messer Leonardo."

"I know that this year you've lent our lord Ludovico almost ten thousand ducats. Rest assured I shan't be asking you for such a sum. I just need a small endowment to see me through until the end of the year, when I'll be receiving various payments. I'm still owed twelve hundred lire by the Confraternity for a painting."

"The one they call the Virgin of the Rocks? I've seen it. A wondrous work. You're a genius, Messer Leonardo."

"You're very kind, but you see, geniuses have to eat too. And so do their apprentices. Not to mention their mothers."

"Then what they say is true? The Caterina who just brought us this excellent meat is your mother?"

"As true as the fact that Christ died on the cross," the aforementioned lady said, entering the room. "Excellent meat, indeed. And my beloved son won't even try it. Would you like some more wine?"

"No, thank you kindly, signora."

Portinari waited a few seconds after the woman had left.

"Do you know how a bank works, Messer Leonardo?"

"Of course, I do. You borrow at twelve percent and lend at fifteen. And the remaining three percent is your income."

"It's a little more complicated than that. The fact is, I manage the money of a large portion of Milan. All the storekeepers on Via degli Armorari are my clients. I even have clients among the carders of Lodi."

"I'm delighted to hear it. It means your business is doing well, so you can lend five hundred ducats to an artist who is a fellow townsman of yours."

"My business is indeed doing well. I manage a very large amount of money. Much larger than I actually possess. You see, Messer Leonardo, a bank is like a juggler. It keeps other people's money up in the air, and every time I touch a coin that belongs to somebody else, a little of it rubs off on my hand. But even when I keep ten dishes in the air, I only ever hold one in my hand, and that one isn't even mine."

Which, objectively speaking, was actually true. Although it had a turnover of about one hundred thousand ducats, the branch's capital was about one tenth of that—barely ten thousand. The fact remains that this was the little speech Accerrito Portinari churned out whenever he had to refuse someone a loan. At this point, Accerrito usually explained to the wretch of the day that he couldn't just lend money to anybody, it had to be in in return for specific guarantees. His present interlocutor being a genius, he naturally had no need to say that explicitly.

"You're telling me you can't just lend money to anyone who comes along," Leonardo said, still smiling. "I understand you. But I'm not anyone who came along. You know me well. I have much more than my modest clothes to offer you as guarantee. I have my studio and my paintings. You know me well, Messer Accerrito."

"Which is why I could never behave like a usurer with you, Messer Leonardo. Five hundred ducats, and you're offering me as a guarantee paintings that are worth ten times as much."

"If anyone had the means to buy them, of course," Leonardo said, shaking his head. "You're quite right, my works are valuable, and that's why few can afford them."

"True. This isn't Florence, where people like beautiful things and pay good money for them."

"Trust me, they like them here too. But people don't have the money, so they borrow the funds to buy them. Everybody borrows here, even the Duke."

Accerrito Portinari gave a malicious half smile. "Which duke are you referring to, Messer Leonardo? Be careful, here in Milan nothing is clear. Do you mean the Duke of Bari—that is, Ludovico il Moro—or the Duke of Milan, the dear Gian Galeazzo? By the way, did you know you're mentioned in a new poem on that very subject? I heard it sung on the Navigli the other day."

And in a lovely tenor voice Portinari sang:

Leonardo was summoned as a matter of urgency
By Gian Galeazzo, stark naked, and Donna Isabella.
What we need, and it's quite an emergency,
Is a machine to harden my husband's little feller.

The unfortunate conjugal situation of Gian Galeazzo Sforza and Isabella of Aragon was, given the lack of privacy mentioned earlier, known to all Milan. For many months now, Duke Gian Galeazzo, who was not yet twenty, had been unable to consummate his marriage to his lawful wedded wife Isabella, although it was unclear whether this was because of actual *impotentia coeundi*—as court physician and astrologer Ambrogio Varese da Rosate maintained—or because of an inopportune, unfavorable alignment of the stars—as the young duke himself swore again and again—or because Gian Galeazzo felt physical attraction only for the well-built page boys with whom he would linger behind heavy drapes—as the rest of the city, including the suburbs, claimed. Be that as it may, the marriage had not been validated with a proper little fuck as God intended, which was why Ludovico il Moro and Cardinal Ascanio Sforza had used their influence to force Gian Galeazzo to fulfill his duties. It is a mortal sin not to consummate a marriage, his uncles told him quite brutally, so if you don't want to go to hell, make sure you overcome your natural bashfulness with regard to pussy and do your duty, or else the marriage will be annulled, your bride's dowry will have to be returned, and we'll lose tens of thousands of ducats, not to mention losing face.

In the meantime, Caterina had come into the room and started clearing the few dishes from the table. Barely ten seconds: long enough to hear Portinari's song and notice that her son's facial expression had changed to one of concern.

"Alas, that is not in my power, Messer Accerrito," Leonardo said, looking away. "I have various mechanisms to increase a person's strength, but I certainly can't change his will or inclinations. And even if I could, I assure you I wouldn't want to."

"Come now, Messer Leonardo, don't make that face. Everyone knows by now that Gian Galeazzo's a buggerer, even the French, so it's hardly a state secret. And while we're on the subject, Messer Leonardo . . . you know it's burning at the stake for sodomites in this city. Galeazzo Maria instituted that law and it's never been repealed. This isn't Florence, where certain things are tolerated."

"What are you trying to say, Messer Accerrito?"

"I'm merely trying to give you a piece of advice. People talk. We're not in Florence here. Ah, my beautiful Florence . . . I don't know about you, but I miss it so much . . ."

"Can I ask you something, Messer Accerrito?" Caterina said in a garrulous tone.

"Please do, Donna Caterina."

"If you're so homesick for Florence, why don't you go back there?"

* * *

"Because it's doesn't seem opportune, that's why. You need me. Massimiliano needs me. Whenever I don't see him for a few days I find him altered."

"Thank you for your concern," Ludovico il Moro said, "but I still think it would be of great comfort to your father and sister if you returned to your birthplace for a while. And to you, too."

Without looking at Ludovico, Beatrice went to the child. Under the stern eyes of a woman dressed in black and the attentive gaze of a man in red, the little boy was crawling, dirtying his hands with the aromatic herbs the servants had strewn on the floor to mask the stuffy smell that prevailed in the bedrooms.

"Come, Massimiliano . . ."

Beatrice nimbly reached out with her arms, lifted the child in the air, and held him out in front of her, at arm's length. The woman in black simply watched the babe being picked up, although this in no way discharged her of her own responsibility. She was Teodora, Massimiliano's nurse, and she took care of him twenty-four hours a day, including the three or four minutes when he was allowed into the presence of his parents.

Beatrice d'Este was eighteen years old at the time, but a modern observer would have thought she was twice that. It was partly the child, and partly the double chin and baby fat that had refused to go away after his birth, and which the Duchess of Bari usually tried to conceal by wearing large, loose dresses with gold and silver vertical stripes: for although, as previously mentioned, being slightly overweight was the mark of an elevated social status, even back in those days it was something men could allow themselves much more than women.

That day, however, the Duchess was wearing a brown cloth dress with puffed sleeves, and, on her head, instead of the usual pearl ornament, she had a black silk cap with long white veils. She was in mourning, her mother, Eleanor of Aragon, having recently died, which was the reason Ludovico il Moro had been trying to persuade his wife to visit her family in Ferrara for the past few days, hoping she might find some peace.

"My father would find comfort enough if only you gave him what you promised. As for my own comfort, I can assure you that all I want is to be the wife of the Duke of Milan."

"Beatrice, my most beloved wife, you know perfectly well that the decision is not entirely up to me. Putting your father in command of the French troops would seem the ideal choice to me, too, but the stars do not appear to agree. I was discussing it with Magistro Ambrogio only this morning. Isn't that so, Magistro?"

"The stars have spoken quite clearly, Your Lordship," Ambrogio said in a deep, dark voice that seemed to come straight up from the floor. It was the voice of a man who knows that what he says derives not from his own beliefs, but from his knowledge. Or at least, so he believes. "Mercury is under the malign influence of the stars, and this is a terrible moment for those whose fate is tied to that planet, such as those born under the sign of Scorpio."

"Pietrobono, on the other hand," Beatrice cut in, her voice rising an entire octave, "says that October and the cold, damp weather are ideal conditions for the strength of Scorpio to express itself. My father is therefore at a moment of maximum vigor."

Almost surprised, Magistro Ambrogio raised an eyebrow and directed his gaze to the Lord of Milan.

I am Ambrogio Varese da Rosate, the gaze said. Physician, pediatrician, astrologer, dentist, and Your Lordship's political and military advisor. Is your wife really confusing me with some common or garden variety Pietrobono?

After a moment's silence, Magistro Ambrogio looked again at Beatrice. "The moment is most inauspicious for your excellent father, Your Ladyship, as demonstrated by the recent loss of your most beloved mother. An irreparable loss for him and for the Duchy, and entirely sudden and unpredictable, except for the stars and those who can read the stars."

This was one of the things that Magistro Ambrogio, being a thoroughbred astrologer, excelled at: remembering, and reminding others of, all the events that confirmed, or had confirmed, his predictions, and downplaying or failing to mention those he had resoundingly screwed up.

Il Moro got to his feet. He too looked at his wife, who kept staring at Magistro Ambrogio like someone who would have known exactly how to reply to him if, as usual, there hadn't been other people in the room.

"Moreover, my most beloved wife, you must appreciate the fact that I cannot make this decision without consulting my allies. In this war, we cannot ignore the wishes of the French. On the contrary . . . Ah, dear Galeazzo, greetings. Come in, come in. Did you hear what I was saying?"

"I did, somewhat," Galeazzo Sanseverino replied like the gentleman he was, seeing that he had been standing in the doorway for five minutes, waiting for permission to enter. Although they were friends, it was the other who was lord and ruler of Milan. "Unfortunately, we'll need to convince our allies, and that won't be easy."

He stretched out his gloved hand, in which he held a letter that smelled strongly of incense. A letter from France. Not because the French usually scented their letters, but because Magistro Ambrogio, fearing the plague, had given orders that all missives from filthy places prone to contagion, like the countries beyond the Alps, were to be fumigated.

Ludovico took the letter, opened it, and read it attentively, while behind him, pretending to play with her son, Beatrice tried to look over his shoulder.

"It's from the Duke of Commynes. He informs us that he is going to cross the Alps and will be in Milan in the next few days to meet with His Most Christian Majesty's inspector, Perron de Basche. He asks for hospitality during his stay in Milan."

"Who is this Perron de Basche?" Beatrice asked in an uninterested tone as fake as a three-sesterce bank note.

"He's the inspector appointed to travel the length of Italy from Naples on up in order to assess the strength of the Neapolitan army and the condition of the allies. We're preparing for war, my dear Galeazzo."

"So it would seem. We should discuss this. Shall I wait for you at the stables?"

"There's no need, my dear Galeazzo. I have no secrets from my wife."

Galeazzo's noble face did not betray an ounce of his disappointment at having to remain in the room. Since her mother's death, Beatrice had taken her meals in her room, in the presence of Ludovico and Galeazzo, in a grim, silent atmosphere—although this morning Duchess Beatrice was much more cheerful than she had been over the previous weeks. Galeazzo, a man of action, an outdoors man, couldn't bear any more of this mourning period and was trying in every way possible to avoid the Duke and Duchess's apartments and the oppressive cloud that hung over them, and not just metaphorically: what the olfactory atmosphere in that room must have been like—well, the very fact that Galeazzo preferred the stables surely says it all.

"Whatever the case may be, our concern, for the time

being, is where to lodge them. I think it would be appropriate for them to stay here in the castle."

"And we'll have to give them a proper welcome, don't you think?" Beatrice said, all chirpy again and glimpsing an opportunity to wear something sparkling instead of mourning clothes. "We'll have to throw a lavish feast to honor our ally. Something like what Botta did, remember? With all the pagan deities announcing the courses . . ."

While his wife talked, Ludovico was thinking, rubbing his mouth and nose with his joined hands, as though praying to his own brain to come up with an idea.

"I don't know, my dear wife. The French have rather coarse tastes. They do not possess the refined palate of the Milanese or the Neapolitans. I was thinking . . . do we have a French-speaking dwarf?"

"What a splendid idea!" Beatrice exclaimed, smiling at the child and cheerfully lifting him up again. "Of course, a lovely spectacle with dwarves and jugglers! Well done, Your Lordship. You're so, so clever. That would be perfect for the French. See how intelligent your *papà* is, Massimiliano?"

Massimiliano (a.k.a. Ercole Massimiliano Sforza, eldest child of Beatrice and Ludovico, although his mother always used his middle name, and if you suspect she did so in order to pander to the Austrian emperor, then you're quite right) gave a happy gurgle and looked at Galeazzo Sanseverino, who was also smiling.

"I think that's an excellent idea," Galeazzo said approvingly, turning back to il Moro and nodding enthusiastically. "Our chamberlain should be told. Shall I call him?"

"Yes, Galeazzo. We must honor our guest as is fitting. We don't want to appear rude, do we?"

* * *

"You were rather rude, Caterina."

"You're right," Caterina said, still moving about the room, "but when someone's rude to me I'm rude right back." Accerrito Portinari had only just left, with goodbyes shorter than the hellos on his arrival. "You invite him to lunch, feed him the best veal in Milan, and that usurer not only denies you any damned help at all, but starts talking about burning at the stake? Usurers should be burned at the stake too, doesn't he know that?"

"Too? And who else?"

For a few seconds, she continued to pace around, cleaning here and there with a rag. Then, not without effort, she sat down opposite her son.

"I'm no fool, Leonardo."

"I know that only too well, Mother. I'm your son. If a black man impregnates a white woman, the child is born gray. But if the child is born black, then both parents must have been black, don't you think?"

"Listen, Leonardo. When you were in Florence, I heard you'd indulged in some licentious acts, but I paid no heed. People can be nasty, even about their own kind, so imagine with the son of a servant. But now that I'm here I see—"

"What do you see, Mother?"

"I see that boy, Salaì, loitering about the house. He doesn't paint, he doesn't prepare the colors, he does nothing, actually, but he lives with you in your own home."

"It's not true that he does nothing, He's a highly-skilled thief." Leonardo looked at Caterina with a raised eyebrow. Just then, Salaì popped his head through the door, probably sensing that he was being talked about. "Joking aside, Mother, when a boy joins a workshop he always starts with the most menial tasks. When I first joined Verrocchio, I'd clean out the hen coops."

Yes, you heard correctly. In those days, every artist had a henhouse, and not for nutritional reasons. In Leonardo's time, the technique of oil painting had not yet been fully mastered: in 15th-century Florence, tempera was often used, which meant mixing—*temperando* in Latin (Leonardo knew no Latin, but the technique worked all the same)—the pigments with a binding agent like egg yolk, which, once dry, would form a protective protein lattice that would cling to the surface and trap the colors *in aeternum*. Since it would take four hundred and fifty years before the nearest supermarket was opened, every artist—in order to have fresh eggs available—did the most obvious thing, that is, kept a henhouse at home. And that's where an apprentice would normally begin: keeping the henhouse clean. Only later would he graduate to tasks better suited to his talent: breaking the eggs, skinning rabbits, grinding pigments, and so forth. It would take quite a while before he could lay a brush on a board.

This explanation might be interesting to the modern man, but definitely not to Caterina, who knew perfectly well how an artist's workshop operated, including what happened when the artist would take his apprentice into the backroom.

She sighed. "Listen, Leonardo. You almost never go to Mass, and so be it."

"Why should I go to Mass? I would if the preacher read what's written in the Gospel. But all I hear are preachers who mistake their own brains' delirium for the will of God. Like Friar Savonarola in Florence and Friar Gioacchino here in Milan."

"Last year, Friar Savonarola said that a disaster was about to befall Florence and three days later Lorenzo de' Medici died."

"And we needed the voice of God to tell us that? Lorenzo had gout, he couldn't stand up, he was as swollen as a goatskin." Leonardo motioned to Salaì with an open hand, and the boy came to him and curled up in his lap like a kitten.

"Well, even I can predict that this scoundrel is going to steal something in the next three days. You just have to know him."

"It wasn't me, Messer Leonardo! You must have done the accounts wrong last time."

"You hear that, Mother? That's Salaì's cry. The dog goes *woof woof,* the cat goes *miaow miaow*, and Salaì goes 'It wasn't me.'" Leonardo gave the boy a slap on the back of his neck that was more a caress than a blow. "And the preacher goes 'God's will, God's will.' Each has his own cry."

"Careful what you say, son. Perdition isn't punished only by God, but also by men. You got away with it in Florence because a little Medici cousin was with you and if they'd condemned him they'd have condemned you, too. But this is Milan, not Florence. Be careful what you say and what you do."

"And what is it I do that's so reprehensible, Mother?"

"You know, Leonardo."

"Well, Mother, if I already know, I won't feel embarrassed if you tell me."

Caterina fell silent and twisted the rag in her hands.

"Are you referring to the fact that I do unnatural things, as our friend Portinari put it?"

Still saying nothing, Caterina nodded almost imperceptibly.

"You're right, Mother. I do unnatural things. Or rather, to be precise, I do one unnatural thing and one only. And you know what that is?" Leonardo lovingly stroked Salaì's hair, and the boy moved his head like a purring cat, stretching his neck toward his master. "I don't eat meat. I don't feed on the remains of animals that are inferior to me, whether killed by me or someone else, as most animals do in nature. Stuffing oneself with the flesh of weaker animals is a natural thing, and not only do I not do it, I abhor it."

Having gotten Salaì off him with a slap on the back, Leonardo stood up from the table, visibly annoyed by all that had happened after lunch. He stretched and smoothed his pink cloth garment.

"I abhor it but allow it to those I love, so much so that I brought you a piece of meat to make stock, meatballs or whatever you wish. I didn't eat it, because that's what makes me happy, and you did, because that's what makes you happy." Having reached the door, Leonardo turned, smiling. "Similarly, I shan't stop you tomorrow from going to hear your beloved Friar Gioacchino blather on about hells, apocalypses, earthquakes, and locusts. Now, with your permission, I'm going to bed. And even without your permission, I'm going to bed anyway."

By Candlelight

The thumb ran down the horse's thigh to where the muscle became a tendon and vanished from sight. Behind the thumb, half a meter away, was Leonardo, calm and focused. Here's the muscle. It suggests movement. You need it, but it's not enough. Still, it's easier than painting. Sculpting is definitely easier than painting. You're in three dimensions, so all you have to do is copy what you see and feel and you're fine. There must be a reason why the paintings of the Ancient Greeks looked ridiculous, while their statues were majestic. It's easier to do things in three dimensions, right? But it takes skill to do them in two. You need shading, and perspective. But which perspective? From your right eye or your left? All those artists dealt with how a scene appears to the eye, but humans have two eyes. Maybe that's why we can't see the boundaries of things very well. Or maybe it's because there are no boundaries.

* * *

Leonardo roused himself. The clay would be soft and malleable for another half-hour at most. He had to be quick. Here, now. Touch it here, then there. You see? It works. You can see it and feel it.

Where's the boundary between me and you, horse? Is it here, where my hand is touching you? But that's the boundary of my touch. If I press, it changes. And how can I distinguish you, horse, from a heap of new clay, with nothing but touch?

If I move away I don't touch you but I can smell you. A nice smell of clay and water, of soil and coolness. And if somebody touches you, gives you a tap, I can hear the sound. Until I move too far away and can't hear it any more. Could that be where the boundary is between you and me, horse? But if I open my eyes, I can see you. And if I move away, I keep seeing you, and you remain in my eyes until you vanish on the horizon. Then is the horizon the boundary between me and you, horse?

* * *

Leonardo looked around and glanced at the wax candle in a corner, which had burned down a good couple of inches since he had first lit it. That meant he had been working for four hours. Soon it would be time to go back to bed and get some sleep. An hour and a half, maybe two. Until matins. Five days to go before delivering the work. There was still the tail to be done, but there was time. And there was clay, which would become a tail, shaped by my own hands, by Leonardo, son of Ser Piero, Leonardo who came from Vinci to Milan, and Heaven knows how long I'll stay in Milan. Maybe we'll stay here together for ever, my beautiful horse. I'll see you every day.

And if I don't see you, because I'll have gone away, too bad. You're so well made that I might come across a traveler who tells me about you, who describes you, tells me about your curves, and even shows me a drawing. It's not the same as seeing you, it's beyond that. I can picture you in my mind, just as you are, or even more beautiful. That way, you would truly be my horse.

Then perhaps there really is no boundary between me and you, horse. Just as there is no boundary between me and il Moro, in whose service I have to work even when he's not here.

Or between me and Salaì—may God protect him and punish him. I worry about him when he's not around. So where's the boundary, the separation? Yes, I love that boy. Like the son I'll never have.

FOUR

T
he sun had not yet risen beyond the castle walls when the body was discovered.

The pitch darkness of deepest night had already begun raising its curtain in the last few minutes, ready to present the spectacle of another brand-new day. But you couldn't see much inside the castle, and even in the courtyard known as the Piazzale delle Armi visibility was quite low.

That was why Remigio Trevanotti, one of the castle servants, did not immediately realize the nature of the object he had tripped over, an object that should not have been there in the first place, given that His Lordship had ordered that the courtyard be kept clear of objects lying on the ground at all hours of the day or night. It was a kind of bundle with an odd texture, almost like a sack containing large river stones stuck together with mastic. That was Remigio Trevanotti's initial impression as he got back on his feet, cursing because it was now his job to remove this heavy package.

It was only when he handled it, trying to find the best way to load it on his shoulder, that he realized the bundle contained a man.

A man too cold and stiff still to be alive.

* * *

"Dead?"

"Dead, Your Lordship."

"Stabbed?"

"It would not seem so, Your Lordship."

"Then how did he die?"

"It's not clear, Your Lordship."

"Could it be *that*?"

"It could be that, Your Lordship."

"Do we know him?"

"I've seen him before, Your Lordship."

The voice was that of Bergonzio Botta, not only Ludovico's tax collector but also sometimes the master of ceremonies at his morning audiences.

"He was one of the supplicants requesting an audience yesterday morning. Your Lordship did not have time to hear him. He came by the castle again yesterday afternoon to request another audience."

"Do you remember his name?"

"I must have written it on the list. I'll go and get it right away, Your Lordship."

"Go, Bergonzio. But first send for Magistro Ambrogio."

* * *

While the servants were laying the corpse out on the table, Magistro Ambrogio Varese da Rosate walked around it, swinging a thurible in which incense and lemon leaves were burning. Incense because its warm, fragrant fumes were believed to dispel the winds that carried contagion, and lemon leaves because Magistro Ambrogio liked the smell.

Having laid the body down, the servants stood by the table, their eyes shifting from the dead man to the physician, their feet pointing more toward the door than in front of them.

"Undress the poor wretch, may God have mercy on his soul."

The servants did so, with the quick, strained movements

typical of those who are scared out of their wits, and within a very short time left on the table a naked, dead, and very pale man.

Ambrogio da Rosate began circling the corpse, as slowly as a falcon searching for prey.

Ambrogio da Rosate, too, was searching for prey. Or, rather, a sign. Any sign. But there were no signs on this body, of any kind. No signs of stabbing, no marks from a dagger. No bleeding from the mouth, the nose, the ears . . .

"Turn him over."

. . . or any other orifices of the body.

Ambrogio continued walking in circles, absorbed in thought, while the servants stood motionless, hoping they would soon be allowed to leave the room.

Nor any sign of poisoning from substances different than arsenic, so fashionable in those days.

No bruises or blemishes suggesting a beating, a brawl. or a violent contact with some blunt instrument.

No congestion in the face or neck that would make one suspect an apoplectic fit. Besides, Magistro Ambrogio thought, if he had died from a stroke, why take the trouble of wrapping him in a sack and carrying him into the middle of the Piazzale delle armi? What was there about a poor fellow who'd died of a stroke that would need to be concealed?

No boils, bumps, or other ostentatious signs of the disease that had overwhelmed half the continent over a hundred years earlier—those livid weals, those venomous fungi that would pop up under people's clothes and meant one thing only. *That*, as Ludovico had said and Bergonzio Botta had replied. A disease so terrible that no one at court called it by its name and everybody feared it. Servants, cooks, and armigers feared it, and even Magistro Ambrogio Varese da Rosate, an expert in the art of the stars but perfectly well aware of not being anything as eternal as they were, feared it.

And the man who had ordered him to examine the body feared it, too.

"Have you finished, Magistro Ambrogio?"

"I'm not sure," Ambrogio replied in a slow, deep voice. "I'm very, very much afraid we've only just begun."

"What do you mean, Magistro Ambrogio?"

Ambrogio da Rosate turned to the servant, heedless of the difference in their roles. His face was impassive, but there was dismay in his eyes. "Whatever this man may have died from, it's an illness that's never been seen before."

* * *

"Are you sure, Magistro Ambrogio?"

"I confess my ignorance, Your Lordship. I've never come across this disease on the body of any man or woman, or in the pages of any of my treatises."

"So it's not the plague, then," Beatrice said with a hint of hope in her voice.

"I can state that with absolute certainty, Your Ladyship," Ambrogio da Rosate replied, while behind the ducal pair, a servant, hearing the disease named so explicitly, made a quick sign of the cross with a furtive tap on his balls between the Father and the Holy Ghost.

"Nevertheless it kills," Ludovico said, his hands joined in front of his face. "And it kills fast. Messer Bergonzio, you told me you saw this man alive yesterday. When exactly?"

Bergonzio Botta, official collector of tributes for His Lordship in the provinces of Lodi, Como, and Vigevano, was not a timid man. Although he went around escorted by a handful of armigers, it was, so they said, purely and strictly for reasons of personal safety—a safety that was also jeopardized by lightning, plague, poisonings, and all the other calamities that, in Bergonzio's opinion, were seriously underestimated by most of his fellow men. Anyhow, as we were saying, Bergonzio Botta was not a timid man: he was a genuine chickenshit. As Ludovico addressed him, he was actually counting the hours since he had encountered that young man, a mere five paces away, ten at the most, and wondering if the slight dizziness he was feeling might be a first symptom of possible contagion.

"At the ninth hour, Your Lordship," Botto replied.

"And how did he look, Messer Bergonzio?"

"Well, exactly as you saw him. A blond young man, about thirty . . ."

Ambrogio da Rosate, who had understood the question, tried rephrasing it. "Was he shaking? Did he look flushed with fever? Was he pale?"

"On the contrary, he was sound as a bell. Or at least he seemed to be. I'm not a physician, but he looked perfectly healthy."

Ludovico il Moro, his face as dark as his name, looked at Ambrogio da Rosate.

"I've never come across a disease like this, Your Lordship," Ambrogio admitted.

"Could he have been poisoned?"

"I see nothing on the body that would lead me to that conclusion, Your Lordship. There is not the rash and bleeding associated with cantarella or aqua tofana. Every poison that enters our bodies leaves a trace, Your Lordship."

"Every poison leaves a trace." Il Moro repeated Ambrogio's words out loud, as though he either found them particularly interesting or knew them to be true from personal experience. "I see, Magistro Ambrogio. Now tell me: what do the stars say about this?"

"I would need to consult my instruments, if Your Lordship will give me leave."

"Yes, go, Magistro Ambrogio."

After a deep, slow, dignified bow, Ambrogio da Rosate did exactly that. Ludovico let a few seconds pass in silence after the door had been shut, while Bergonzio Botta took his own pulse under his heavy dark cloth sleeve, trying to figure out if by any chance he was coming down with a fever.

"I need your assistance, Messer Bergonzio," Ludovico said.

"At your service, Your Lordship."

"Send for Messer Leonardo."

"I shall fetch him myself, if Your Lordship will allow."

"Messer Bergonzio, do you still go around with your escort?"

"Of course, Your Lordship. Six valiant men, armed and well fed. Messer Leonardo will be at no risk."

Ludovico rolled his eyes. "Messer Bergonzio, what would the populace think if I were to send a tax collector surrounded by armed henchmen to fetch my most talented engineer and artist?"

"That he . . . I mean that there are issues between you and him, payment issues possibly . . ."

"I see that even you can use your head if you force yourself, Messer Bergonzio. Send one of your men, on his own and unarmed, to fetch Leonardo. Let him come alone, without fanfare or henchmen. And conduct him straight to the hospital room."

"As Your Lordship wishes," Messer Bergonzio, muttered, beginning to feel unwell in earnest.

* * *

"I'd quite like this, too, you know, having an east-facing room," Leonardo said, looking through the window, which had no cloth covering.

Outside, the sun, only apparently static in the sky, was actually rising, clothing with fresh light laden with promises the room and everything in it, including the dozens of coats of arms hanging on the walls, symbols of families of noble lineage, as motionless as befits a nobleman before a lord. And what a lord: Ludovico il Moro, master of Milan, who, they said, had the Pope as his chaplain and the Emperor as his butler. Il Moro was standing in the middle of the most luminous room in his castle: a sumptuous, open, elegant tableau. Too bad about the corpse lying bare-assed on the table in the middle of the room.

"Yes, I'd like it very much. Do you see, Your Lordship, how it provides a totally different perspective? The morning light is the most honest."

I'd quite like an east-facing room too, Ludovico might have replied in normal circumstances, that is, with no infectious corpses in the vicinity. But I, effectively the regent and lord of the city, have to live in the Rochetta, in small, dark, west-facing rooms, until my useless nephew Gian Galeazzo kicks the bucket—although that's something Ludovico would never have said.

"The corpse hasn't been brought here so that you might paint it, Messer Leonardo," Ludovico said curtly. "Magistro Ambrogio claims that the winds that carry the plague spread from east to west, and leaving it thus exposed we put the city at lesser risk of contagion."

You mustn't laugh, modern reader. Ambrogio da Rosate was merely complying with the medical knowledge of the time, which stated that it was the winds, and not bacteria, that carried disease, and that it was also the winds that swept them away, so much so that hospitals back then had doors facing the Vatican, to allow the Holy Spirit easier entry. Leonardo, therefore, found nothing strange in this detail. In another one, however, yes.

"The plague?"

Raising an eyebrow, Leonardo approached the body, which raised no objection.

"He doesn't appear to have died from the plague," Leonardo said confidently. "For a corpse, I'd say he looks quite healthy and blooming. Forgive my flippancy, Your Lordship, but prior to dying, this man was in excellent health."

"That's precisely our problem. He doesn't actually look dead. Magistro Ambrogio says he has no idea what could have caused this man's death. He rules out poisoning or premeditated murder, but what could have caused this man's heart to stop, he says he doesn't know."

"Magistro Ambrogio says he doesn't know. Ah."

Had he been among his family members or in his workshop, he would have blurted out something about Ambrogio da Rosate usually knowing everything, but not in front of il Moro. Of all the duke's counselors, the astrologer was the one whose word was never questioned. He continued:

"If Magistro Ambrogio, the most talented physician and surgeon in the peninsula, said that, then what could a painter like I possibly have to add?"

"Magistro Ambrogio has only seen him from the outside. I'd like you to look at the inside."

"The inside?"

"Is it not true, Messer Leonardo, that you take an interest in anatomy and that, in order to make your paintings and your work more realistic, you usually strip the bodies even more, removing the skin and drawing what they look like then?"

Leonardo stopped breathing. But only for a moment.

In those days, human anatomy was more akin to necromancy than to life drawing. There was a vague, incomplete knowledge of where the organs were positioned, and if something was missing it was replaced by astrological symbols as useful as a screwdriver made of modelling clay. There was a reason for this: dissecting corpses was not easy. Not forbidden, but not easy either. Dissecting horses, dogs, and pigs was feasible. Dissecting a woman was not very hard: after all, as everybody knew, women had no souls, so quartering them in order to inspect their internal organs was not so unseemly or so compromising, as far as eternal life was concerned. But men were a different can of worms. Finding an intact male corpse and gutting it to look inside was neither easy nor without risk for anyone who was not a physician. Leonardo did it, but was not very happy for it to be known, partly because ecclesiastical courts were quick to misunderstand certain things.

"My knowledge of anatomy, Your Lordship, is based on the many cadavers I saw in Florence, including the similarities between men and animals, which makes me conclude that there are analogies and differences between them. You see—"

"Listen to me, Leonardo. I don't give a damn what you do with cadavers, just as long as you don't manufacture your own raw material from living Christians. I'm neither my brother the cardinal nor his friend who's sitting on the throne of Rome. I am, however, the regent of this city, so I'm more concerned with the living than the dead, and with avoiding their joining the ranks of the dead. I need your help."

"If Your Lordship will forgive me again, I already have a lot of work, including, at the top of my list, the bronze horse in memory of your father, so to me every minute is precious."

"I understand, Messer Leonardo. You work very hard and are paid very little. By many people, myself included. Very well, Messer Leonardo. I thank you for coming so promptly, and now I will let you return to your business. This is a time of crisis, isn't it?"

"Alas, yes, Your Lordship. It's no time for mirth. There's little money around and those who have it hold on to it even when they've pledged it."

"I know you're still owed a large payment by the monks of the Immaculate Conception at San Francesco Grande."

"Twelve hundred lire, alas. Both I and the kind De Predis."

"That's extremely unfair," Ludovico said, nodding sympathetically. "You will be paid tomorrow. You have my word."

That was what Leonardo found annoying about Ludovico. He never explicitly promised anything in return for something else. He just made you feel indebted. As though wanting to reiterate that he was the master, that you knew it perfectly well, and that he would still be the master even if you did not take it as understood.

"Your Lordship is too kind. I wonder if . . ."

"Go on."

"If you would like me to, I could at least take a look at this poor wretch, even if only from the outside. Magistro Ambrogio is wise and skilled, but his eyesight isn't what it used to be."

"Please, go ahead."

With barely a hint of hesitation, Leonardo put a hand on the shoulder of the body to test its firmness. Then, with a resolute and much more expert gesture than his previous words had suggested, he put an arm around the waist of the corpse and, almost effortlessly, turned it on its back.

He studied it for a few seconds, staring at it intensely.

"No external marks," he said.

"No," Ludovico replied. "Externally, no marks."

Theoretically, il Moro had said the same thing as Leonardo. In practice, there was a big difference in meaning, one that at this point was hard to ignore.

Just as it was hard not to see that something in Leonardo's expression had altered. It was still serious, but his face no longer had the customary lightness that made those who met him happy. As though he had noticed something that had escaped the duke's astrologer, but wasn't entirely certain.

The two men were silent for a few more seconds.

"I shall require a few things," Leonardo said in a practical tone, breaking the silence.

"I'll send you my chamberlain immediately."

"Thank you," Leonardo replied, not weighing down his answer with unnecessary titles and possessive pronouns. "Also please have Giacomo Salaì fetched from my workshop. And don't let anybody in apart from those two."

FIVE

"Very well," Ludovico said in a low voice, looking around, "let those two in."

The room wasn't at all as bright as the one in which he had left Leonardo. In fact, it was the darkest, most secluded room in the castle. He had chosen it deliberately, hoping his guests would appreciate it.

It was a corner room, without windows, where the only ventilation was provided by a chimney flue that could barely draw away the smoke from the wood that burned there constantly, from fall to spring.

From the door, the castellan nodded, then turned, opened the door wide, and announced in a loud voice:

"His Most Excellent Lordship Philippe Duke of Commynes and Signor Perron de Basche request admission to your Lordship's presence."

"Come in, my dear Duke, come in," Ludovico said, practically stepping over the castellan with his far from formal greeting, and motioning to him to leave them alone. "We've been very much looking forward to seeing you. How are you, my dear Philippe?"

"With God's help and His Most Christian Majesty's favor, very well, Your Lordship," the duke replied, bowing slightly. "And how are you?"

"Well, very well. I must first of all apologize for the delay in receiving you properly, but we've had a small mishap and I've had to intervene personally."

"Your Lordship is too kind, deigning to receive us in person like this," Perron de Basche replied, in an accent that was in no way French but, rather, vaguely Umbrian. The ambassador had in fact been born in Orvieto, but had been in the service of the French for so long that he considered himself Transalpine in every respect. "You must have a thousand other things to do."

"All of them less important than the one we need to discuss, my dear Perron and my dear Duke," Ludovico replied, looking at the two ambassadors. "And that is precisely why I decided to receive you in this place, and alone. I am eager to hear an initial report on the situation from Signor de Basche, and this is the most secluded room in my modest castle. Please, let us sit down."

And Ludovico motioned to the solid chestnut table that dominated the middle of the room, supported by a heavy central foot with a square base, and carved with floral patterns and the inscription HERCULES DVX FERRARIAE DONAVIT: a wedding present from Ludovico's father-in-law, and one of the most gratefully received. A lord's best friend, Ercole had said, slapping the table top. When you sit down to talk at a table like this, you can be sure people will listen.

The Duke of Commynes and Perron de Basche looked at one another. As seasoned diplomats, they both knew that it was never advisable to discuss delicate situations in detail when you've only just arrived and are tired, hungry, and all shaken up after hours of galloping.

Realizing their embarrassment, Ludovico smiled and opened his hands. "Needless to say, this room is at your full disposal so that you can discuss your business in private, and then relate to me in detail over the next two days how much His Most Christian Majesty requires, so that we may then talk about it properly. For now, I would like to know what the situation below the Alps is, and if it is still favorable to our purpose."

The two ambassadors heaved sighs of relief. Perron de Basche was about to say something when the duke got in first by putting a hand on his shoulder.

"We thank Your Lordship for his hospitality. May I be so bold as to remind Your Lordship that my two aides-de-camp, Robinot and Mattenet, are in the quarters reserved for the retinue? If we could possibly meet with them . . ."

"As you wish. You may go to them in their quarters, but I think it would be more fitting to your rank that they should come to you. I will instruct the servants to allow them access to your rooms."

"Your Lordship is most kind," the duke said, taking a seat. "So, Perron, please deliver your report to His Lordship, and to me, too. We haven't had the chance to exchange a single word yet."

"Your Lordship was inquiring about the situation. I would say that it is more than favorable. Florence is just as I told you last June. The Council of the Seventy holds an ambiguous position, but that's not what matters. What matters is the will of the people, and the people are completely on the side of His Most Christian Majesty, our king."

"And what does Piero say?"

"Forgive my candor, but Piero is of no consequence. At the moment, the most important man in Florence is Brother Girolamo Savonarola. And Savonarola calls Charles VIII God's envoy, who will punish anyone who soils his hands with the devil's excrement."

Ludovico nodded gravely.

It often happens that heads of state—powerful, enlightened men, authentic visionaries able to combine genius and common sense—are punished with an idiot first-born who has neither. Nowadays, this is usually a private matter, but in the Renaissance, when power was handed down from father to son, it could be a public catastrophe. And so when Lorenzo—not yet known as the Magnificent—died, he was succeeded by his son Piero, who was immediately nicknamed the Unfortunate. Strong but stupid: in other words, the opposite of his father.

"I don't have much to add to what we discussed in June," Perron de Basche continued tendentiously, as though about to proceed down the Italian peninsula realm by realm. "If the situation has altered, then it has altered for the better, as I was saying. If we want to cross Italy and enter the Kingdom of Aragon, there's no better time. The Pope who has just died was displeased because the Aragons in Naples didn't pay their tithes, and the new one, the Borgia, seems more interested in a woman named Vannozza than in our movements . . ."

"Good," il Moro quickly cut in. "Duke, Signor, this is music to my ears. As sweet as the music of your Josquin des Prez. If you wish, you can soon hear one of his most recent compositions. Thank you for the time you have granted me before you have even had the opportunity to take refreshments and rest. I shall expect you at dinner this evening. We will have a rich banquet and even richer delight from our court acrobats. In the meantime, feel free to use my castle and your rooms entirely as you wish. My respects, gentlemen."

And with this he stood up and walked to the door.

The Duke of Commynes pondered for a few seconds, then turned to his almost-countryman.

"Perron."

"Yes, Duke?"

"What do you think?"

"We're in for a treat, Duke. I was afraid that at dinner we'd have to listen to a rosary of motets by Josquin des Prez. I much prefer the acrobats. At least we'll stay awake."

"Oh, I agree, Perron. But that wasn't what I meant."

"What, then?"

"Didn't Ludovico strike you as nervous?"

* * *

"Of course I'm nervous, Galeazzo. So would you be. I have a dead man who died of nobody knows what in my own court-yard, that's already unpleasant enough."

"What does Magistro Ambrogio say?"

"Magistro Ambrogio says it's not the plague, but I also want to hear Messer Leonardo's opinion. I'm not afraid of what I know, Galeazzo. It's what I don't know that scares me. When I see two things happen in rapid succession, I can't help but wonder if by any chance the second was caused by the first."

"The second? What was the first?"

"The first, I now discover, is that the gentleman who was so lacking in decorum as to kick the bucket in my courtyard had requested an audience with me only yesterday."

"Are you sure?"

"I asked Botta to check the lists." Ludovico opened a yel-lowish sheet of paper covered in tiny, precise handwriting. Typical of a miser like Botta, Galeazzo Sanseverino thought. True, paper is expensive, but this is going too far. "Rambaldo Chiti, a painter and printer. He comes to see me, and the next day he dies."

"And is this a reason to worry? Listen to me, Ludovico. How many people request an audience with you every week?"

"Oh, many. Dozens and dozens."

"And how many people die every week here in Milan?"

"Yes, you're right, Galeazzo. Even so . . . Ah, here he is. Yes, yes, do come in, Magistro Ambrogio."

Ambrogio da Rosate crossed the room majestically, his face even more funereal than usual. He looked the very image of a bird of ill omen.

"At Your Lordship's service."

"So tell me, Magistro Ambrogio. What do the stars say?"

"It's a disease, Your Lordship. The position of Mars leaves

no room for doubt. There's a clear threat to the city, but it definitely does not come from war or violence. It comes from inside the city itself."

"A disease? And what disease would that be?"

"That, the stars don't say, Your Lordship."

"Hmmm," Galeazzo, said with a doubtful expression. "It seems to me that being so far up, they surely must know quite a lot."

"Captain, Magistro Ambrogio is doing what he knows best," Ludovico replied in a conciliatory tone.

"In other words, talking nonsense," Galeazzo retorted. "If I were you—"

"*I* am me, Galeazzo," Ludovico answered, calmly but distantly. "It is you who are perhaps not in control of what you're saying."

There followed a few moments of understandable awkwardness, during which Ludovico placed his hands on the armrests of his chair and Galeazzo stared at a dot on the wall to avoid meeting the eyes of both his father-in-law and the astrologer.

"Thank you for your invaluable oracle, Magistro Ambrogio. You may go now. Galeazzo, please run and ascertain the condition of the dead man. I need hardly tell you, gentlemen, not to talk about this even between yourselves, except in my presence."

* * *

"Of course, of course. We shan't talk about it to a living soul."

"Good. And now it's time to act, not talk. How do you propose to do this?"

The Duke of Commynes's two aides-de-camp looked at each other before speaking.

"We must first see the man we need to deal with," one of them, the shorter one, said. His name was Robinot and he was a stout little man with a woolen hat that concealed a scabby head, and who had a total of seven or eight teeth left even though he wasn't all that old, somewhere between twenty-five and fifty, to be precise. "But I don't think there'll be any problems. If I understood your description correctly, he's a man of average build man and prone to absent-mindedness."

"And if there are any problems, then *whack!*" said the other one, a big, dark-haired lad with very pale skin, sky-blue eyes, and the determined expression of someone who knows what he has to do, provided he's told beforehand. Not the sharpest tool in the box, this Jaufré Mattenet. Tall, slim, good-looking, well-built—the exact opposite of his sidekick—but also rather silly.

"*Whack?*" Commynes said, looking gravely at the young man. "No, my friend. If there's a problem, you just walk away. Remember, not a single hair on Messer Leonardo's head must be touched. You must get your result as carefully and discreetly as possible."

"Trust me, Master Commynes," Robinot said. "I could swipe the duchess's bonnet and she wouldn't even notice. So a notebook's no problem. You see, the important thing is that its owner should be distracted, engaged in something else that draws his attention. We can even do it tonight, at dinner. Tell me, is this Leonardo a big eater?"

"No, not at all. He eats no meat and is a man of remarkable restraint."

"I see. Is he given to drink? Does he like to pour himself one cup too many?"

"I don't think so. And bear in mind that at formal dinners it's the servants who pour the wine. You won't be able to top him up to your heart's content."

"That's too bad." Robinot seemed absorbed in thought for

a moment. "Will there be a performance during dinner? Acrobats, jugglers, mummers, jesters? Could he be engrossed in watching them?"

"Possible, but difficult. From what I know, the staging of such entertainment is often assigned to him. As a matter of fact, he usually goes around the tables and entertains the most honored guests with his jokes. He's an extremely affable man. Actually, I think he's the most affable man in all of Milan."

"Where Bacchus can't go, Venus flies to the rescue," Robinot said. "Could you bring to dinner a whore he doesn't know, perhaps from outside the castle?"

The Duke of Commynes shook his head. "I couldn't, and it wouldn't be any use anyway. I couldn't because at dinners with ambassadors il Moro admits only women from his court. And it wouldn't be any use because Messer Leonardo has Venetian tastes and isn't tempted by women, period. Perhaps not by men either, so they say."

"All right. In that case, Duke, you need to make him talk. When he approaches you, you must try to make him talk, and agree with him even when he talks the greatest nonsense in the world."

"Messer Leonardo is unlikely to talk nonsense," Perron de Basche remarked, looking up at the ceiling.

"Better still. Try to win him over in any way you can, Duke." Robinot smiled, which made him look even more unsightly. That happens when more than twenty of your thirty-two teeth are missing. "When people talk, they forget about the rest of the world. You could pull out one of their molars and they wouldn't even notice if they're busy talking about themselves. All men are like that, all of them. And if this fellow is a man, then there has to be some way of tricking him. Even if his name is Leonardo da Vinci."

* * *

"Leonardo da Vinci?"

"He's still inside, Captain," the guard at the door of the room said, standing aside.

Without a word, Galeazzo walked in and saw Leonardo standing by the table, grave-faced.

"My respects, Messer Leonardo. Have you finished examining the corpse?"

"Just this minute, at His Lordship's request," Leonardo replied, still with that grave expression on his face. It was unusual to see him looking so grim.

Galeazzo Sanseverino looked around. On the table, the corpse lay dismembered, its chest cavity open and the organs lying around it, like garments pulled from a drawer in haste. A sight that would have made anybody's stomach turn, and indeed poor Salaì looked pale and deeply upset.

"So, young Giacomo, men aren't so beautiful on the inside, are they?"

"No, Signor Galeazzo," the boy replied, walking past him with a quick bow.

"Please don't throw up on me, I'm wearing new clothes." Galeazzo watched as the youth, looking like death warmed over, put away the tools. The little rascal. It had been two or three years since he had filched his pouch, with half a lira inside it, but Galeazzo Sanseverino was not the kind to forget something easily, whether it was good or bad. And that little rascal, likeable as he was, was definitely on the bad side. "So, Messer Leonardo, what can you tell me? What disease killed this poor wretch?"

"What can I say, Captain?" Leonardo replied, wiping his hands with a rag. How they had managed it wasn't clear but, whereas Salaì was covered in blood and other things from top to toe, Leonardo was still as neat and clean as when he had first walked in. "What disease, you ask? It's a disease that's very difficult to avoid, Captain."

"*That?*"

"Worse, Captain. Much worse. Human wickedness." Leonardo threw the rag down on the table, next to the corpse. "This poor man, you see, was murdered."

"Murdered?" Galeazzo said in surprise.

"Murdered. Suffocated, to be precise. Death by lack of air in the lungs."

"But if you will excuse me, Messer Leonardo, that's impossible. I have more than once seen what a strangled man looks like, and they certainly don't look this peaceful." Galeazzo failed to mention that he had strangled a couple of gentlemen himself—it didn't seem relevant at the moment. "Their tongues, eyes, faces—"

"Forgive me, I may have been unclear. I didn't say strangled or throttled. I said suffocated."

"Of course, Messer Leonardo. But even so, if something had been rammed down the poor man's mouth, his eyes would have been twisted, and—"

"No, no. Nothing like that. There's no trace of fiber between his teeth, nor was his mouth forced open. And there are no bruises. Forgive me, Captain, but I think something different happened."

"Something different? What, for Heaven's sake?"

"Ah. What, you ask me? Well, it's not at all easy to explain. I think we should go together to His Lordship."

From the Writing Desk of Giacomo Trotti

To Ercole d'Este, Duke of Ferrara, ferre

My Most Illustrious and Highly Esteemed Lord,
A sumptuous dinner cum *much pomp was held last evening to welcome the French ambassadors,* id est *the Duke of Comminè* et *a certain Signor Perrone de' Baschi,* et *large quantities of food and wine were served that were a pleasure to behold,* et *indeed a large number of peasants came to the castle to watch and cheer.*

Giacomo Trotti put down his pen and massaged his hand by rubbing it against his thigh. It was late October and already very chilly at this time of day, so removing his gloves in order to write was quite a torture.

The ambassador of Ferrara liked to wake early in the morning and write to his master about the previous day's events with a cool mind and detached calm. A low-key, informal letter that would be dispatched by that morning's horse post at about the time of terce. That is why the letter had been marked *ferre*, carry, and not *cito*, make haste.

Between courses, a few young men performed ball games and leaps, and the dwarf Catrozzo made everyone laugh uproariously, both voluntarily et etiam *involuntarily, because in order to jest with the jumpers, he had to climb on the table using the sleeve of one of the French party, who let go of him abruptly, causing Catrozzo to fall off the table and go crashing to the ground, much to the hilarity of the guests.*

The Duke of Comminè sat beside Leonardo di Ser Piero and talked of many things in genere et in spetie, *chiefly about matters of money. Comminè wished to know how much Leonardo was being paid,* etiam *how often,* et *I think this was a way of finding out about the state of His Lordship Ludovico's affairs* et *how he would be able to wage war.*

The ambassador of Ferrara put down the goose quill again, got up from the writing desk, went to the window, and pushed the cloth aside.

Outside, the pink dawn was caressing the darkness away, tinging it with blue, apart from a few meaningless clouds here and there.

Giacomo Trotti had never understood how some people could predict the weather by looking at the sky, how they could say "it's going to rain tomorrow," "it'll be sunny again in two or three days," or "it smells like snow." To Trotti, the clouds, the sky and the winds were silent details, whose dynamics had uncertain, deceptive, and unavoidable consequences.

What Trotti was good at was reading men.

Grasping their intentions. From the way they moved. From what they said and how they said it. Especially by how these two things compared, whether they matched and were appropriate to the context.

And Trotti would have bet his life that the two Frenchmen were there to ask for a loan. The repeated compliments, the forced admiration, all that praise that seemed to leave large oily stains on il Moro's clothes. Besides, it was no secret that what Ludovico could not achieve with his power he achieved with his money. As for the rest—the embassies, the preparations, the speeches of the aides-de-camp—they were just excuses. These men were here to beg for money, no doubt about it. But it was still too soon to unsettle Ercole or to alarm him about the financial affairs of his son-in-law and beloved daughter. Tomorrow, if he turned out to be correct, he would be more specific.

At one point during dinner, Messer Leonardo took offense, perhaps because the interrogation had become annoying, or perhaps because the henchmen of Comminè spilled a bucket of wine on his favorite garment, et *then made matters worse by trying to help him clean himself, so much so that I heard* cum *clarity Messer Leonardo, who is usually gentle and sweet-natured, speak words to him that I believe are used in Tuscany, telling him to go to a place that decency and my respect for Your Excellency prevents me from naming.*

I also had the impression that Ludovico was equally cold toward Leonardo, something for which I do not know the reason, although I can hazard a guess that it might be in connection with the ongoing issue of the famous bronze horse, which has caused a deterioration in relations between the two men.

Once again, Giacomo Trotti looked at the sky. The clouds might have moved, or maybe not. Later, it might rain, or maybe not. At any rate, there was nothing he could do about it. Where men were concerned, though, he could intervene. He could hear, listen, understand, wait, and act. Or, even better, let them act. All it took was a word here, a nod there, a well-timed silence. A kind of social lubricant, that was what Giacomo Trotti considered himself to be. Not a pottery vase among iron vases, which could be crushed at any moment, but oil between two parts of a machine, of a mechanism, one of those levers Messer Leonardo was so good at devising. And because he was so fluid, not only did he not crumble but, on the contrary, he was able to make it possible for both parts of the machine, each solid and powerful in itself, to work in tandem, however different their functions.

Rather like money. Money, too, had always been a lubricant for Giacomo Trotti. A convenient remedy for making a trade more equal. I have something worth ten, you have something worth six, give me four and the deal is done. That's why it works. That was how Trotti had always viewed money. And when money runs out, the mechanism breaks down. Which was probably the reason for the frostiness between Ludovico and Leonardo da Vinci.

But there might be another reason for this regrettable situation. Fertur that the body of one Rambaldo Chiti, a painter, was discovered at the castle et that Chiti died of a divine curse. This could well be causing great distress to Ludovico, who, as Your Excellency knows, is prone to superstition and to seeing ill omens everywhere. Whatever the reason, the atmosphere in the castle is not good, and although the dinner included an abundance of wine, it lacked merriment and ended much earlier than usual.

After dinner, I saw Ludovico lead Beatrice away with caresses and demonstrations of affection and your Most Illustrious daughter reciprocate as she happily followed him to the Rochetta rooms. Countess Bergamini, also—as Your Excellency recalls—known as Cecilia Gallerani, was not at the dinner, nor have I seen her of late. The castle is so large and so well guarded that I do not always have the opportunity to keep a close eye on its master or what is around him.

And that's pretty clear to those who get it. I haven't yet been able to ascertain, my dear Ercole, whether your daughter is being cheated on, but rest assured that if il Moro wants to cheat on her, he will. Regardless of me, of your daughter, or of you, Ercole, Duke of Ferrara.

As ever, I commend myself to your benevolence.
Mediolano, XX octubris 1493
Servus Jacomo Trotti

Six

Messer Leonardo, what a pleasure to see you."

"Countess, Cecilia, the pleasure is mine. Thank you for taking the trouble to see me so quickly."

Walking beneath the open galley, Cecilia had now come close enough to Leonardo to realize that he was frowning. Around them, the inner courtyard of Palazzo Carmagnola was peaceful and quiet, the exact opposite of the Piazzale at Porta Giovia.

"Don't mention it," Cecilia Gallerani said, taking Leonardo's stiff, cold hands in her own, which were warm and soft. "Rather, I hope there is nothing alarming about the reasons for your visit. I was expecting you tomorrow, for the music. What brings you here with such urgency?"

"I would rather discuss it in a secluded place, Countess."

"Is it something that happened at the castle?" Tersilla asked. She was one of Cecilia's ladies-in-waiting, the most affable in manner but also the most petulant.

"Tersilla, don't annoy Messer Leonardo . . ."

"It's about that man found dead in the Piazzale delle Armi, isn't it? Is it true he died by the wrath of God?"

"Who told you these things, Tersilla?"

"Everybody knows," Tersilla said with a shrug. "It's all anybody was talking about here in the Broletto today, and Friar Gioacchino also mentioned him in his sermon. They saw Magistro Ambrogio cross the castle in a huge rush, getting dressed as he went."

"You see, Messer Leonardo, it's as I've always told you," Cecilia said, chuckling. "It's impossible to keep a secret in the castle. There are always too many people about, too many people haunting the place. When I was still living at the castle, there was even an ape who would wander about the Piazzale delle Armi dressed as an armiger."

"He's still there," Leonardo said. "His Lordship says he's more disciplined than half his servants, and from what I hear he has a point."

"Come, then. Tersilla, Messer Leonardo and I are going into the blue hall. Do not disturb us for any reason."

"As you wish, Countess."

* * *

"So, Messer Leonardo," Cecilia said, chuckling again. "Did someone die in the castle by divine will?"

"Far from it," Leonardo replied, sinking into the highly uncomfortable wood and fabric seat he preferred, for reasons that were somewhat unclear, to the soft leather armchairs available everywhere else in the hall. "It's convenient to invoke divine wrath whenever there's something we don't understand. We used to do it about eclipses, thousands of years ago. Then we learned that the motions of the stars can be predicted. But then, since we didn't understand anything and couldn't predict anything other than the motions of the stars, we convinced ourselves that from the motions of the stars we could work out men's destinies. It's rather like that joke about a man searching in a puddle in an alley beneath a torch attached to a wall. What are you looking for, my good man? I'm looking for a ducat I lost, he replies. And did you lose it in that puddle? No, he replies, I dropped it over there, in a puddle in the middle of the alley. So why are you looking for it here? Because there's light here, the man replies, pointing to the torch."

Cecilia gave an affected laugh, her hand on her throat. Then she looked at Leonardo. "Do you have something against the Duke's astrologer, by any chance?"

"A pompous ass," Leonardo replied. "Only good at spouting hollow words. And I'm also afraid I've committed a grave indelicacy."

"So tell me. Tell me about the dead man. First of all, what did he die of?"

* * *

"He was murdered, Your Lordship."

"Murdered?"

"Suffocated, to be precise."

Ludovico glanced at Galeazzo, who returned a blank look. "He doesn't look like a strangled man."

"Of course not. The man was suffocated by mechanical constriction."

"Please explain this fully, Messer Leonardo."

"You see, Your Lordship, a man breathes by mechanically letting the air into his thorax, in other words by expanding his chest and increasing its volume." Leonardo put his hands on his chest and took a deep breath, emphasizing the movement of his ribs with his palms. "The movements of water and air are similar in nature, as both tend to fill any receptacle you place around them. But there's a difference between air and water: one can be compressed, squashed, reduced in volume, while the other cannot. You can blow a little into a pig's bladder, tie it with a string, and squeeze it in your hands until it grows so small it becomes very resistant to more compression and you can't go any farther. But that's not possible if the bladder is full of water. And just as air can be squashed, so a body full of air can be compressed. But if there's an orifice through which it can escape, the air is expelled and never gets back in."

After thinking this over for a moment, Ludovico looked at Leonardo again. "I don't think you've fully explained yourself, Messer Leonardo."

"I think that poor wretch's chest was constricted in a corset, a doublet, which compressed and squeezed his chest so tightly that it expelled all the air from his body and prevented him from broadening it to let more in."

"What leads you to this conclusion?"

"When I dissected the body, I saw that the ribs and ribcage were fractured. Not in the bones, but in the soft joints that link the ribs to the spinal column and to the bone that acts as a shield to the heart. As if something had pressed in on him from all directions."

Ludovico joined his hands, raised them in front of his mouth, and rubbed them together. A few seconds later, he looked up again. "And can one die from something like that?"

"Yes, Your Lordship, just as one can die by drowning or in any other accident that deprives one of air."

"Magistro Ambrogio, what do you think?"

Ambrogio da Rosate lifted his chin almost imperceptibly and indicated the vault of the ceiling with his hand. "The stars point to a death from disease, Messer Leonardo. The position of Mars leaves no room for doubt."

"I am happy for you that you are able to read so many things in the stars, Magistro Ambrogio," Leonardo said, opening his hands. "The stars barely show me where north is."

"Your observations concern the body, a mere mortal object," Ambrogio replied gravely. "Mine concern the stars, the first and most obvious manifestation of the Eternal. I hope you're not trying to compare what you see in a body with what you see in the stars."

"Forgive me, Magistro Ambrogio, but yesterday you, too, examined the body to see if there were any signs of disease or violence."

"Since we have the body, it's the first thing to do to get an idea of what happened. But in order to obtain certainty, and to connect the past and the future, it's necessary to consider the stars. The stars never lie."

If Ambrogio da Rosate and Leonardo had been alone at dinner, Leonardo would probably have launched into a disquisition on the peculiar etymology of the verb "to consider," which in fact, with his poor knowledge of Latin, he had thought might be translated as *cum sideribus*: "with the stars." But since they weren't in a pub, but in front of the Lord of Milan, and since that crimson-clad clothes horse thought he could disparage his science, Leonardo took it very badly. Where knowledge was concerned, Ser Piero's son held it in much higher esteem than he held himself.

"I understand." Leonardo turned to Ludovico with the air of someone forced to hear that the moon is made of cheese. "Like that Dominican friar who told His Lordship your brother was born under the influence of the stars and predicted that he would conquer the Peloponnese, Asia, Africa, and the whole of *Mare Nostrum*. What was his name? Annio da Viterbo?"

As everybody knows, Leonardo was a genius. It therefore did not take him long, barely one billionth of the time Jupiter takes to complete a revolution around the sun, to realize that he'd just committed the mistake of the century.

To remind Ludovico il Moro that his brother, Galeazzo Maria, had believed in the horoscope provided by an astrologer monk who'd told him he would conquer the world was not a clever move, especially since the same Galeazzo Maria had been stabbed to death less than three years later in that same Milan from which he had never budged.

"If you wish to do true honor to the memory of my family, you would do well to hurry up and finish the monument I commissioned you to build several years ago, rather than doubting the words of Magistro Ambrogio."

* * *

"So he didn't believe you?" Cecilia shook her head grace-fully. "My poor Leonardo, you really did say the wrong thing at the wrong time. When will you learn that there are certain topics Ludovico can't abide?"

"I don't think I ever will, Countess Cecilia. That's why I'm here to ask for your help."

* * *

"So why doesn't he put my father in command of the troops? Ercole is the bravest, most valiant man south of the Alps and, from what I hear, north of them, too. Of His Most Cretinous Majesty King Charles's henchmen, only the Duke of Orleans is a worthy warrior."

"My Lady, I would advise you to speak more softly when you touch on subjects pertaining to foreign policy."

Beatrice d'Este stopped abruptly, looking slightly vexed. Of course, Trotti was her father's ambassador in Milan, a prudent, experienced man, but Beatrice was unable to appreciate these qualities. All she could see was a bald, annoying little old man who was always feeling the cold, always agreed with everyone, but then did what he pleased.

"I am in my palace, after all."

Not quite your palace, my girl, Trotti thought. If you were the mistress of the place, you'd live in the large east wing, not here in the Rochetta, in these tiny rooms filled with luxuries but no light. And where it's freezing cold.

"That's precisely what worries me, my Lady. We're in the Castello Sforzesco. Here, even the floors have ears."

"In any case, you said you will shortly be having an audi-ence with my husband. Why don't you ask him straight out to appoint my father commander-in-chief?"

Giacomo Trotti looked at the girl like someone who knows he can turn to a person of superior intelligence. "My Lady, you know only too well that in matters such as these, the most important thing is to keep a balance between the powers at play, so that the outcome may be as close to what His Most Illustrious Lordship—the Duke your husband—wishes.

Giacomo Trotti waited for a length of time we would nowadays quantify as one tenth of a second, but which nobody back then would have dreamed it was possible to measure.

If Beatrice had been as intelligent as Trotti's expression was trying to make her believe, there would have been no need to explain anything.

The point for il Moro was not to invade Naples but to keep the Duke of Orléans out of his noble way long enough. In order to launch and carry out the invasion, King Charles VIII needed the steadfast commitment of the Duke of Orléans, given the fact that on his own he was unable to pull a finger out of his ass, let alone win a war.

Busy crossing Italy in order to invade Naples, the Duke of Orléans would certainly not be able to wage war on Ludovico il Moro and then claim the title of Lord of Milan.

The war needed to last long enough for Il Moro to be acknowledged as Duke of Milan by Maximilian I and acclaimed by the people.

Now, as we have already said, Beatrice's father, Ercole I d'Este, was not just any minor lord. He was a man who had waged and won wars for real. Above all, he was someone who had actually learned military strategy and tactics in Naples. Putting at Orléans's side a worthy, intelligent, brave man like Ercole d'Este, one who, in addition, was familiar with the enemy, would considerably shorten the war. And this, given il Moro's purpose, was tantamount to his slamming a hoe down on his own feet.

Since Beatrice was only pretending to think, Trotti continued:

"A river in flood cannot be stopped but only channeled. When His Illustrious Lordship bursts the dam of the Alps, the French river will flood Naples. And to get the waters to flow where we want them to, we need levees, not shepherds."

"You're very poetic, Messer Giacomo. You almost sound like Messer Leonardo."

Trotti stood there, silent and still. One of the things he excelled at and that had made him the perfect ambassador. He always knew when it was inadvisable to expose himself.

"I don't like Messer Leonardo. He's always smiling. He's always calm and cheerful like . . ."

"Like who, my Lady?"

"Like someone who knows that things will turn out well for him even if they turn out badly. Do you think he's trustworthy, Ambassador?"

"I'm not as privy to life in the castle as you are, my Lady. I see Messer Leonardo on Thursdays, when—"

Beatrice d'Este huffed and turned away. "When you go to hear music and discuss incomprehensible things at the Milanese whore's house, of course. I wonder what she'll be wearing tomorrow. Probably three dresses one on top of the other. She's so skinny, she'd look dead otherwise."

"I can assure you that the last few times I saw the Lady Gallerani, she wasn't wearing any new garments or adornments."

"Do you think she'd be so foolish as to wear them when you're around, Messer Giacomo? She may be a slut, but she's not a fool. Keep your eyes peeled, Ambassador. I'm not asking you, I'm ordering you."

* * *

"Then what are Your Lordship's orders?"

Ludovico turned to Galeazzo, aware that he, too, had a good

mind and that his opinion should be taken into account, although not as much as that of the ducal astrologer.

"What do you think, Captain?"

Galeazzo Sanseverino nodded, as though to show that he appreciated the attention. "If Magistro Ambrogio is right, Your Lordship, this wretch died from a disease. If so, everybody who lives near Chiti's house will have been exposed to the same winds. It would be advisable to go to his workshop, close and bolt all the doors and windows, and evacuate all the surrounding houses as a precautionary measure."

If, however, this wizard has been talking nonsense, then Rambaldo Chiti was murdered, as Messer Leonardo says. And if that's the case, it'd be worth going to his house and rummaging around to try and find out who he was, who he associated with, and why somebody decided not only to kill him but also to dump him in the middle of the castle courtyard.

"Do you think this is advisable, Magistro Ambrogio?"

"I agree with Captain Sanseverino, Your Lordship."

"Very well. Galeazzo, send for the captain of justice and tell him to find this poor Rambaldo Chiti's house and close it up. But don't move the neighboring population out. For now, this would only alarm them needlessly."

"If Your Lordship will allow me, I should like to go with the captain of justice."

Or, in modern lingo: Do you know how scared I am of the disease this idiot is convinced has killed the wretch? The square root of zero.

"Of course you are allowed, Messer Galeazzo. By all means go, and may God watch over you. Chamberlain, what do we have now?"

"Ambassador Giacomo Trotti, envoy of Ercole, Duke of Ferrara."

"Good. Gentlemen, leave us, and show Ambassador Trotti in."

* * *

"You do understand that, as an ambassador, it is my duty, not just in my own interest but on instructions from my master, to ask you such unpleasant questions."

Giacomo Trotti stood before Ludovico il Moro, who was sitting in his high-backed chair. Even so, it was il Moro who was in an uncomfortable position at that moment. Trotti's question was not the kind you could circumvent.

"May I ask how you found out, Messer Giacomo?"

The first rule of a good politician: Always answer a question with another question.

"The rumor is starting to spread across Milan, Your Lordship. Even this morning at terce, Friar Gioacchino da Brenno mentioned it in his sermon."

"Friar Gioacchino?"

That's all I needed, Ludovico thought, trying to conceal his annoyance. But Trotti noticed it for sure.

"What did Friar Gioacchino say exactly?"

Something I could send him on a visit to the papal prisons for, perhaps? Something that would teach him to bother with the Lord's business, meaning the Lord of Milan, not the one up in Heaven?

"He said that divine wrath has struck this city, and that this death is the work and will of the Almighty, just like Lorenzo de' Medici's death in Florence. That the devil's excrement, money, has taken possession of this city, and that the Almighty will chase the merchants from the temple, starting with the leader of these merchants."

"And that would be me, according to Friar Gioacchino?"

"I would never dare suggest that. So is the unhappy news true?"

Giacomo Trotti, too, was a good politician.

"I'm afraid it is. A man, a poor painter, was found dead in

the Piazzale delle Armi yesterday during lauds. Magistro Ambrogio is convinced the cause of death is natural but unknown to him. Messer Leonardo, on the other hand, claims the man was murdered. As you can appreciate, both theories worry me far more than divine wrath."

Ludovico did not deem it appropriate to mention that the dead man had requested an audience the day before turning up dead. As a reason to worry, a corpse in the courtyard was already more than sufficient.

"I understand you well, Your Lordship."

"I know you are a clever, careful man, Messer Giacomo. That is why I should like your opinion."

"I am at your Lordship's service."

"At the banquet yesterday, I saw Messer Leonardo talking with the two French ambassadors, and at a certain point I had the impression he became angry. That's quite unusual for Messer Leonardo. Do you know what they were talking about, or what happened?"

"Nothing serious, Your Lordship. One of the envoys in the Duke of Commynes's retinue spilled a large quantity of wine over Leonardo's clothes in a truly odd way, almost as though on purpose rather than out of clumsiness. Until then, the conversation had been about money."

"Money?"

"Apparently, the French were very interested in how much Leonardo earns, and how Your Lordship pays him."

"Ah."

"If I may be so bold, Your Lordship . . ."

Ludovico opened his arms in a gesture of impatient welcome. "As a matter of fact, I would appreciate it, Ambassador. You know how much I respect your judgment."

Giacomo Trotti closed his eyes and gave an almost imperceptible bow. Then, having cleared his throat, he said, "Winter is almost upon us, which is not the best time to start a war by crossing the Alps. I think the French gentlemen are here primarily to ask for money. Their questions, I believe, are just a way of finding out how much Your Lordship is able to draw from the treasury to lend the French for their war effort."

Ludovico smiled. Whenever the ambassador of Ferrara opened his mouth, he spoke sense. And in this case, as Ludovico knew perfectly well, Trotti was absolutely right.

"I think as you do, Messer Giacomo. But there is another possibility, and I would genuinely like to make sure I am not wrong."

"If I understand correctly, Your Lordship requires my humble services to get to the bottom of this conundrum."

"Precisely, Messer Giacomo." Ludovico leaned his torso and head out of the chair, reducing the distance between himself and the ambassador. "In not just my interest, but ours, I have a mission for you."

* * *

"Do as you see fit. Meanwhile, you've been given a mission and all you've managed to do so far is make yourself look ridiculous."

"You're right. You're absolutely right, Duke."

"I don't care about being right!" The Duke of Commynes slammed a hand down on the table, probably causing himself an injury, but not letting it show. "I need that notebook, Robinot."

Robinot stood before the duke, head down, having removed his cap in deference and then put it back on again in obedience ("oh, do cover up that worm-eaten skull of yours, you're repulsive" were the duke's exact words). Behind him, listening without the least intention of opening his mouth—grateful for once that he wasn't the one speaking and that he was of less consequence—stood Mattenet.

"But of course, of course. As I was telling Your Lordship, it's always a matter of trial and error. Now we can rule out being dextrous in a crowded place, and we must act in the dark."

"That may well be the case, Robinot," Perron de Basche added, snickering. "Partly because Leonardo is hardly likely to let you anywhere near him again if he recognizes you. What on earth possessed you to use the rabbit?"

* * *

"I'd heard that live rabbits are used at elegant banquets to wipe one's hands, so when I saw them in the hall and saw other guests do that, I thought I could use one to distract Leonardo. I thought he would—"

"You thought it would be a good idea to rub Messer Leonardo with a live rabbit to wipe away the wine. I saw you. As a matter of fact, many people saw you." It wasn't clear whether the Duke of Commynes was more annoyed by the lack of notebooks or the lack of good manners. "Rabbits can be patted, Robinot, which is how you wipe the grease from your fingers, but they can't be used as cloths, for God's sake! It would be like cleaning your teeth with a fork! Now get out of here and try to think of something better."

"By Your Lordship's leave . . ."

The two petty thieves left, closing the door carefully behind them. Perron de Basche turned to the duke.

"So you also agree that we absolutely have to get our hands on that notebook."

The duke, who was blowing on his hand, nodded before replying. "Without a doubt. I had the distinct impression yesterday that Messer Leonardo cannot be corrupted in any way. He works for il Moro, period."

"Or else he knows that, for all our promises, we couldn't

pay him as much as Ludovico pays him," Signor de Basche remarked. "Which brings us back to our primary aim. We have to put our request to Ludovico. We need thirty thousand ducats, and we need them quickly."

SEVEN

Horse. A beautiful horse. It almost looks like Galeazzo's Sicilian. But this one's more beautiful. The legs are too thin. But the muscles are well in evidence. It's the muscles that give the impression of movement. The muscle tense, the leg flexed, making for strength. And the proportions. If you make the horse's leg as long as it actually is, the statue will look motionless. Remember, you must make it a little longer than in real life. The back leg shorter, contracted, pushing. The front leg longer, thrusting. But that's design. Muscles are art. The horse has to be smooth, and the muscles well in evidence. Today I'm going to try sand with rabbit hair and egg yolk. Hmm.

"Everything alright, Messere? Forgive me, I was lost in thought . . . Oh, is it you, Ambassador? What a surprise! I hope you didn't hurt yourself."

"Not at all, Messer Leonardo, not at all," Giacomo Trotti reassured him, having just been almost mowed down by a Leonardo da Vinci in full stream-of-consciousness mode while crossing the street and having avoided falling on the ground only by some miracle. After all, he was a seventy-year-old man, albeit well-padded, who had collided with a rather robust forty-year-old. "What about you, are you all right?"

"Perfectly all right. It is I who must apologize, but you know how it is, I sometimes get distracted and don't look where I'm going. It's fortunate I collided with you and not with one of those carts that scamper around everywhere. It did happen to me once. I was practically run over by a cart and to top it off was insulted by the lady driving it. The height of embarrassment, I can assure you."

"Don't give it a second thought." Trotti put a hand on Leonardo's arm. "It happens to me too, more often than it should to a man my age. Where are you going, somewhere nice?"

"Not far from here, near the animal market."

"I'm going that way too. Will you allow me to walk with you?"

"Gladly." Leonardo smiled. "Perhaps if there are two of us, we'll be more careful."

Trotti also smiled, internally. The first problem, making contact with Leonardo in such a way that it would appear accidental, had been solved. Ludovico had said it explicitly: Make sure he doesn't feel he's being investigated.

"Do you need to buy an animal?"

"No, not at all," Leonardo replied, apparently lost in his own thoughts again. The man had an almost disturbing tendency to become distracted. "I'm going to see an old friend from whom I think I can obtain something I need. And who won't charge me very much, since this stuff is usually expensive."

"Well, good-quality stuff always costs a lot. Living in Milan, one always has less money than one would need. When I lived in Ferrara, I would spend in a week what I spend here in a day."

Coming from Trotti, this might sound as if it had no ulterior motive. The ambassador of Ferrara was known to have few equals—Gallerani's husband included—as a miser. But, in actual fact, Trotti was trying to bait the hook.

I want to know if Leonardo can be corrupted, Ludovico had told Trotti loud and clear. I suspect—in fact, I'm certain— that the French want his plans and there are many reasons why Leonardo might complain about the money he isn't receiving from me or from others. They could buy them, or they could buy him. I want you to find out if it's possible. Go, ask, interrogate. Discreetly but skillfully, you're good at that.

And that's exactly what Giacomo Trotti was doing.

* * *

"Money wouldn't be a problem," Leonardo said. "I mean it wouldn't if I had enough of it."

"Apparently nobody has enough," Trotti remarked. "Even the two French gentlemen who arrived yesterday keep complaining about it."

"Don't mention them," Leonardo replied, shaking his head. "They spent half of last night's dinner talking about money and how much I earned." He chuckled. "I'd earn a sufficient amount, I told them, if I didn't have to keep buying new clothes to replace those stained with wine thanks to other people's clumsiness."

Leonardo smoothed the front of his garment with that compulsive gesture Trotti had often seen him make, as though he were afraid he was still dirty.

"Too much importance is given to money, Messer Giacomo. Many people are so sure it has a substance of its own that they keep it at home and constantly admire it as though it were a painting or a jewel. But money is not a substance, it has no body of its own."

Meanwhile, they had reached the square next to the Cathedral site. It was here that the animal market was held. All kinds of creatures, from hens to cows, from rabbits to little birds, along with an abundance of species not for sale, such as flies. Leonardo slowed down and looked around. Good old Trotti, who was losing his breath, managed to pump more air into his organ pipes.

"So what's money for you, then?"

"Good question. You see, Messer Giacomo, I am an *omo*

sanza lettere, an unlettered man who knows no Latin, and when I start to explain things I often end up getting lost in a maze. So I'll start with an example, if I may."

Saying this, Leonardo deviated slightly from his path and walked up to a seller of little birds, who was carrying his merchandise in cages hanging from rods, like balancing poles, and was hunched over under the weight of all these birds and, above all, their cages.

"Good day to you, my good man."

"Your humble servant, Messere," the man said in a voice that resembled that of his merchandise. "Matteo, the bird man, is here for you. What are you looking for? We have green and yellow parrots, or, if you like music, we have nightingales that sing better than any musical instrument."

"Wonderful," Leonardo said, looking as sincere as he could. "Now, Messer Giacomo, do you think it's fair for such splendid natural creations to be in cages, helpless, just so we city men can enjoy their song? Tell me, my good man, how much do you want for this pair of nightingales?"

"Five deniers for these, Messere. But it's money well spent. They have voices like angels."

"I don't doubt it, my dear man," Leonardo said, putting his hand in his pouch. "Here you are."

"And here you are," the man replied, untying the cage with the two nightingales from the pole and handing it to Leonardo. "You'll need to build them a larger home if you want to keep them in your house."

"Don't worry, Messere. There'll be no need."

He opened the cage and proffered a finger to one of the little creatures, which immediately climbed onto it. Leonardo pulled out his hand and raised it, like an inexperienced falconer trying to train a toy hawk. All at once, the bird took off, flapping its wings and circling over the crowd before vanishing above the houses just a few seconds later.

Giacomo Trotti turned to Leonardo, who had been looking up, following the bird's flight with a mixture of complicity and glee. Meanwhile, seeing that the cage was open, the second bird had also left without anybody noticing.

"Marvelous, isn't it? I've always dreamed of devoting myself to the study of bird flight. I may be able to get down to it one day, once I'm done with this blessed bronze horse. So, Messer Giacomo. Did you see?"

"Yes, I saw. You spent five deniers for nothing."

"For nothing? Forgive me, my friend, but I gave a pair of nightingales their freedom and was able to observe and experience all that derived from that. Their happiness, my happiness, and your astonishment. In such a situation, in which thoughts turn to hope, I transformed thought into flight, almost as if I were God Almighty. Do you think that a trifle?'

"You're right, of course. When a man buys good wine, he certainly doesn't buy it so that he can keep it and look at it. One doesn't buy wine as such, one hopes to buy wellbeing, the pleasant feeling of intoxication." Giacomo Trotti nodded pensively. "I understand you, Messer Leonardo. You think the way I do. Money is an ambassador, a fluid. A means to obtain what one wants. At this point, though, forgive me, but you can't tell me you don't care about the amount of money. Even in your case, the more money you have, the more possibilities of doing whatever makes you happy."

"My dear Trotti, I don't think I've been clear enough. Just now, that bird seller and I concluded a transaction. I gave him five little pieces of metal, and he gave me two nightingales. We both agree on the meaning of those five little pieces of metal. You see, money is a language. It works not because it has a nature of its own, but because we humans all agree in granting it the same power. And it's a more powerful language than all our words and sentences."

"Naturally, because everybody understands it."

"On the contrary, it's because it's a secret code."

"A secret code?"

"Of course. Think about it, Messer Giacomo. Try shooting an arrow at the heart of a man or an ape. The same thing happens. Both the man and the ape die. Try giving them food, a piece of fruit for example. Both the man and the ape will eat it. But try putting a ducat in the ape's paw and expect it to give you back the same fruit you gave it earlier."

"It would tear my arm off."

"Almost certainly. And yet if it understood what it had been given, it'd be able to buy a hundred similar pieces of fruit." Leonardo stopped and turned to Trotti. "Money, like language, is a secret code through which people reach agreement, and it's totally incomprehensible to anybody who isn't human."

"Like the language of nature, you mean."

"Even more powerful, because even more secret. You can train a dog by resorting to language. You can say 'down,' 'sit,' and other words. But try giving it a ducat and it's bound to swallow it." Leonardo turned determinedly onto Via degli Armorari, with the relaxed gait of one who has almost reached his destination. "And that's why we humans are the most powerful beings alive, and why we have dominion over all the other animals in creation. Lions, pigs, apes, dogs . . ." He smiled. ". . . and even horses. And yet horses have the upper hand over us in the end. Worth thinking about, for the time being. I've arrived, Messer Giacomo."

Giacomo Trotti looked around.

At the time we are referring to, Milan was one of the manufacturing cities *par excellence*. All sorts of things were manufactured there.

Fabrics, brocade in particular, woven with fine gold thread, but also any other kind of Lombard silk cloth or wool from the Cotswolds, which, after being processed in Milanese workshops, acquired beauty but kept its warmth and softness.

Garments, from the humblest rags of servants to the *cioppa* and *camora* worn by ladies of the court, to the high fashion of dukes and duchesses, whose clothes were designed by the finest artists, including Leonardo, who had himself created those worn by Beatrice at the famous Festa del Paradiso.

Stackable, convertible furniture, such as writing desks that turned into dining tables, carrying dark wood inlays with the warning NE GRAVIORA FERAM—don't overload me with heavy stuff.

And, above all, armor. Every kind of armor and arms, whatever the shape or use, and not necessarily for martial purposes, in fact almost never. It's true that back in those days, arms and armor were objects of high fashion and not just of war, and they were commonly worn in the city center during a parade. An object created with quite another intention would be shown off just for the pleasure of displaying the extent of one's wealth and suggesting a superior attitude toward exploration and bravery: a little like driving an SUV in a restricted traffic area nowadays.

Consequently, many successful craft workshops had blossomed in a very specific area of the city, and, thanks to their good taste, these craftsmen had imposed the prestige and exclusivity of Italian-made brands even on the complicated world of halberds. This was the area in which Leonardo and Trotti now were: Via degli Scudari, the absolute kingdom of luxury arms dealers.

Now it's true that Leonardo was a forerunner of dandyism, and could hold his own in terms of elegance, but Trotti really couldn't picture him in armor.

"Are you planning to buy yourself a suit of armor, Messer Leonardo?"

"Oh, no, of course not, Messer Giacomo. I'm here to talk to an artisan who's an expert on metals. Are you busy?"

"On the contrary, I'll be glad to accompany you."

"In that case, let's go. Come." And Leonardo slipped into a dark doorway that led to a small open gallery, from whose cell-like rooms came a whiff of acidic heat and the clang of mallets striking iron. Leonardo looked into the first of these rooms.

"I'm looking for Master Antonio."

The youth at the anvil, covered in soot and sweat, squinted to make out the visitor's identity. Having recognized him, he put down his mallet and left the room without saying a word.

A few seconds later, from the room in the center of the gallery, there emerged a giant of a man, as massive, Trotti thought, as a four-seasons wardrobe, dressed in green and gold, who came toward Leonardo with a broad smile on his face.

"Messer Leonardo, what an enormous pleasure! To what do I owe the honor of your visit?"

"It is you who honor me with your welcome, Master Antonio." Then he turned to his companion. "Giacomo Trotti, Ambassador of Ercole, Duke of Ferrara. Master Antonio Missaglia."

Giacomo Trotti bowed.

So did Antonio Missaglia.

It was said that Milanese armor manufacturers had become dominant throughout Europe. Thanks to their good taste, it was said, but not exclusively: it was also by virtue of efficient technological solutions and good old-fashioned competition. Even back then, there were such things as brands, and every armor manufacturer would conspicuously impress his stamp on the metal. And the most prestigious by far was that of the Missaglias.

Missaglia garments would be paraded by the kings of France, Maximilian I, the Aragonese sovereigns of Naples, and many other *parvenus* with no kingdoms to defend or tournaments to fight, but only money to spend. Hearing "May I present Antonio Missaglia" in 1493 Milan was like hearing nowadays "Let me introduce Giorgio Armani."

"It's a pleasure and an honor," Trotti said. "I didn't realize you two were acquainted."

"Messer Leonardo has done me the honor of his friendship since shortly after he moved to Milan, Your Excellency," Missaglia replied, displaying a large arc of black teeth through his white beard. "In fact, I feel somewhat ridiculous being called *master* by him. If there's a master here, it's him."

"You're far too kind, Master Antonio," Leonardo said with a half-smile, as though to let it be known that he agreed with this point but didn't wish to insist on it. "Master Antonio has taught me many things about metals, how to forge them, how to hammer them. We made Galeazzo Sanseverino's armor together."

"An almost mint gold suit of armor. You thought it, I made it." Antonio Missaglia laughed like someone who has gotten away with murder. "And luckily somebody paid for it."

"And who put in the most work?" Trotti asked, looking around.

"Oh, it was easy for me. Working with gold is a dream in comparison with iron. But keeping a rider in his saddle with all that weight is no small feat. Gold is soft and easy to hammer. But it's heavy. Heavier than iron and bronze, which weigh more or less the same."

Trotti raised a finger, like a schoolboy. "Excuse me, Master Antonio, but since I have this rare opportunity to ask you questions, there's something I'm curious about. May I . . . ?"

"I hope I can answer you, Your Excellency."

"I've always heard it said that cannons for use in war cannot be made from iron because they'd be too heavy and difficult to transport. But you now tell me that iron and bronze weigh the same. So I don't understand how these two things can be reconciled."

"Bronze may weigh the same, but it's much stronger." Missaglia raised a hand that in shape and size looked like a chopping block. "You see, Excellency, you have three choices." Missaglia took a thumb the size of a ham between two fingers. "*Primero*, you can make a cannon from inch-thick bronze, transport it with horses, and use it in battle." Missaglia grabbed his forefinger. "*Secundo*, you can make a cannon from inch-thick iron, transport it with the same effort, but you *couldn't* use it in battle. It would explode in your face at the first shot." Missaglia squeezed his middle finger. "*Terzero*, you can make a cannon from two-inch-thick iron and use it in battle but it would be very costly to transport it onto the battlefield. It would be much heavier than a bronze one of the same size. Moreover, bronze melts and becomes liquid much more easily. You need half the heat or almost. Bronze is a great material but it can't be used for armor. It's too hard to hammer. It's fine for cannons, though. And for statues, am I right, Master Leonardo?"

Just for a change, Leonardo was lost in his own thoughts, his brow furrowed, his eyes downcast. Quite justifiably, no doubt, since what Massiglia was saying was something he knew only too well. After a few seconds' silence he roused himself, and the deep furrow on his brow faded.

"You're quite right, Master Antonio. And that's why I'm here. You see, I'm doing a few little tests for the casting of the monumental horse in memory of His Lordship the late duke, and I need a small quantity of copper to melt into bronze. Three or four sheets at most."

"Anything you need, Master Leonardo. Do you also require tin to bind it?"

"No, I still have enough for another two or three castings. The thing is, Master Antonio, I need you to give me this copper on credit. I don't have the money to pay you right now, but I'm expecting a large sum from the Confraternity for the panel and—"

As Trotti took a few steps away to lessen the embarrassment,

Missaglia raised his hands, casting a shadow over a hectare of courtyard behind him.

"Oh, for goodness' sake, Master Leonardo. For you, this and more. As long as you promise not to pay me in lead." Missaglia laughed, but stopped immediately on seeing Leonardo turn the color of wine. "I'm jesting, of course, Master Leonardo. I'll send for some copper right away. In Milan, it's other people who are bad payers. Do come back whenever you wish, you're always welcome here."

* * *

"Oh, Galeazzo, welcome. Have you been to that poor fellow Rambaldo Chiti's abode?"

Ludovico il Moro was sitting on the bed, playing cards with Beatrice, who, judging by the mound of little silver deniers in her lap, was winning. And, judging by His Lordship's face, this wasn't due solely to his wife's luck and/or skill.

"As Your Lordship instructed." Galeazzo lifted his chin, and it was almost impossible not to notice that his eyes were glistening. This was almost more evident than the large wooden chest he was holding, and which seemed to weigh a great deal. "We closed and bolted the doors and windows and piled the clothes and blankets we found in the house into a cart that's just outside here."

"Good." Ludovico slowly put down a card, and Beatrice snatched it at lightning speed and slipped it in among the ones she had in her hand. "Now make sure to burn them with wood and coal, aromatic herbs and incense. Magistro Ambrogio says these things are essential for removing the contagion, which goes way up high with the smoke and can't be carried on the winds anymore."

"We'll do that. But I think you'd like to know what else we found and how we found it."

"I don't follow you, Captain."

"First of all, Rambaldo Chiti's home was very poor. Very poor, like its owner's clothes and his few possessions. But these few things were in such a mess, in such a state of upheaval that it's impossible to think someone could live in a place like that. It was worse than a whorehouse on a drunken night, if I may be allowed to use such a licentious expression in Your Lordship's presence."

This was a kind of signal agreed between Galeazzo and Ludovico. Whenever Galeazzo used an improper word then apologized for it, it meant that he wished to be alone with il Moro.

"That's quite all right, my dear Galeazzo. But even so, it may be best if your ears do not hear such grim stories, my most beloved wife."

This was said with gentle words and in a gentle tone, of course. But it was rare for il Moro to ask to be left alone, and when it happened it was only right and proper that he should be obeyed at once. With a smile and a flourish, Beatrice d'Este left the room, no doubt to see the kid for the daily four- or five-minute parental care slot. But not before gathering in her encircling hand the little silver coins lying in her skirts.

"So, tell me, Galeazzo. It seems you weren't the first to enter that wretch's home."

"No, the house had been turned upside down, from top to bottom, if one can use the words 'from top to bottom' about a couple of shabby rooms. We weren't the first, but we were the luckiest."

Galeazzo took the wooden chest he was holding and put it down on the floor, in front of Ludovico.

"Whoever went into the house didn't search it thoroughly. There was an anvil next to the bed, a large block of wood. The block was hollow but well filled so that you wouldn't notice the hollowness from the sound."

"And how did you notice it?"

"What would a painter be doing with an anvil? Why would such a poor man keep such a bulky object in such a small room?" As he spoke, Galeazzo opened the chest and took out a long iron shoe horn. "Because he needed it. Do you know what this is?"

"No, I don't. It reminds me of something but I'm not sure what."

"Perhaps it'll become clearer if I also show you these," Galeazzo said, taking two silver rods from the chest.

"Holy Mother of God." Ludovico's eyes moved to the object. "An iron channel for fusing metals. Chiti was a forger."

"So it would seem," Galeazzo confirmed. "There were a few planchet marks on the anvil, as though someone had struck coins on it. In addition, the chest contains files, pliers, and a copper plate, as well as a small crucible."

"Is there also money in the log?"

"Not coins, no, but money, yes. And that's what I wanted to talk to you about."

"Fancy that," Ludovico said as Galeazzo bent over the chest again and rummaged through it. "Our little scoundrel Chiti could have been murdered by someone in his shady circles. Messer Leonardo might have been right after all."

Galeazzo, grabbing hold of what he was looking for, shook his head. "Be patient for a second, Ludovico. We're going to talk about Messer Leonardo now."

* * *

"So, Messer Leonardo, we've arrived. I wonder if I might ask you a favor."

"Do tell, Messer Giacomo," Leonardo said, opening his front door. "My modest rooms are at your disposal."

"Thank you, Leonardo. You see, I have a sudden urge to relieve myself, and I was wondering if . . ."

"Most certainly, Messer Giacomo," Leonardo replied, gesturing to the stairs. "Feel free to use my room as you wish. You will find everything you need in the bottom drawer next to my bed. Good evening, Caterina."

"I'm in the kitchen, Leonardo," Trotti heard as he climbed the stairs.

Having opened the door, Trotti looked around. Still looking around, he opened the drawer Leonardo had mentioned and pulled out a heavy brass chamber pot.

Giacomo Trotti was, after all, seventy years old, so asking to use the chamber pot in someone else's house was never solely an excuse for being able to look around at his leisure; but while using it, with all the care a seventy-year-old must apply in such cases to coordinate as best he can his poor eyesight and his over-enlarged prostate, Trotti did in fact take a look around.

The room was an ordinary room, which could have been anybody's except for the numerous sheets of paper scattered all over the place, in an order that was an order only in the owner's head. No blowpipes, no glass receptacles, no metallurgical tools or other alchemist's apparatus, although these might be in his workshop. What could be here, at most, was the odd note. It was hard to get a clear idea, and impossible to start looking through the papers, especially since they were written right to left, which made them incomprehensible unless one had a fair amount of time at one's disposal. And Trotti did not have that much time. Prostate or not, he couldn't spend a quarter of an hour alone in somebody else's room.

Having put the chamber pot back, after emptying it out the window with a polite but stentorian warning, Trotti tidied his clothes, left the room, and went back downstairs.

"Well, Messer Leonardo, I thank you for your company . . ." he began, but stopped on entering the kitchen and seeing Caterina sitting at the table with a basket of beans in front of her, shelling them with a solemn air. When she saw

Trotti, she put down the pod and stood up, brushing hulls from her skirt.

"Forgive me, Messere, my son's had to go out in a great rush. A servant from the castle arrived with the order to escort him to His Lordship Ludovico Sforza. He apologizes for not saying goodbye to you."

"No matter," Trotti replied, opening his hands to show that it was no big deal. "It is I who must thank you, and I must also thank your son for granting me a little of his precious time."

"Ah, time. Leonardo never has enough of it. He carves it out and looks for it in every way he can. He sleeps for an hour and a half then wakes for four. And he's always doing a thousand things."

"So he also works at night, does he?"

"Most definitely. And as if it weren't bad enough that he works at home, which just means that he loses sleep, he also goes out."

"Goes out? At night?"

"Yessir, signore. I'm old, you know, so if I wake up at night I can't get back to sleep. It's three times now that I've noticed he wasn't at home during the night, and that he came back shortly before matins. I told him it's dangerous to roam around the city at night, but he won't listen. If His Lordship Ludovico asks me, he says, I have to do it."

"Ludovico? And what does he have to do for His Lordship at night?"

"You don't know? Neither do I." Caterina rubbed her hands on her apron and threw a quick glance at the table and the pyramid of beans still to be hulled. "Now please excuse me, signore, but I have to return to my chores. There's so much to do and no one to give me a hand. Actually, if by any chance you see a young man in a white jacket and blue and white tights out there in the street, give him a shout and send him in here."

* * *

"Messer Leonardo da Vinci is here, Your Lordship."

"Show him in, castellan, show him in."

The castellan admitted Leonardo to the Room of the Chevrons, where three people were waiting for him: Ludovico il Moro, Galeazzo Sanseverino, and young Marquess Stanga.

Leonardo's heart felt lighter as soon as he saw the latter. Despite his ridiculous name – *Beanpole* – he was a very serious character: superintendent of the Court treasury, in other words, the official paymaster. The man who gave out the coins, as people said in those parts. And his presence in this room could only mean one thing. That Ludovico had received the money straight from the Confraternity and was about to put an end to his financial tribulations.

"Here you are, Messer Leonardo. Come. We have important news for you. Stanga, you may leave us. We've finished for today."

"As Your Lordship wishes," the man replied with the hint of a bow, and started to walk away, leaving Leonardo in the company of il Moro and Galeazzo, but much more alone than earlier.

"So, Messer Leonardo. As I was saying, we have important news. Come in, come in. What are you carrying in that satchel?"

"Copper plates, Your Lordship. To do a few small-scale tests for the casting of the horse. Master Antonio Missaglia most generously gave them to me."

On this subject, may I remind Your Lordship that you promised me a payment and now I see Stanga is dismissed. I would like to know why you summoned me here. Because it was you who summoned me and I've already had a lousy day. I've thought this, Your Lordship, I'm not saying it. Copper plates on credit, and then Missaglia. Who puts me in a difficult situation with bronze and lead. You summoned me. Alright, now they'll pay me. I see Stanga and you send Stanga away. Why am I here?

"Well, now. Our Leonardo is a hard worker. He does one thing and thinks another ten. I'd give a penny for your thoughts every now and then."

Every now and then but not now. You wouldn't like them.

"As I was saying, Messer Leonardo, there's important news. Captain Galeazzo has had the dead man Rambaldo Chiti's rooms emptied and examined. They found it in a terrible state, a dreadful mess. As though somebody had already been looking through Chiti's things."

"Which, if I might say so, Your Lordship, supports my theory that Chiti was murdered. Have they found anything interesting?"

"Many things, Messer Leonardo, many. Or rather, whoever searched first didn't find anything, whereas our good Galeazzo found these, carefully hidden in an anvil. Do you know what they are?"

"Files, planchets, clay. Pliers. Burins. An iron rod for casting. The tools of a jeweler, or a forger."

"Precisely, Leonardo. Are you well? You look pale."

"I'm well, Your Lordship. I've had a hard day."

"And it's not yet over, Messer Leonardo. I have two other things to show you."

Ludovico took a few papers from Galeazzo's hands and opened one. It was a sheet of very fine Florentine paper, with tidy, precise handwriting.

Year of Our Lord 1493, on the 24th day of June, in Florence

1,000 Florins

As is customary, this letter entitles Messer Rambaldo

Chiti to one thousand florins, at the rate of one thousand and twenty-five ducats per florin, on behalf of Messer Accerrito Portinati and associates in Milan. Christ be with you.

Beneath, a signature. A signature Leonardo knew. But it wasn't the signature that mattered, it was the whole letter.

When a banker received a letter of credit, he was supposed to return in cash the amount stated in the letter. Naturally, every bank manager has a specimen of the handwriting of all his colleagues from the other branches. And when we talk about the Medici Bank, or banks affiliated to it, we are talking about branches all over Europe, from Rome to London, by way of Bruges.

The letter of credit was the cornerstone of the continent's business, protecting its owner from thieves or from journeys made arduous through the need to take with you a cart full of money. You deposit the money in Florence, you take the letter, you go to London and get back the money deposited at the current exchange rate: there's a small loss in monetary terms but a huge gain in safety.

Leonardo looked at the sheet of paper in bewilderment. "I don't understand."

"Neither do I. This is a letter of credit for a thousand ducats, in the possession of a miserable wretch who worked as a painter. But at least that makes two of us who don't understand. As for the second document I'm about to show you, perhaps you'll understand it better than I."

And Ludovico showed Leonardo a second sheet of paper. A sheet showing a number of drawings, along with numbers, and covered in tiny handwriting that was indeed almost impossible to understand.

Not surprisingly. It was written from right to left.

EIGHT

Rambaldo Chiti was one of my apprentices. He was introduced by the client of a good friend, Giovanni Portinari, who asked me to take him into my home and my workshop, which I did."

Ludovico was listening, motionless, his hands clasped one on top of the other in front of his mouth, as though to show that for as long as Leonardo spoke, he was all eyes and ears, and everything in between.

"Rambaldo was good, he had talent, he was a quick learner, bright and well-mannered. I was pleased with him, and he soon started giving me a hand with my work."

Leonardo sighed slowly, looking down at the floor. There was no need to look up to realize that Ludovico was there and hadn't yet changed position.

"Then, one day, two years ago, Master Antonio Missaglia sent for me. He said he'd found fake coins in his payment drawers. Lead ducats thinly plated in gold, perfect copies that were quite deceptive until you weighed them on hydrostatic scales. He suspected a few of his customers. So he asked me to mark the money I gave my apprentices."

Beside Ludovico, Galeazzo seemed to be following both of them alternately, watching Ludovico while Leonardo was speaking, then looking at Leonardo whenever the latter caught his breath and gathered his thoughts.

"A month later Master Antonio called for me. That morning, I'd given Rambaldo Chiti four ducats and marked them.

But the ducats I saw him deliver with his own hand at the fifth hour had no mark. It was something that could not be ignored."

Leonardo opened his hands. Ludovico did not move a muscle. It was extraordinary how a creature so still could at the same time be so obviously alive.

"After apologizing most profusely to Master Antonio, I took Chiti home and asked him to explain the process he'd used. I shan't go into too much detail, but it's exactly what you found written on the paper you showed me earlier, the procedure used to coat lead with gold. The procedures and timings were clearly marked, because if you don't follow them to the letter, the result is a disaster. It was the same procedure Master Antonio and I had considered at first for making the armor of the most illustrious Captain Sanseverino, using light metals and giving them the appearance of gold."

Leonardo took a deep breath.

"You can understand my dismay and embarrassment, Your Illustrious Lordship. I'd taught that rascal the skill myself, and now I could see it was being used to make fake coins and palm them off on one of my dearest friends in Milan. I was so ashamed and disgusted by what he had done that I didn't even chide him. I threw him out of my house and wrote to the few friends I have who are experts in the art of metal, Sangallo, Francesco di Giorgio, and Pollaiuolo, telling them not to let the wretch in if he ever came knocking at their doors, because they would be letting disaster in."

Ludovico moved his hands away from his face and lowered them. Leonardo fell silent.

"You should have reported him to me and the Secret Council," Ludovico said in a sharp tone.

"You would have put him to death, Your Lordship."

"I would have done my duty as lord regent of this city. I would have stopped fake coins from circulating and deterred anybody who dared try it again. I would have done what had to be done. It is you, Leonardo, who didn't do what you should have."

Ludovico got to his feet, towering over the room and those present, a lord in form and substance.

"It is you who should have done your duty as a citizen. A city isn't held up only by the strength of its outer walls, Leonardo, but also by the trust of those who live and work in it. This letter, Leonardo, works because I trust the man who sent it, and I am sure he is able to honor the request. Thanks to this trust we can trade with the whole of Europe, sell our silks in Bruges, our arms in Paris, our wool in Frankfurt. But if I didn't trust the man who writes it, it would be scrap paper."

Leonardo and Galeazzo remained silent as Ludovico started to walk around the room in circles, still speaking.

"A city of honest people would be an ideal city to live in, but it's a fact that people are not honest. Show me a hundred citizens and ask me if most of them are good men, and I'll say yes. Out of a hundred men, ninety or perhaps even more would never do any harm. But it takes only one, Leonardo, to spoil that hundred, just as it takes only a spoonful of excrement in a barrel of wine to make it undrinkable. It's my duty as a lord to keep those honest ninety safe and sound, not to concern myself with the one who has erred. It's the only way to maintain trust. Now tell me, Leonardo: when you saw Rambaldo Chiti's corpse, did you recognize him?"

"Yes, Your Lordship."

"And was it after you recognized him that you took the decision to examine his mortal remains in order to determine the cause of his death?"

"Yes, Your Lordship."

"Were you thinking to tell me eventually that you'd known the dead man?"

"I'm not sure, Your Lordship."

"What do you mean?"

"I was afraid you would misinterpret my relationship with the wretched fellow. That you would think I had been and still was his accomplice and associate in the revolting business he was practicing."

"Which is exactly what I may be thinking right now. Even more so now, as a matter of fact. I may be thinking that you were minting fake coins with your apprentice until quite recently and that, after he left, you found yourself short of money. Now tell me, Leonardo, why should I trust you?"

"For a few reasons I shall give you, if Your Lordship has the patience and benevolence to hear me out."

It was his tone more than anything else that surprised Galeazzo. He had kept his eyes on Leonardo since the beginning of the conversation and could see that as Ludovico spoke to him he had seemed to acquire a certain serenity, a serenity he did not lose. And now he had spoken in a respectful but calm tone, like someone who not only knows he is in the right but knows he can prove that he is in the right: two things that don't always go together.

"Then tell me. I'm listening."

"First of all, there are the letters I sent my few peers, which I mentioned earlier. They are reputable artisans and engineers as well as conscientious people, and I trust they've kept my letters, just as I keep theirs."

"All right. And then?"

"Secondly, I myself told you, and insisted on the fact, that Rambaldo Chiti was murdered and did not die of a disease or thanks to divine wrath, as others told you. It would be truly foolish of me, Your Lordship, to fall into a trap I myself had set."

"Very well, I grant you that. Is there anything else you wish to say to me?"

"Two things. The first is that I entrust myself to the

impartiality you have shown so many times, especially in the case of the two Germans in Capiago."

At the end of May, two Germans living in Capiago near Lake Como, Jacob de Pesserer and Jos Crancz, had been arrested with their servants, accused of being forgers. Their house had been searched and all its contents confiscated and inventoried, and the inventory examined personally by il Moro, who, with Leonardo's help in fact, had concluded that the two men were not forgers, but alchemists. And not naive alchemists trying to obtain gold by mixing lead and urine, as was often the case, instead of using zinc bisulfide which, as everyone knew by now, was the most promising method of obtaining gold. They had a well-developed laboratory, but there were no minting dies, no mallets, no blunt objects. The two men had been released on June 11th, with an edict signed by il Moro in person, after eleven days of prison and none of torture. There weren't many places where this happened at the end of the 15th century.

"And the second thing?"

"The second, Your Lordship, is that I have evidence that Chiti was not only a counterfeiter, and the letter of credit you showed me earlier is a fake."

* * *

"You see, Your Lordship, the letter is signed by Bencio Serristori, Accerrito Portinari's associate and my good friend in Florence. It's clearly dated the twenty-fourth of June this year."

"Yes, I can see that. So?"

"Well, Your Lordship, the twenty-fourth of June is the Feast of Saint John the Baptist in Florence. Nobody works on the day of the patron saint. And, from what I knew of Bencio Serristori, he would never have left home—or, above all, a lavishly set table—on the Feast of Saint John to go to the bank."

"Knew?"

"That's right, Your Lordship, Bencio Serristori died in Florence on the first day of July this year. My mother Caterina, who has recently come to stay with me, told me this along with other news she brought from Florence."

Ludovico joined his hands in front of his face and began rubbing his chin up and down with the knuckles of his index fingers. Not a very duke-like pose but more than essential at that moment. Ludovico was thinking.

In order to be paid, a letter of credit had to match the specimen of handwriting and the signature every bank manager kept with him. If Chiti had forged that letter, it meant he had access to a specimen of a real letter. But where could he have obtained it?

And, above all, where was this specimen?

"So you knew this Signor Serristori well?"

"As I told you, we were each other's guest in Florence."

"And do you have any idea who did business with him here in Milan?"

"There are a few I remember, Your Lordship, but I cannot guarantee there aren't more of them."

Il Moro's knuckles continued to rub his chin. A fake letter of credit. The real one is missing. And the man who most likely fabricated it is murdered in that absurd manner and dumped in the middle of my castle. In the center of his city. I have to get to the bottom of this.

"Messer Leonardo, draw up a list of the Milanese names you know to have had dealings with your friend Serristori."

"As Your Lordship wishes. May I therefore hope for Your Lordship's forgiveness and trust?"

"Of my forgiveness, my Christian forgiveness, you can always be certain, Messer Leonardo. As for my trust, we'll see if you can earn it. Remember that we have made some very specific agreements and I am still waiting for proof of your craftsmanship."

Il Moro's eyes traveled in an indescribable but perceptible fashion to Leonardo's face.

Eyes that said: And I don't just mean the bronze horse.

To which the eyes facing him replied: I know that perfectly well.

* * *

"I must get to the bottom of this matter, Galeazzo. I don't know what's going on, but I don't like it."

"I don't understand it either, Ludovico. What I understand least of all is why somebody should have dumped that body in the middle of the piazzale, like a cat bringing a dead bird home. I don't understand why they did it, and what they expect from it."

"You wonder why, Galeazzo, because you think like a soldier. I am a ruler, so what I wonder is: *Who?* I wonder who it was. Which is why I don't know whom to trust or how much I can trust."

Galeazzo and Ludovico were now alone in the large room, waiting for the members of the Secret Council to be admitted and for the day's audiences to begin. These were not supplicants, not people who wished to speak with il Moro, but people who had been summoned and with whom il Moro wished to speak, in a safe place and in the presence of witnesses.

"You simply have to, Ludovico. If you're thinking of Leonardo, his behavior would make no sense if he had something to hide from you. In any case, you either trust him or you don't."

"You sound very sure."

Galeazzo shook his head a millimeter, looking into the distance. "As you yourself said, Ludovico, I think like a soldier. If you asked me to take that cannon ball and shoot it at an enemy line that was facing me, what would I reply?"

"You'd call me crazy. And you'd send for a cannon."

"But the cannon might blow up in my face."

Ludovico smiled. "You couldn't win the battle without the cannon."

Still serious, Galeazzo continued speaking, while looking into the distance. "And you can't get to the bottom of this business without Leonardo. The distance between Milan and Florence is too great for you on your own and without the information he already possesses."

"Which might be false or incomplete."

"Ludovico, just as I am a warrior, you are a politician. I know how to fight and you know how to trust the right people. Do so and keep doing so. It makes no sense for you to trust Leonardo with some secrets and not with others."

"What do you mean?"

"I wasn't born yesterday, Ludovico. You and Leonardo are plotting something secret together. I'm good at picking up when two people are talking around something a third party isn't supposed to know."

"Galeazzo, do you trust me?"

"Of course, Ludovico."

"Then keep trusting me. This has nothing to do with you." Ludovico heaved a sigh that expelled the carbon dioxide from his chest, but not the tension. "Very well, then. Admit the councilors and the first man we summoned. Who do we have now?"

* * *

"The Prior of the Congregation of the Poor of Jesus, Father Diodato da Siena, and Brother Gioacchino da Brenno, of the same Congregation," the castellan announced in a firm voice.

"Come in, come in, Father," Ludovico said, keeping his seat. "Brother Gioacchino, do step forward. I'm curious to meet the Jesuit preacher who's on all Milanese lips."

"You could have come to Mass, Your Lordship, if you were so curious."

Of the many qualities Friar Gioacchino da Brenno might have possessed, friendliness wasn't exactly the most obvious. And nor was attractiveness. A little man like so many others, with a monastic tonsure verging on incipient baldness, compensated for by two thick, bushy eyebrows and generous tufts of hair sprouting from his ears.

When he heard these words, Father Diodato gave Ludovico a look such as a cocker spaniel would give his mistress after breaking her genuine Ming vase.

"Your Lordship must forgive Brother Gioacchino's impetuousness. He comes from the wooded moorlands of our Val Camonica and isn't accustomed to speaking with lords."

"On the other hand, they tell me he is very good at talking to peasants."

"I beg Your Lordship to forgive me if I have been coarse," the friar said, not smiling. "I am merely a humble Jesuate, a servant of the Lord, unused to the pomp of your proud residence."

"I'm happy to see that you carry your humility with the pride it deserves," Ludovico replied, smiling. "And I would be even happier to hear what you think of the way this city is being run."

Friar Gioacchino looked at Father Diodato.

Mind what you say, his superior warned. He's testing you.

"Your Lordship, I would never dare—"

"Do so in front of me? I don't see why not. You do it in front of the subjects of Duke Gian Galeazzo, whose guardian I am, and in front of the foreigners who come to Milan, of which I am regent."

"Your Lordship," Father Diodato intervened, "Friar Gioacchino is a man of vehement sermons but an honest heart. He would never say anything that went against the Holy

Scriptures, and I am sure this is your chief concern, as you most charitably proved by pardoning and acquitting Friar Giuliano da Muggia."

Father Diodato da Siena was not prior of one of the most powerful congregations in Europe by chance. And just as he had warned his friar, so now he was warning Ludovico. Politely, respectfully, but pointedly. My dear Moro, you may be Lord of Milan but I'm telling you loud and clear, even while making big humble, imploring eyes at you, that to the Church you're nothing.

"Of course, Father. I am not a cleric like my brother Ascanio, but I too am familiar with the Holy Scriptures. I believe that in more than one of the Holy Gospels, it is written 'Render unto Caesar the things that are Caesar's.' If it's written in the Holy Gospel, then it's an instruction that should be respected by every good Christian, don't you think?"

With this, il Moro had been equally clear. I'm no man of the cloth but my brother just happens to be a cardinal. And he is perfectly capable of requesting the intervention of the Roman authorities if he were to feel, or I were to point out to him, that you are saying something the Scriptures do not sanction, my dear little friend with the bushy ears.

"I respect the Holy Scriptures and everything written in them," Gioacchino replied in a guttural voice, "but not everything is written in the Holy Scriptures, Your Lordship. And the people don't know what's not written in them unless one tells them. It's not written in the Holy Scriptures that the wrath of the Lord has smitten Milan, and yet it has happened."

"Which is precisely what I wanted to ask you. The reason this happened. I'm told you say it's because of the poor governance of the city. Very well. Since the government is made up of people, I expect you to give me the names of these people. Names and surnames, that's what I need in order to take action against them."

Taken aback, the friar looked at his superior. Forget about being a Jesuate and become a Benedictine for a few minutes, Father Diodato's face told him.

"You're in the right place. This is the Secret Council, which deals with affairs of State, and these are my councilors." Ludovico smiled. "You have nothing to fear."

The second and third sentences, the friar's eyes seemed to say, were not exactly consistent with each other.

"I am not in a position to name names, Your Lordship, but only to allude to the general conduct of this city, where money has now become the cause and aim of every act and every interest. What I preach—"

"What you preach, you can do outside. This is a government council and I am asking you to give me the names of those who are governing this city badly so that I can prosecute them. Are you able to provide me with some of these names?"

Father Diodato once again tried to intervene. "Your Lordship, as Friar Gioacchino has already said—"

"Yes or no?" Ludovico continued, looking at the friar and not paying the slightest attention to the prior.

"I am not, Your Lordship."

"In that case I apologize for summoning you," Ludovico said, opening his hands with a benevolent air. "We've both wasted our time. Castellan, be so good as to escort Father Diodato and Brother Gioacchino out. Whose turn is it now?"

* * *

"His Excellency Philippe, Duke of Commynes, and Signor Perron de Basche."

"Come in, come in, Your Excellency. Welcome, Signor de Basche. I hope all is well and that the castle is to your liking."

"Your hospitality is even more exquisite than we could have hoped for, Your Lordship. And thank you for summoning us to this audience, since we ourselves have a question to submit to Your Lordship's counsel."

"In that case, Your Excellency and Signor de Basche, I shan't waste any precious time. My summons concerns the situation of His Most Christian Majesty King Charles VIII's army as it is now. Please bring me up to date."

"The situation is excellent, Your Lordship. We have twenty thousand men at arms under the orders of His Excellency the Duke of Orléans. His Majesty's fleet now consists of thirty armed galleys, thirty galleons, and ten gulets ready to set sail for Naples."

"I am pleased to hear it. With that and the famous cannons your army possesses, I would say you are in an excellent state of preparedness. So we can begin."

"We can begin as soon as we have the last thing we need, Your Lordship. The means to transport the cannons across the Alps."

"In order to arm the galleys," Perron de Basche now said, "His Most Christian Majesty has been forced to commit not only the State treasury but also his family's reserves."

We beg the forgiveness of readers not philologically inclined, but an explanation is necessary here: "to commit" in this case meant not "to exploit within an inch of its life" but, literally, "to pawn." In fact, Charles VIII had pawned his personal belongings, houses, castles, and other real estate, not all of it strictly his, and obtained the money required for the expedition at a staggering rate of interest of seventy-two percent per annum, or 72% if you prefer figures to numbers—in any case, a lot. How good King Charles would be at waging war, the French nobility had no way of knowing, but they hoped he would be better at it than he was at doing business.

"I understand, Duke. You therefore need my support."

"Yes, Your Lordship."

"I understand. Given the estimated number of cannons and

foot soldiers, and the horses they already have as well as those they need, and the suitable means of transport, as I have been informed by Belgioioso . . ."—here Il Moro pretended to make a complicated mental calculation—". . . you will need some tens of thousands of ducats."

The Duke of Commynes felt his stomach smile at him and grow light. From what he knew of il Moro, when he started to count, it meant yes. "The figure we need, Your Lordship, is thirty thousand ducats."

Il Moro slowly nodded, as if drawing comfort from the fact that the required sum matched the figure he had tried to estimate.

"Castellan, send for the treasurer. Let's see if we can meet the needs of our valuable ally, gentlemen."

By Candlelight

My Most Excellent Lord, whom I alone may call mine,

today, having spoken with Master Antonio, I made a small trial cast of a horse in copper and tin. I cast the animal lying on its side, since the lack of depth and the water table prevent it from being cast standing upright or turned in any way.

It was my firm belief until today that the most important factor when fusing the metal and casting the horse was the force of the pressure exerted by the molten metal, and that, as described by Archimedes, a body immersed in liquid is given a thrust equivalent to the weight of the liquid it shifts. This pressure is exerted not only in an upward direction but on all the sides, since by its nature liquid tries to resume the form that is most consonant with it, and if it is thrust too high it wants to come back down, and in order to come back down it applies pressure. Just as a little boat placed in a tub rests on the water, the water inside the tub rises then tries to come down and, in order to do so, also thrusts against the sides of the tub as well as the hull of the boat.

If this liquid is molten metal, then it is much heavier than water and when it weighs down on the form of the horse, which is inside the molten metal, its thrust is of such force that it can crack the outer crust that lends it its form.

Having cast the horse, I wanted to let it cool down in icy water, but since Salajno had broken the large bowl and since in the medium-sized one there was a slumbering cat that I did not want to disturb, I had to pour the water on the horse directly from a pitcher, imagining that the ebullition of the water would make it evaporate immediately and not get the floor wet. To let it flow more easily, I decided to wet the horse by pouring the water on the lying horse, as I plan to do with the life-size monument.

Once it had cooled, I tapped on it with a mallet to see if it emitted a dull sound, an indication of cracks or rifts, or a clear, limpid sound, and noticed that it made a different sound depending on whether it was being tapped on the head or toward the tail. To hear it better, I tapped longer and at one stage gave it rather too vigorous a tap, so that the horse split in two, precisely down the middle, along the join between the right and the left parts. I picked it up and felt that the left part seemed lighter than the right, even though the sizes appeared the very opposite, that is, the right was lighter than the left. This was confirmed when I immersed both pieces in water to measure their volume. I took both parts and weighed them on the assay balance. The right one weighed two hundredths of a pound more than the left one, even though it was only half a fingernail of water smaller in volume.

I imagine this happened because copper takes longer to cool than tin when they are in a pure state, and requires a higher heat in order to melt. Cooling it with water in the lying position, I cooled it more on the right side, in such a way, however, that the water evaporated quickly, and almost failed to flow over the left side. And so the tin mixed with copper retreated from the cold side, pushed away by the copper, and since copper is heavier than tin, it so happened that the right side of the horse contains more copper than the left, and that is why it is denser and thus heavier, although smaller in volume.

If you want the horse to remain solid along the joins, which need to carry the most weight, make sure they contain more copper than tin. In any case, make sure they cool down first and to do that pour water around the joins, as I tell you. Then put pipes around the form, placing many of them next to the joins, so that the water flows through them first, more than anywhere else.

I bid you farewell until we next meet, ever yours,

Leonardo.

From the Desk of Giacomo Trotti

To Ercole d'Este, Duke of Ferrara, ferre cito

My Most Illustrious, Respected Lord,

Hodie *I spent the morning in the pleasant company of Messer Leonardo da Vinci, having been asked by the Most Illustrious Signor Lodovico to try and investigate the aforementioned Messer Leonardo in relation to his money, since he fears the French might take it away from him before or during or after the war. It seems to me that Signor Lodovico is paying close attention to the way in which Leonardo is conducting himself, and that his suspicions are not unfounded or unreasonable. He claims that* ipso *Leonardo is restless and anxious, and I myself have witnessed this. Even so, I do believe Ludovico is not being entirely frank* cum *me and that he wishes to place Leonardo* sub observatione, *but cannot truly believe that Leonardo has no money, whereas I believe the opposite, as I am about to tell you.*

Daylight was still a long way from conquering the sky, but Giacomo Trotti had not slept that night. It was partly the cold, partly the fact that he had not been able to sleep since he had turned sixty, and partly the fact that he was tense. Tense because he thought he had realized something. Something very important. He had realized it, of that he was certain. And now he was not sure how best to act.

*

While I was cum *the same Leonardo in the house of the Most Illustrious armorer Antonio Missaglia, the latter jested that Leonardo was quite capable of paying him* cum *lead. His words,* verbatim, *were "As long as you don't promise to pay me with lead." The said Leonardo suddenly turned as red as a brazier and Missaglia immediately changed the subject. I surmised that the said Misssaglia has known Leonardo for a long time and that they are very familiar with one another.*

Everyone recognizes that Leonardo is skilled at many arts and sciences, tam clare quam obscure, *and very talented at fusing and transmuting metals, as Your Excellency well knows.*

And everyone truly did know that. He had spent the whole day with Leonardo, talking about metals, and it was clear that Leonardo was a great expert. What, however, was secret was the notebook Leonardo never parted with, always checking frantically that he had it on him, finding any excuse, from smoothing his garment to tapping his belly, to check that he still had it.

And another secret was what he was doing for Ludovico. He didn't know what it was, but whatever it was, it certainly wasn't something that could be done in broad daylight.

That day, during the customary evening interview with il Moro, he had tried asking him, in a casual manner.

"Of course, Messer Leonardo is a very absent-minded kind of person," Trotti had said, just throwing it out there. "I wonder how he manages to walk safely in the streets."

"I always try to have him accompanied by a person able to guide him," il Moro had replied, smiling and shaking his head. "Otherwise, Messer Leonardo would be quite capable of getting lost between his kitchen and his bedroom."

"Do you have him accompanied even when he goes out at night?"

"I don't think Messer Leonardo goes out at night," Ludovico had said, his pupils contracting. "Or rather, I hope for his sake that he doesn't."

Ludovico il Moro was skilled at lying, and did it naturally.

But Giacomo Trotti was an old fox.

Those two, Leonardo and Ludovico, were plotting something together. Something nobody was supposed to know about, not even Trotti.

Much fuss is made in Mediolanum *about Leonardo's knowledge and the great esteem in which Ludovico holds him, even though* ipso *Leonardo is reluctant to finish any kind of work and* excepto *redesigning Vigevano and painting a few beautiful panels, he has done nothing useful for Sforza for many years now.*

Messer Leonardo complains a great deal about the fact that the Most Illustrious Ludovico pays him seldom and badly, and the reason is apparently not that Ludovico is as stingy in giving as he is lavish in praise, but that the State coffers are empty. According to the said Leonardo, the dowry required by His Highness Emperor Maximilian is so high that it has stripped the Duchy of every penny.

Nonetheless, just hodie *I spoke with Messer Marquess Stanga, who said, with much disdain, that he has been ordered to provide letters of credit worth thirty thousand gold ducats for His Most Christian Majesty, the King of the French.*

The lines he would have to write now were of huge importance.

They had to be clear and balanced, because the theory Trotti was submitting to the ears of Duke Ercole was extraordinary, although not impossible by the notions of the day. Quite the contrary. At the same time, it was essential to advance it with all possible caution in order to avoid being considered crazy; and in this respect, the fact of being Giacomo Trotti, and of having the reputation he had accumulated over many years of service at the side of the Estes, carried some considerable weight.

A few months earlier, Trotti had imparted the news that an unknown Genoese navigator had rigged out four caravels—since, as his colleague Annibale Gennaro had written, *the world being round, it was bound to revolve*—and discovered a large island inhabited by half-naked people with olive skin. Many in Ferrara had laughed, until the day it became clear that what Trotti was saying was entirely true.

Picking up his pen again, Trotti twice tried to draft the sentence he had in mind on an odd piece of paper, which he then, even with how much paper cost in those days, scrunched up and set alight with the flame of the candle. Then, sure of what he had to write, he picked up the pen yet again and resumed the letter.

It is my belief, Excellency, that it is not impossible Leonardo has discovered or is about to discover a way to transmute lead into pure gold. And this would give sufficient et item *ample reason to hold him in such high esteem.*

Giacomo Trotti thought again about his conversation with Ludovico, and about his reaction when he told him that Leonardo had squandered five deniers to set two nightingales free. Instead of being outraged, instead of expressing astonishment that someone who complained of having little money should throw it away so foolishly, Ludovico had laughed. He had laughed, and said something even more alarming.

"Oh, has he done it again? You're not the first to tell me this. My dear Trotti, that's the way Leonardo is."

My dear Trotti, that's the way Leonardo is. That had been the explanation. Of course. The possibility of turning lead into gold—that could be the explanation. Of so many things.

Of Leonardo's lack of concern about his apparent shortage of money.

Of Ludovico's poise in dealing with absurd expenses, approving a thirty-thousand-ducat loan without batting an eyelid, promising his niece in marriage to Maximilian and providing a dowry worth four hundred thousand ducats.

Trotti sighed and put the pen down.

* * *

Banks have always lent to rulers because rulers rule, and so can always pay back their loans, either in money or in concessions, such as tax revenues.

That was why, almost one hundred and fifty years earlier, Florentine bankers had been quite happy to bankroll the king of England, Edward III, having as a guarantee the revenues from the tax on wool. Only, the war King Edward had given new momentum was the Hundred Years' War, which was to last at least a hundred and twenty years and would result, first and foremost, in the collapse of the wool market.

Trotti let his gaze drift over his own study and come to rest on Villani's *Chronicles*, the book in which he had studied the history of Florence: aware that history sometimes repeats itself.

That was how the Florentine bankers realized they would never see a penny of the four hundred thousand florins the king owed them. Somebody else, down South, in Naples, realized it a little sooner: King Robert of Anjou, afraid of losing his savings and those of the citizens who had invested in the

Florentine banks of the Bardis and the Peruzzis, immediately sent noblemen and high-ranking prelates to withdraw their deposits.

The result? A crisis. Currency no longer flowed in Florence. Merchants, artisans, and peasants could neither sell nor buy. A dark, bloodcurdling crisis from which Florence would recover only a hundred years later, after going from ninety thousand to forty-five thousand residents. Of course, in the meantime, there had been the plague, which had also done its share, but it had found the Florentines poor, hungry, and weary in spirit as well as in body.

But there had also been something else. The negotiability of shares. Public debt shares, which until then had not been transferable, became negotiable. People began to sell their debts to others, at a reduced rate, hoping they were in a position to redeem them. Because they were bigger, nastier, more arrogant.

Like Ludovico il Moro, who was a statesman and not a banker, but who played the banker with other States. He had his own debts with banks, and yet he lent money left, right, and center.

Il Moro was both a bank and a government. Like a customer paying himself to paint a picture he wanted to own. Trotti felt it wasn't right.

* * *

Launching a war flanked by an ally who was like yourself was reassuring, for the time being. But it might be dangerous in the future. A future that he, an ambassador in the sunset of his life, had neither the duty nor the hope to imagine about, but with which a good ruler absolutely had to concern himself.

He, Giacomo Trotti, had done his duty and had written what he felt he had to write. Now it was for someone else to worry about. Someone with power, as well as the possibility and desire to keep it. Someone like Ercole, Duke of Ferrara,

to whose benevolence I always entrust myself.
Mediolano, XXI octubris 1493
Servus Jacomo Trotti

NINE

M esser Leonardo is here, Countess."

"Ah, Messer Leonardo, welcome. I was hoping you would pay us a visit."

"Forgive me, do forgive me. I was held up at the castle longer than I had anticipated, over some most unpleasant issues, and as you know His Lordship does not like a job to be abandoned halfway."

Cecilia Gallerani, Countess Bergamini, took Leonardo da Vinci by the elbow and led him to the salon.

"Come in, come in. We'll be starting the music in another hour or so, but not before His Most Christian Majesty's envoys arrive, as they told me they would very much like to attend the performance. In the meantime, we were having a little conversation. You do know my guests this afternoon, don't you? Father Diodato da Siena, prior of the Congregation of the Poor of Jesus . . ."

"Most honored," Leonardo said with a slight nod at the older Jesuate, a man with a graying beard and a kind expression.

". . . Friar Gioacchino da Brenno, of the same Congregation . . ."

"Most honored," the artist/engineer/architect/genius continued, nodding at the younger monk, a man with thinning black hair and the face of an asshole.

". . . and Messer Josquin des Prez."

"Oh, such an honor, such an honor," Leonardo replied, smiling with noticeably greater sincerity, going up to the man with open arms, and giving him an affectionate hug. "Messer Josquin, it is truly an honor to make your acquaintance, just as listening to your music is genuine relief to the soul. You are able to touch the cords of the human heart and mind like no one else."

Josquin des Prez smiled briefly, like somebody who is accustomed to certain compliments and knows he deserves them. He was a strong, fair-haired man who bore a vague resemblance to Galeazzo Sanseverino, until you saw his hands—white, slender, and used to pen and stave paper, not at all like those of His Lordship Ludovico il Moro's son-in-law, who was more at ease with lines of foot soldiers than lines of music.

"Please, Leonardo, do sit. What is it, Tersilla?"

"Well, Countess, I was wondering . . . if you're about to begin one of your parlor games, might I join in? It's been a dull day, and should the Countess permit, and if I weren't too much of a bother . . ."

Parlor games were among the true attractions of Casa Gallerani. Word games, charades, rebuses, and riddles, the most successful of which were almost always those of Leonardo. Riddles such as "The woods will give birth to offspring that will cause their death" (the handles of shutters), which Cecilia almost always was the first to solve.

"But of course, Tersilla, of course. Only we shan't be playing any word games or charades today, it would be inappropriate in the presence of two men of the Church. Master Josquin was just telling us how he intends to compose one of his next pieces of music. If you wish to stay and keep us company, and you, gentlemen, don't mind . . ."

"On the contrary, we would be delighted to have Madamigella Tersilla's company," said Father Diodato, whose appreciation of female company was not unknown to anyone. "Sadly, I must soon take my leave of you, but would be happy to hear what Master Josquin was explaining."

"It's very simple," the composer said, in a pronounced French accent. "Inspired by the word games to which the Countess has introduced me in these past weeks, I decided that in some cases it's possible to compose a melody by taking the notes from a person's name. The example that came to mind was that of Ercole of the House of Este, which is *Hercules Dux Ferrariae* in Latin. If we divide the syllables and then take the note that contains the vowel written in the syllable, in music Her-Cu-Les Dux Fer-Ra-Ri-Ae can be written as Re-Ut-Re-Ut-Re-Fa-Mi-Re. The melody contains the name of the person to whom the composition is dedicated."

"And do you think anyone could pick up on such concealed praise?"

"It's not really necessary to pick up on it in order to appreciate the composition," Josquin said. "But I would say that, yes, a refined ear might pick up on it, of course."

"What made you think of Ercole d'Este? You're in Milan, after all. Couldn't you do the same with the Lord of Milan?"

"Not with the same outcome. Lu-Do-Vi-Cus would become Ut-Sol-Mi-Ut," Josquin sang in his beautiful tenor voice. "Do you hear? There's no tension. There's no aspiration towards a resolution, it's almost a statement."

"Perhaps you could try it with the *true* Lord of Milan," Friar Gioacchino said sternly.

Everyone present held their breath for a moment.

Ludovico il Moro, let us recall, was not in fact Duke of Milan; the true duke was his beloved nephew, the bumbling Gian Galeazzo, son of his brother Galeazzo Maria, who'd had the terrible idea of getting himself murdered, when young Gian Galeazzo was only seven years old, by refusing to wear a surplice of chain mail because it didn't match his new tunic—

in Milan, people did insane things for the sake of fashion even as far back as the late 15th century. The Duchy was left in the incapable hands of Bona of Savoy, Ludovico's hugely meddling and conceited sister-in-law, who was convinced she could rule after her husband's death, in place of her young son. Ludovico had tried very hard to persuade Bona to trust him instead of listening to her counsellor Cicco Simonetta. This process of persuasion had been lengthy and difficult, and at one stage had required the beheading of Simonetta, just to make sure he stopped talking when he wasn't asked, and the imprisonment of Bona herself in the highest room of the farthest tower in the most remote corner of the castle. But in the end, il Moro's argument had prevailed and stability returned to Milan.

There remained the specter of Gian Galeazzo, although, to be honest, he didn't give two hoots about ruling—as long as there were wine and stallions, kindly provided by his uncle, he found life pleasant overall. All the same, he was not il Moro's favorite topic of conversation.

Mentioning Gian Galeazzo in Countess Gallerani's house was definitely inappropriate, far more so than word games in the presence of clerics.

"What do you mean, Brother Gioacchino?" Tersilla asked, electrified at the thought of hearing the most influential preacher of the day cause a scandal in her mistress's house.

"I mean money, Madamigella Tersilla," Friar Gioacchino replied. "Lucre, gold, the means that becomes an end, the devil's excrement everybody yearns to roll in. The true Lord of Milan isn't il Moro but money."

"Money. Sol-do, sol-do" Leonardo said after a moment, in a grave tone. "No, it doesn't sound right. It's a descending fifth. It suggests a conclusion, not a beginning. It's as ugly as tripping over a cat at the top of a staircase."

There was a second of silence. Then Tersilla began to laugh, with a sound akin to the neighing of a horse, and her laugh was so sincere that it infected the salon, like applause spreading through a theater.

Cecilia laughed too, in her elegant, ladylike way, relieved not to have to intervene in light of the turn the conversation had taken.

Father Diodato laughed, covering his mouth and blushing, like someone who shouldn't be joking about some things even though everyone else does.

Josquin des Prez laughed, his eyes narrowed and his mouth open, giving Leonardo, who was also laughing, a slap on the back.

Only Friar Gioacchino was not laughing.

"You see, Brother Gioacchino, musical intervals give sensations that come from their proportion. Depending on the length of the string or pipe that produces them. That's where harmony is born. It's not the actual sound that gives a sensation but their relationship and the concordance in their relationship."

"If you were right, Messer Leonardo," Father Diodato said—beside him, Friar Gioacchino looked like a dog about to snarl—"then the most sublime sound of all should be the one that corresponds to the name of Our Lord. Deus. De-us. Re-Ut."

"If the name of Our Lord were the same in every language in the world, I might agree with your theory. But in the Semitic language, that in which Our Lord God revealed Himself to men, there are actually no vowels."

"That means words and music are distanced from each other," Friar Gioacchino said in a trenchant tone. "And the Lord, who has chosen to distance us from animals by giving us the power of speech and the task of giving names to everything in creation, certainly did not tell us to make music. Man is the master of creation because the Almighty has given him speech and certainly not because he can play a lyre. Even a dog can draw sounds from a harpsichord if it walks over it."

"You can also draw sounds from your own larynx, for that matter."

"Those are sounds, not words."

"Or else they are words we do not understand. No, Brother Gioacchino, I agree that the power of speech allows us to dominate the world, but not that it's a gift from the Lord or that it's what distinguishes us from animals. If that were the case, then why would the Lord have given us something that makes it possible for us to lie?"

Leonardo opened his hands, like someone saying something simple and true.

"Animals don't lie. Men do. That's the true power of our speech, that's what truly distinguishes us from beasts. We can lie. Or rather, we can say things that don't exist. And speak of things that don't exist. I can draw a dog with eight legs, or a man with two heads, but to do so I don't need to have seen them or know they exist."

Leonardo continued, raising his index finger, while Friar Gioacchino watched him as though the artist were suggesting painting Christ in a mini-skirt:

"A great philosopher, a German named Nicholas of Cusa, says that this ability makes man similar to God: this ability to invent things that didn't previously exist and give them a meaning. Every man can give shape, in his own head, to objects that don't exist and persuade others that such objects exist or will exist. Think of dragons, or unicorns."

While Leonardo was speaking, Friar Gioacchino stood up, his face even uglier than the one he normally wore.

"So, Leonardo, are you saying the Lord has given us the ability to lie? That the Almighty's greatest gift to His creation is the lie? That, Messer Leonardo, is blasphemy. Take back what you said."

"I've no intention of doing so, Brother Gioacchino. Say something, then take it back? It would be like digging a hole then filling it again. I already have so little time to do all the things I have to do that wasting it like that would be a sin, don't you think?"

Friar Gioacchino turned to his prior, contempt coming out of his ears (along with hair). "Forgive me, Father, but I have no intention of staying in the same room as a coarse blasphemer."

There was a moment of oppressive silence, interrupted by a servant who appeared at the door.

"Countess . . ."

"Yes, Corso?"

"The musicians of the ducal chapel and the ambassadors of His Most Christian Majesty are here. The Duke of Commynes, Signor Perron de Basche, and two gentlemen whose names I don't know."

"Thank you, Corso. Show them into the music salon."

* * *

"Leonardo, Leonardo, when will you learn to keep quiet?"

Some embroidery in her lap, Cecilia Gallerani was looking at Leonardo and shaking her head. Leonardo was sitting opposite her in his usual little armchair made of wood and canvas, hands joined and resting on his closed knees. Besides them, only Tersilla was in the room. The two clerics had left without a word, Friar Gioacchino with his chin up and Father Diodato apologizing to the hostess, while Josquin des Prez had relocated to the salon to welcome the musicians and the French envoys, with a cocktail of haste and courtesy in equal measure.

"I apologize profusely, Countess, I would never have thought that such intellectual discourse could be taken as a blasphemy against the Almighty. I have been frequenting your salon for months, and I have always appreciated the profound candor and composure of your guests when speaking of philosophy. In fact, I had assumed that Father Diodato was not a newcomer to your gatherings."

"That is indeed so. This wasn't his first time, and he has always shown himself to be a man of intelligence, as well as a staunch defender of the Holy Roman Church, although never inclined to bigotry. Perhaps it was my fault, but I was eager to meet that Friar Gioacchino everyone in the city is talking about. And I wasn't the only one, was I, Tersilla?"

"Not at all, Countess. At the Broletto, his sermons were all that people were talking about. But I didn't think he would be so . . . so . . . "

"I know, I know," Leonardo said, turning the palm of his hand upward. "It always satisfies our sense of justice to hear attacks aimed at the wicked, as long as those deemed wicked are other people. But he's precisely the kind of Christian who hasn't read the parable in the Gospel and who, blinded by the beam in his own eye, chose to see the mote in my reasoning. As though there weren't already enough wickedness within the walls of Milan without the need to make up some more."

"Are you referring to that poor man who was smitten by divine wrath?"

"Divine wrath had nothing to do with it, my dear Tersilla. That man died suffocated at the hand of man, and for less than noble motives, I believe. Just as I believe the thing may drive me to ruin unless I can find an explanation for that act."

Tersilla blushed deeply while Cecilia shuddered—a verb that must always be used when describing a lady's reaction in a historical novel. Especially if it is set during the Renaissance.

"Are you serious?"

"Alas, Countess, the man who was deprived of his senses was a wretched workshop apprentice of mine."

"An apprentice of yours?"

"He used to be. His name was Rambaldo Chiti."

"Rambaldo Chiti. I don't know him. Did you ever mention him to me?"

"Not by name, Countess."

"Now I understand. He was that villain who paid with fake coins on your behalf, wasn't he?"

"He and none other, Countess. I have reason to believe that, as I may already have told you, he continued with that evil trade of his and counterfeited a letter of credit that was found in his possession. That's why I was at His Lordship's after dinner today, with the Most Illustrious Bergonzio Botta."

"Most Illustrious, Messer Leonardo?" Tersilla said, her eyes narrowed. "Forgive me, but using such words for one of those predatory dogs who make a living from scraping every penny they can from the pockets of artisans with heavy taxes—"

"Tersilla!"

"Forgive me, Countess, but that's what the city calls them. Predatory dogs. If they were decent people, they wouldn't need to travel with escorts."

"Please leave us, Tersilla."

"As you wish, Countess."

Tersilla stood up, eyes shining and bosom heaving, gathered her skirts, and left the room, quietly closing the door behind her. Cecilia leaned slightly toward her guest.

"Forgive my lady in waiting's boldness, Messer Leonardo. She's a good young woman who's had unpleasant experiences in her family. A year of floods that ruined a harvest, and her dowry went up in smoke. I took her in with me to look after little Cesare. My little emperor, as I call him."

"I understand. And how comes it that you relieved her of this duty?"

"How do you know I did?"

"Your Cesare, Countess, has just turned two. A child that

age needs his nanny at every hour of the day, and yet for some months now I've seen Madamigella Tersilla tending to you and not to him."

Yes, indeed. Cesare Sforza, the illegitimate son of Cecilia and Ludovico, had turned two only in May. True, they said he was a precocious little tot, so much so that when he turns six his father will try to get him appointed Archbishop of Milan, but four years earlier little Cesare wasn't doing much beyond eating and the opposite, and anybody given responsibility for his wellbeing had to be on duty from lauds to vespers.

"You're right," Cecilia said, blushing slightly. "You see, Tersilla is a good young woman, although a little bit of a flirt with men, but she comes from a family outside the walls and grew up somewhat coarsely. She often speaks in a licentious and at times imprudent manner, as you heard. I don't wish my little boy to grow up hearing vulgar words like those you've just heard, and for which I once again beg your forgiveness."

"I don't see why sincerity should require forgiveness. Everybody here in Milan can see that the Duchy has increased taxes excessively, and as for the new duty on salt . . ."

Cecilia sighed, as a woman might sigh on seeing her former high school sweetheart walk by with his wife, a pot belly, and a comb-over. "You will never hear me speak ill of His Lordship Ludovico il Moro, Messer Leonardo. Let us get back to you, please."

"I apologize, Countess. I didn't mean to . . . Anyway, the thing is, the banker whose letter was counterfeited was a friend of mine in Florence and—"

"Was? Is he dead?"

"Yes, Countess, he died last summer. For Chiti to have faked his signature and handwriting, someone here in Milan must have had a sample, a letter of credit that could have been used as a model. Botta and I tried to make a list of the people here in Milan with whom he wrote to me that he'd had dealings. You probably know some of them yourself: they're wool workers or carders, like Giovanni Barraccio and Clemente Vulzio—"

"I know Barraccio well. I get blankets and cloaks from him."

"—or else jewel and gemstone merchants, like Candido Bertone, or traders in needles and tools for working brocade and silk, like Costante at Porta Ticinese. Anyway, we're trying to find out if any of these people have mislaid one of these letters or had one stolen from them. This very day, the captain of justice will call on these people and ask them for an account of their credit transactions, and tomorrow go to Accerrito Portinari's bank to look at the books and see if they match."

"And what about you?"

"Right now I shall come with you to listen to some good music and try to take my mind off things."

* * *

"It's no use. He won't take his mind off it."

"If he won't take his mind off it, then we must think of something else," Robinot said. "In the meantime, keep an eye on him."

Around them, the music room was enveloped in the confident, powerful harmonies produced by the singers of the ducal chapel—high and low waves that each member added to and subtracted from in an ebb and flow that became one vast sea of sonorous beauty, thanks to Josquin's confident direction.

Behind him as he led the singers, seeming almost to compress and shift the air as he wished, more than twenty people sat with rapt attention, although some more than others. Among the less attentive ones were Leonardo, who clearly was attending the concert more in body than in brain, and the Duke of Commynes's two henchmen, who, at an appropriate distance from their master, were discussing their objective in low voices.

"I still think we could do it the old way," Mattenet said, although there was doubt in his tone. "A nice dark alley and . . . *whack!*"

"Listen, you shit-filled brain, I'll whack that thing dangling between your legs," Robinot said, still muttering through his half-open mouth. "You heard our master Commynes. He mustn't be hurt in any way."

"Our master Commynes can talk. I'd like to see him in our shoes. Instead of which, there he is, between two beautiful ladies. Do you see the one on the right?"

Robinot glanced over at his master and saw Tersilla, sitting next to him, her little foot swaying lazily from left to right.

"Yes, I see her."

"She's undressing me with her eyes."

"Forget it. We need to think about work."

"I am thinking about it. And she's thinking about it too. How much longer is this thing going to drag on?"

As though to confirm Mattenet's words, the young lady turned and threw the young Frenchman a very Italian look, which spoke without the need for words. Then, after a languid moment, she turned back toward the singers.

"What did I tell you? Did you see that?"

Robinot turned and looked at his sidekick. Tall and straight, with broad shoulders, narrow hips, and all his teeth still in his mouth, displayed now in a young, mocking smile. All in all, a fine-looking youth.

Robinot studied him for a moment, then let his eyes wander slowly around the room, a slow, ravaged smile spreading across his face.

Just then, the music came to an end and applause washed over the musicians. Josquin bowed to the small but densely-packed group of listeners.

While everybody was applauding, Robinot went up to the Duke of Commynes, brought his mouth close to his ear, and whispered something. Almost immediately, the duke turned to his repellent aide, smiled, and nodded slowly. Then, drawing his lips close to Tersilla's ear, he whispered into it. The lady in waiting, casting a fleeting glance in Mattenet's direction, blushed and covered her face with her fan, although she was unable to conceal her smile.

Meanwhile, the Duke of Commynes also looked, and nodded with even more conviction, as though proud of his second aide's handsomeness.

Robinot rubbed his hands and returned to his companion.

"Well? What did the Duke say?"

"I'll tell you now."

* * *

"No."

"It's the only way."

"Not on your life."

"The Duke agrees. He thinks it's a brilliant idea."

"That's good of him! It's easy to be a hero when it's someone else's hide on the line. No, no, and no."

"Listen, these are the Duke's orders. The Duke has given me his word that if you come back with the notebook, the lady in waiting will be yours."

"And if I come back without the notebook?"

"Then it'll mean Messer Leonardo will have screwed you twice. And the third time the Duke will do it himself." Robinot nudged his accomplice with his elbow and handed him a goblet full of wine. "Come on, stop making a fuss. Leonardo's alone. Use your charm and ask him if he'd like company on his way home."

Mattenet looked around. A few meters away, the Duke of

Commynes met his gaze and raised an eyebrow, then turned his eyes to Leonardo, who was alone, his back against a pillar, looking thoughtful, like someone who has better things to do.

Mattenet took the goblet without enthusiasm, raised it to his lips, emptied it in two gulps, and returned it to his companion without looking at him.

"When I come back, I'll kill you."

TEN

D o you really run the risk of losing all this?"

"Alas, yes, Messer Leonardo," Father Diodato replied, eyes downcast. "I don't know when exactly it'll happen, but we're in the Lord's hands. And His Lordship's."

Leonardo nodded slowly, still looking at the frescoes in the large refectory. Just to make it clear, they were nothing special, what we would nowadays call "late 15th-century Lombard school," more appropriate for a degree thesis than a paying public. Bernardino Butinone and Bernardo Zenale, as well as the odd niche and makeover by a spurious hand that Leonardo was able to recognize with just one look, and no desire to give it a second.

And yet it was obvious that the good Father Diodato was worried. Not so much at the thought of losing the frescoes, which he had partly commissioned himself, but at the prospect of losing the pictorial support—in other words, the building.

"His Lordship's new law is very clear," Father Diodato continued. "Anybody wishing to expand and enlarge his place of commerce or manufacture may expropriate the buildings adjacent to his own establishment, unless they are already a part of other places of commerce or manufacture."

"But you're also in commerce, unless I'm mistaken," Leonardo said, his eyes still wandering over the frescoes. Recent frescoes.

Leonardo didn't like the fresco technique. Too quick, too

decisive. It didn't give you time to think again, to correct, to add shade and gradation.

"Oh, very little," Father Diodato said. "We're small-scale artisans. We produce brandy, and pigments for painting, as well you know. Fortunately, when our fellow brother Eligio da Varramista led a secular life, he was accustomed to keeping double-entry books, and he keeps a close watch on every item of expenditure in order to avoid wasting money. And Friar Eligio is much more careful and punctilious in his practice than any other of our brothers. But our Congregation was created precisely to oppose the commerce in everything inside the Holy Roman Church. We're too small as merchants, and of too little importance as a religious Congregation."

Leonardo nodded absent-mindedly while still looking around.

The monastery of the Poor of Jesus, dedicated to Saint Jerome, stood in Porta Vercellina, along the Naviglio. If anyone wished to look for it nowadays, they would go down Corso Magenta until it intersects with Via Carducci (which was in fact once called San Girolamo), then walk along that street until they get to the block between Via Mellerio and Via Marradi, after which they should start digging. Because nothing actually remains of the monastery these days.

"The decision lies with Cardinal Ascanio, il Moro's brother," Father Diodato continued. "And if he decides against us, our monastery will become part of a shoemaker's workshop, and we'll be left with a church that's too large for the few souls who prefer it to San Francesco Grande."

"How many friars does the monastery have at the moment?"

"Almost forty. It's not big, but it's not small either. But let's go back to us, Messer Leonardo. To what do I owe the honor of your visit?"

Leonardo fumbled with his pink headdress, which perfectly

matched his salmon-colored garment and clashed violently with the rest of the refectory.

"I've come by, Father, to apologize if I offended you and Friar Gioacchino last night. It was not my intention to say anything akin to heresy, as I hope you will realize."

Father Diodato shrugged. "There's no need to apologize, Leonardo. On the contrary, it is I who am sorry. Doubly sorry. Firstly, because Friar Gioacchino's reaction was rash and disproportionate. Secondly, because I was very interested in what you were saying. Friar Gioacchino is unable to tell the difference between reasoning and provocation. For him, there are no degrees or shades, everything is black or white. Unlike your painting. I've always been struck by how you make faces emerge from dozens of color glazes."

Leonardo opened his eyes slightly and raised his head. Receiving constant compliments was tiresome—especially if one receives them in lieu of money—but nothing is more flattering to an artist than to feel valued for the very thing that is, according to the artist himself, his true, genuine singularity.

"Well, Father, a good painter has two things to paint, man and the concept of his mind. When we see a man, we don't see a nose, a mouth, a row of teeth. We see an intention, peaceable or malign, an object on which he is concentrating, or the serenity he feels when contemplating his own wellbeing. We can see this in the man's actions and movements, whether these are perceptible or not. A painting does not move, and yet I must make sure that whoever looks at it sees that movement, those intentions." Leonardo smiled. "It would be a serious mistake to paint all that just with clearly-defined, immutable lines. The boundary between one thing and another, between a face and the wall behind it, changes position if I move or if one of those two things moves, because that boundary doesn't exist. It's located only in my eyes and in my intellect."

"Ah, now that's the topic I found fascinating," Father

Diodato said after a few moments' silence. "You maintain that the power of man resides in language, because it allows him to describe things that don't exist."

"All languages draw their power from this. Imagine what hard work it would be for me to construct a scene that gives a worthy representation of the Marriage at Cana." Leonardo pointed to a scene on the surrounding fresco, since that was its theme. "I'd have to get dozens of guests, a table, food, and, finally, be able to turn water into wine. It's too much for me, and I doubt even Bramante would succeed. But let's take a brush, a little whipped egg, a few of your excellent paints, and here we are." With his open palm, Leonardo indicated the wall painted by Zenale. "We're done. It's no small feat, don't you think?"

* * *

"Well, gentlemen, our task is almost done. We have no reason to linger in Milan any longer. I mean no official reason. Do you understand me, Robinot?"

His elbows on the table, the Duke of Commynes was drumming his fingertips against one another. Near the table, Robinot was pacing impatiently up and down.

"I understand perfectly, Duke. As I was saying, Mattenet didn't return to his lodgings last night, and that's a good sign."

"He could have been murdered in the street," Perron de Basche said, looking up. "Or else he could have been struck by divine wrath. Apparently, it's dangerous to walk around Milan these days if one is in a state of sin."

"In that case, this castle should have burned down decades ago, and us along with it. Excuse me, I hear knocking."

The three men fell silent. A few seconds later, they did indeed hear a couple of quick, almost furtive taps at the door. Robinot strode over to it and asked, "Who's there?"

"Me, it's me," Mattenet's voice replied.

* * *

"I understand, Father. You are the prior."

"Precisely, Messer Leonardo. I can appreciate that Friar Gioacchino's behavior upset you, but I can assure you, you have nothing to fear from him."

"So he doesn't mean to write to the bishop and accuse me of heresy?"

"I can't rule that out. What I can rule out is the letter ever being dispatched." Father Diodato looked at Leonardo good-naturedly. "No letter leaves here without my reading it, Messer Leonardo. And none reaches my fellow brothers' hands without undergoing the same fate. When words are written down, they travel far, last over time, and can cause damage. My power, like all power, lies in knowing more than my flock."

Leonardo and Father Deodato were walking around the cloisters, and had already done the complete circuit a couple of times. When they reached the refectory, the prior stopped, looked at Leonardo again, and spoke in a voice as firm as his footwear:

"There's something else Friar Gioacchino is wrong about. You see, Leonardo, it's quite true that my Congregation was founded to oppose the excess of money and commerce, the constant commercialization of the word of the Lord by men of the cloth. That's why we're called the Poor of Jesus."

Leonardo nodded. He knew the story of Colombini, the Sienese merchant who had converted after reading Jacopo da Varagine's *Golden Legend* on the lives of the saints, stripped himself of everything, and begun a life of poverty. He was Sienese, just as all the Congregation's friars were Sienese or Tuscan. Apart from Friar Gioacchino, Leonardo had never known a Lombard Jesuate.

"Money must be shunned, but the true master of Milan is not money. Money is used as a means to power, not for its own sake, as an end. From il Moro, who uses his niece's dowry to get himself acclaimed as duke, to the lowliest of the municipal secretaries, who acquires his position by buying it from his predecessors. The diabolical form they worship isn't money, it's power."

Still speaking, the prior went through the refectory door, Leonardo following him.

"But this power is an ephemeral, mortal power. Only the Almighty can have true power over men. Man, every man, whatever his place in the world, taunts the Almighty and grants himself rights he doesn't have, rights that belong only to God."

"You do the same," Leonardo said in a low voice.

"Yes, I do the same," the prior said, looking around. "But I'm aware of that. I know my mortal nature, which is the reason our power is just an illusion. We're fleeting, we are leaves on the branch farthest from the trunk."

"Yes, father. It's something I've been thinking a great deal about in these last few days."

Father Diodato looked at him with the air, not so much of a friar as of a confessor. "You've no doubt heard of that poor man who was murdered then left in the middle of the castle, may God have mercy on his soul?"

"His name was Chiti. Rambaldo Chiti. An apprentice of mine whom I was forced to send packing several months ago." Still looking at the frescoes, Leonardo took a few steps forward. "Perhaps you knew him too."

"No, I really don't think so. Why do you ask?"

Leonardo shook his head, as though to dismiss a doubt. "I had the impression he lived not far from here, in a room in San Vittore. Although, admittedly, he wasn't the kind to attend Mass."

"From what I hear, Leonardo, you don't attend much either."

* * *

"No, I didn't sleep much either," Mattenet began. There were deep, dark rings under his eyes, as if he'd had hardly any rest. "It got very late, it was already dark even in the widest streets. I tried to make conversation as we walked, but he was obviously absorbed in other thoughts and had accepted my invitation just to be polite."

Sitting opposite him at the table were the Duke of Commynes and Perron de Basche. Robinot was walking around the table, with slow but anxious steps.

"We finally reached his house and I asked him if I could come up with him to see what he was working on. I said I was an admirer of his work and his paintings. He replied that he was very tired and wanted to go to bed. So I took my courage in my hands and said, 'Master, I am here to offer you my body. Do with it as you please.'"

"And what did he say?"

"He looked at me. And smiled."

And that was when Mattenet had started to wonder. Leonardo's smile had actually been incredibly sweet. Not lascivious, not mocking, not sensuous; but sweet, sweet and happy, as though amazed by such a stroke of luck. So sweet and lovely that maybe . . . no, I don't even want to think about it. I like women. I'm here to do my duty.

"And then?"

"He looked at me as if he was seeing me for the first time. From top to toe. Then he opened the door, took me by the hand, and let me in. What the fuck are you laughing at, scabby head?"

"Nothing, nothing," Robinot said. "Please continue."

Mattenet took a deep breath, then rubbed his hands on his pants, back and forth, as though wiping something disgusting off them. "He took me to a room. I think it was his bedroom. There was a bed, and sheets of paper all over the place. He put his hands on my shoulders and slowly unfastened my tunic. He ran his hands over my chest, still smiling. Within a few seconds, I was naked."

"Naked and not sure what to do," the duke said, unable to restrain a smile.

"That's right. Naked and not sure what to do. If I move, I thought, I'll either hug him or punch him. So I let him take the initiative and he . . ."

"And he? What did he do?"

Mattenet put his hands on the table and clung to it, as though about to confess an unspeakable sin. ". . . he drew my portrait."

* * *

Perfect proportions, you see, perfect proportions. One seventh, one fifth. But the center isn't the same, that's the secret. The center isn't the same. The square and the circle mustn't have the same center, or it won't work. I must write this to Francesco di Giorgio immediately.

Leonardo looked at the paper on his desk. A man with open arms and legs close together, standing inside a square, superimposed on the same man with arms spread wide and legs apart, contained inside a circle. Perfectly. Here it is, the perfection of man.

This is what makes a man a man: proportions. It's the same distance from the shoulder to the ulna as from the ulna to the wrist. That way the arm can bend and the hand reach everything within its radius, without blind or unattainable spots, which would exist if the forearm were longer, or shorter, than the section before it. Proportions, proportions. Man has perfect proportions, and this sets us apart from the dog or the horse. And without this perfection, we couldn't. We couldn't pick up objects. We couldn't even stand up. Carry our head, the heaviest, most serious part of the body, so far from the ground. We're the only ones to do that. It's just a matter of proportions. The fly doesn't do it, the elephant doesn't do it . . .

"Leonardo!"

"I'm upstairs, Caterina."

"Can you come down and give me a hand? The eggs need collecting and I'm on my own!"

"I'm coming, I'm coming."

She won't leave me alone, not even once.

* * *

"Not even once!"

Slap.

"Not once, I say!"

Another slap.

"Not once, not once, I say, do you manage to do what you're asked!"

The Duke of Commynes was standing there, blue in the face. In front of him, motionless, Mattenet and Robinot, being assailed by the duke's outburst, as he yelled like a third-division coach, underlining his words with terrifying slaps on the table instead of exclamation marks.

Sitting, or rather, slumped on the table, next to him, Perron de Basche was laughing. He, too, was slamming his fist on the table, tears in his eyes.

"And you, de Basche, stop laughing, for heaven's sake!"

"I can't help it. How could anyone be so dumb—"

Slap. Not on the table this time, but on the back of Perron de Basche's neck, making him slam his gums on the table.

"Enough, fuck it! Enough of this laughing! And enough messing about! Tomorrow, the day after tomorrow at the latest, we have to leave. We have no reason to extend our visit, it'd arouse suspicion. So I want that notebook tonight. Do anything you like, but bring me that notebook!"

"Anything?"

"Anything."

"Even . . ."

The Duke of Commynes brought his face much closer to Robinot's, to within a distance that manners or esthetics would have considered an overstepping of the bounds. "Listen, rock head, and keep my words in your mind. If you don't bring me the notebook, I'll cut off your head. You have to bring me the notebook, and any damage you do to Leonardo I will do to you. Do you understand?"

Robinot slowly turned to look at Mattenet.

This time it really is your problem, Mattenet's eyes said.

* * *

"Leonardo . . ."

"Hmm?"

"Leonardo, is it true?"

Leonardo was sitting at the kitchen table, a sheet of paper in front of him. Hearing his mother's voice for the second time, he had turned and instinctively covered the paper with his right hand. Then he had lifted it and resumed studying it, answering his mother without looking at her.

"Yes, Caterina."

"I didn't even ask you what!"

Leonardo turned again and looked at his mother, laying his left hand on the paper and scrunching it up. The sound seemed to be keeping time with the fire crackling in front of the table. "Something you're worried about, Caterina. You're worried about me. And since I'm worried too, I'm saying yes, it's true. There's good reason to worry."

"Oh, Blessed Mother of God!" Caterina replied, making the sign of the cross. "Did you really have to say those foolish things to a man of the Church?"

"Foolish things? Church? I don't understand, Mother."

"Today, Friar Gioacchino said in his sermon that yesterday, while he was a guest in a noblewoman's house, listening to music, a man who thinks himself a great genius but is nothing but a little fool said that God gave men the power of speech only so they could lie, and that God's greatest gift is the lie."

"Listen, Caterina—"

"Yesterday, you went to listen to music at the house of Countess Bergamini, the one you call Gallerani, il Moro's favorite—"

"She was il Moro's favorite—"

"—and I bet it was you who uttered those absurd blasphemies. Or am I wrong, Leonardo?"

Leonardo stood up from his desk, slowly, the scrunched-up paper in his hand. "You're wrong, Mother. You're wrong, just as he's wrong." Leonardo took the ball of paper between his fingers and threw it into the fire. "Friar Gioacchino da Brenno is so enlightened by Our Lord that he's sometimes blinded and makes mistakes. I was speaking figuratively, and he took me literally."

"Go on, Leonardo, be clever. In the meantime, you're worried too, and rightly so. The man could denounce you and get you into trouble with the Holy Church."

"Of course he could. In fact, he probably already has."

"So what are you planning to do to defend yourself?"

"Me? I don't have to do anything, Mother. Friar Gioacchino can blab all he likes, but we're not in Florence here, Mother, or in Rome, where they burn men as if they were firewood. This is Milan, the home of Ludovico il Moro."

"Then why are you worried?"

Leonardo looked at the fire without seeing it. "That's why, Mother. Precisely because we're in the home of Ludovico il Moro."

"I don't understand you, Leonardo."

Leonardo went up to Caterina, put his hands on her shoulders, and squeezed them gently. "I know you don't. It's better that way, trust me."

* * *

Caterina stared at the door for a moment after Leonardo had left. Then her eyes drifted back to the fireplace, where the flame was licking at the scrunched-up paper her son had thrown in the direction of the fire, narrowly missing it.

Why had he scrunched it up? Because he'd written something improper on it. Something that could have gotten him into trouble. Like that time when he'd written that the sun doesn't move. It was Salaì who'd told her how he and Marco d'Oggiono had teased him for a long time and asked him if by any chance it was the earth that moved, and Leonardo had smiled and shaken his head.

Caterina instinctively went to the fireplace and with a rapid movement lifted the ball of paper out of the hearth. She returned to the table and opened it, spreading it on the table top.

Drawings. A mouse, a cat, an elephant. And a few handwritten lines, which for her were an impenetrable secret. Caterina couldn't read when things were written the right way around, let alone backwards.

"Greetings, Caterina," Salaì said cheerfully, walking in. "What's for dinner tonight? Please don't say turnips again."

"My little Giacomo, are you able to read my son's handwriting?"

"Of course, Caterina."

"Could you tell me what it says here?"

Salaì bent over the paper and frowned. Then he began to spell it out.

> *Take two times two and you get four.*
> *Take three times three and you get nine.*
> *Take four times four and you get sixteen.*
> *Take five times five and you get twenty-five.*
> *And if you divide forty-nine by seven, you get seven.*
> *This will apply to the armor as well as the shell, since it applies to the bone and the cannon.*

Caterina looked at Salaì with some alarm. Then she looked again at the paper, with those drawings of a mouse and an elephant that looked so real it felt almost unnatural to see them standing still.

"Are you pulling my leg, little Giacomo?"

"Not at all, Madonna Caterina, no. It's written exactly as I read it."

"And what on earth does it mean?"

"How should I know?"

THINGS TO DO

Speak with Accerrito the banker to see if he ever receives false letters, and how he recognizes them.

Speak with Captain Galeazzo about how a body can be dumped inside the Piazzale delle Armi in the Castello Sforzesco and how come nobody saw it being done.

Speak again with Master Antonio the armorer about how much strength is required to suffocate a man inside a suit of armor. This time go on your own.

If you understand these three things you will understand how this incident took place, since effects follow causes, just as branches sprout from the trunk, and no tree grows from branches born from the air. The more facts you learn, the easier you will find the cause from which they spring, since all the facts converge in the same trunk and it only takes one for you to see them all, but if the trunk is hidden in dense forest, the more branches you have in order to find it, the better.

I write my duties, and I know my duties, but others do not. A painter's duty is to paint, an armorer's duty is to make armor, a customer's duty is to pay for the work when it has been done to perfection. And a painter's duty is to live and eat and give his apprentices a decent life, because if one cannot eat then one does not live, and if one does not live then one cannot paint. Although I ask myself why I am staying here in Milan, with all the other places there are in the world.

And leave the horse alone for the moment.

ELEVEN

S o, then. Every branch of a river carries water to the main river, and every branch of a tree is connected to the trunk.

If you see a tree growing and forking, and measure the diameter of its trunk and the diameter of the two forks, you'll find that their sum is equal to the diameter of the trunk. At any height, if you take the branches at that altitude and make them into a bundle, this bundle will be as thick as the trunk.

If two branches meet in one point, this point must be thicker at its base than the branches. It has never been seen that branches sprouting from a trunk are thicker than the trunk itself. It's the same for man. If you join his fingers, they are as wide as the palm of his hand, if you put his legs together, they are as wide as his hips, and if you lift his arms next to his head, all of this, arms and head, is as wide as his chest.

* * *

The man sitting next to Leonardo looked at him with a puzzled expression, and only then did Leonardo notice that he had raised his arms beside his head, his hands together, like a diver on an Olympic springboard. Solemnly, pretending to assess the nature of some pain in his joints, Leonardo lowered his arms and sighed.

He had been waiting for almost half an hour. And during

that half-hour, in a room in Porta Comasina adorned with a carved marble door, his brain had wandered off, as usual. And, as usual, it constantly veered away from the main problem, and Leonardo was obliged to force it back to the Problem with a capital P. That was when he noticed. Because sometimes his mind would get lost in such a powerful and promising thought that it took great commitment even just to realize that he was fantasizing. Even though, in actual fact, this wandering around branches had a reason. If two branches meet at a point, that point must be as thick as the sum of both branches. And therefore it must be thicker than each of the two branches taken alone. And given that this point is certainly—

"Messer Leonardo da Vinci?"

"Yes," Leonardo said, getting to his feet.

"This way. Messer Accerrito will receive you in person."

* * *

"Ah, Leonardo, what a pleasure. Come in, come in. Forgive the wait, but it's been a very busy morning, or rather, a very busy couple of days. In fact, you must forgive me, but I can't give you very long."

"Do not fret, Messer Accerrito. I am not accustomed to insisting in the face of refusal. I am not here to ask for money. The coin I ask is much more precious."

And here Messer Accerrito gave a little shudder, a mixture of anxiety and annoyance.

"It isn't hard currency I wish to speak about but the softer kind." Leonardo smiled, thoroughly pleased at his interlocutor's obvious discomfort. "You are a wizard, but in a way that doesn't upset the authority of the Church and its courts. You turn paper into coins, and vice-versa. I therefore ask of you only this: a few answers."

"Gladly, if I can provide them," Accerrito said, increasingly troubled. "But bear in mind that in matters of credit, silence is golden."

"I am sure it is. Gold is gold, and paper is paper. Turning paper into gold when one doesn't have the possibility to do so may not upset the Holy Mother Church, but it certainly annoys His Lordship Ludovico il Moro."

Accerrito turned slightly pale. The punishment for forgers, as well as for those who circulated false coins knowing their origin, was death. "Very well," Accerrito said, swallowing. "Ask me a specific, concise question and I will give you a concise, specific answer."

"Alas, alas, you are an optimist, Messer Accerrito. Often, the more specific the question, the more difficult, more nebulous the reply. But let us not digress. The first question is: Have you ever had anything to do with fake letters of credit?"

Accerrito Portinari appeared to hold his breath for a second. His eyes swept over his desk, as though it might provide him with a reply. "Why do you ask?"

"Because the wretched man who was murdered, and then left in the Piazzale d'Armi, Rambaldo Chiti, had a letter of credit signed by Bencio Serristori in his room. A fake letter."

"How do you know it was fake?"

"It was signed and dated the twenty-fourth of June."

Accerrito Portinari was silent for a moment, then burst into hearty, almost hysterical laughter. It took him several seconds to calm down. "The twenty-fourth of June? Imagine that! Bencio working on the Feast of Saint John! What forger would be foolish enough to commit such a stupid error?"

"I think it was Chiti himself, Messer Accerrito."

Accerrito's face darkened. "But wasn't this Chiti one of your apprentices?"

"He was. I threw him out a long time ago, when I discovered what a scoundrel he was. But forgive me, Accerrito, you haven't yet answered my question."

Accerrito Portinari linked his fingers in front of his face, then lowered his hands to his belly and leaned back in his chair. "Have I ever had anything to do with phoney letters of credit, you ask? Yes, it's possible. In fact, it's almost certain."

"And what do you do when you receive one you think is fake?"

"I pay it."

"You pay it?"

"Of course. Unless it's obviously fake, as in the case you mention. Or unless the figure is an exorbitant one, in which case I would have been informed in advance by a personal letter that a branch has granted Messer So-and-so a credit of twenty thousand ducats, say, and in that case I would have sufficient time to scrape the money together."

"Wouldn't it be better for you to investigate so as to ascertain whether or not it's fake?"

"It would be even better for me if people didn't lose faith in the credit system. You see, Messer Leonardo, if I started asking pointless questions about every letter of credit I think is fake, people would stop using our bank and go elsewhere. Letters of credit are used by travelers, by strangers who don't have time to stay long. I can't tell them to stay in Milan for a week, they'd tell me to go to hell."

"And couldn't someone other than the holder cash it?"

"Only if authorized by the holder. That's a brand-new service, and my bank is one of the first to offer it." Accerrito smiled, then his face darkened again. "As it happens, that's my problem this morning. One of my customers has died, and even before his body has had time to turn cold, I'm surrounded by heirs who want to know if he had money in his account, and if so how much, and I have to work out who among them is entitled to ask me that. The poor man was murdered, and these people are at my door armed with rocks, clamoring for money. So if you'll excuse me, I must—"

"But of course, Messer Accerrito, of course. Murdered, you say?"

"Stabbed while leaving an inn. Inexplicable."

"Perhaps he had gambling problems? Or there was an altercation over a woman?"

"Hardly. He was an elderly, respectable man, the kind who always do things properly. Poor Signor Barraccio."

"Barraccio? Not Giovanni Barraccio?"

"Yes, him. The wool merchant. Did you know him?"

* * *

"Yes, of course, I know him," Cecilia Gallerani said, looking at Leonardo with disbelief in her eyes. "We were talking of him only yesterday afternoon. And you're telling me he's dead?"

"Murdered, Countess. Stabbed outside an inn."

"That's terrible. Oh, Holy Mother of God, a man so . . . so . . ."

"Respectable?"

"Yes, Messer Leonardo. A good man, generous, hard-working. I find it hard to believe that someone could have quarreled with him to the point of stabbing him. Did you come all the way here in such a rush to tell me this?"

"Yes, Countess. You see, Giovanni Barraccio's name was mentioned yesterday because he was one of the people I knew who'd had dealings with my friend the banker whose letter of credit was forged . . . What?"

Leonardo's astonishment was not unjustified. Cecilia had suddenly squeezed his arm with her right hand, in an unexpected, inappropriate, but nevertheless not at all unpleasant contact.

"A letter of credit? Listen, Messer Leonardo. Last summer, in mid-August, I met with Giovanni Barraccio to order a few things.

We talked a little, as usual, and he asked me if by any chance I had ever used a letter of credit. I told him I had never had either the need or the opportunity, but that if I could help him I would gladly do so. He then asked me if one of these letters was still valid even if the person who had issued it was dead."

Leonardo didn't say anything. Which didn't mean he had nothing to say. But Cecilia did not need to be led.

"I replied that I didn't understand these things, but that I knew more than one person who might perhaps help him. I gave him the name of one in particular. You and I both know him. And now you tell me that Messer Barraccio has been killed."

"Pardon me, Countess, I have a very specific idea of the person to whom you are referring, but I would like my suspicions to be confirmed."

"So you also have a name in mind?"

"A very specific name, Countess. Shall I say it or will you?"

Cecilia blushed and looked away. A mantle of embarrassment had fallen around them, as tangible and heavy as one of Master Antonio Missaglia's suits of armor, but even harder to take off.

"We look like two people in love, Messer Leonardo."

Leonardo, who until that moment had been the same color as his garment, now became indistinguishable from his hat.

"Forgive me, Countess, it was not my intention to make you feel uncomfortable. I sometimes forget who I am and whom I am addressing. It had better be I who utters the name."

* * *

"Accerrito Portinari, director of the bank at Porta Comasina."

"Come in, come in, Messer Portinari," Ludovico said, remaining seated. "How are you?"

Accerrito Portinari looked around. He had never felt uneasy in this room. On the contrary. It was one of the places where power was exercised. But today, Ludovico, the members of the Council, and even the chevrons decorating the walls seemed to be looking at him with a blend of annoyance and suspicion.

"I am well, Your Lordship, quite well."

"And how is business? I hope being back in your original head office is proving beneficial, both to your morale and to your customers."

"As it happens, that's what I've come to speak about with Your Lordship. Two things happened today. Two distinct things that may not be distinct after all."

"Please explain yourself, Portinari."

"Well, I've received many requests for money by letter of credit today."

"That's good, isn't it? It is the nature of your work, after all."

"Yes, it's good, except for one thing. There's something strange about these letters."

"In what way strange?"

"Well, they're all signed by the same banker. A Florentine banker, Bencio Serristori."

"Bencio Serristori," Ludovico said, turning the name over in his mouth like one of those aniseed candies his wife liked so much but that he found disgusting and ate only so as not to upset her. "That's quite a coincidence."

"Yes, it is. It sometimes happens that two letters from the same banker arrive on the same day. There's an explanation for that. People travel together from Marseilles, Konstanz, or Bruges, to be safer, and arrive at the same time."

"But what we have here is more than two letters, if I understand correctly."

"Yes, Your Lordship. And all signed by a banker who died in the middle of the summer. Florence is a long way from here, so it's not easy to check our records, especially if the banker who signed these letters died months ago."

"He died?" Ludovico said, feigning surprise.

"Yes, he died. Do you see what I mean?"

"You fear these letters might be fakes."

"I more than fear it, Your Lordship. Moreover, this is the worst possible time to deal with such an emergency. I am swamped with the collection of promissory notes and loans. And on top of that . . ."

"On top of that?"

"Today at about terce, Messer Leonardo da Vinci, who is a friend, came to see me. We've known each other since our Florence days, when I was a young man and he was a boy, and when he moved to Milan I was one of his first associates."

"I'm sure you and Leonardo are well acquainted," Ludovico said curtly, although in truth he had a vague sense that Accerrito was exaggerating somewhat. They didn't seem to him like two people who could be on such familiar terms. In the past, perhaps, but not now.

"Well, today Leonardo came to me and asked if during my banking career I had ever had anything to do with fake letters of credit. He told me he feared they had been produced by someone named Rambaldo Chiti, a former apprentice of his, whom Leonardo said he dismissed after experiencing his iniquity. If I understood correctly, this Chiti is the very person who was found dead in your Piazzale delle Armi."

Ludovico looked Accerrito Portinari up and down, from top to toe. Until that day, he had always thought of the manager of the Milanese branch of the Medici Bank as a toad. Except that toads weren't supposed to have scales.

"The Piazzale isn't mine, it belongs to the castle, and the castle belongs to the Duchy of Milan," Ludovico said, looking around. "As for the rest, I cannot deny that what you're saying is true."

"That, Your Lordship, is all I came to tell. There have been far too many coincidences in my bank today, and I felt it my duty to report them to you, just the way they happened."

"Thank you, Messer Portinari." Ludovico gave a signal and the servant at the door rapped on it with his knuckles. The door was opened from the outside and the castellan came in. "Castellan, wait before you show the next supplicant in. Good evening, Messer Portinari."

"May God protect Your Lordship."

While Accerrito Portinari slithered away, Ludovico joined his hands together in front of his face and began to rub.

Leonardo was a Florentine. Bencio Serristori was a Florentine. The Medici Bank was Florentine. Who could have had the facility to obtain a letter of credit from a Florentine banker? Someone who had ongoing contact with Florence. Like Leonardo. But.

But really, Leonardo? Were we talking about the same man? Could Ludovico have been so grossly wrong about him?

Ludovico raised his eyes and met those of Galeazzo Sanseverino.

It's possible, Galeazzo's eyes said. I don't believe it, but it's possible.

"Captain, would you please go fetch Messer Leonardo?" Then, more loudly: "Castellan, today's audience is suspended."

"There are just two more people, Your Lordship."

"Tell them to come back tomorrow. We will hold a supplementary session to hear those who were left out."

"They claim it's important, Your Lordship."

"Everything's important to an interested party, even the smoke from their neighbor's chimney," Ludovico said, standing up and gathering his garment around his legs as he turned. "Tell them to come back tomorrow or go to hell."

"Tell me yourself, if you're able to," a polite but firm voice said. A woman's voice.

Ludovico turned again and noticed a few blushing faces among his dignitaries.

On the threshold, dignified and haughty, stood Cecilia Gallerani. Beside her, Leonardo da Vinci.

* * *

"Countess, dear Cecilia. Why come see me as a supplicant?"

"Because today *I am* a supplicant, Your Lordship," Cecilia replied, with flushed cheeks and narrowed eyes. "Today I come to you as a Milanese and a subject of the Duke of Milan and of those who have power in this city. Messer Leonardo and I have extremely important news to impart to you, so that justice may be done and the city not fall into ruin."

"Really?" Ludovico said, trying to make light of it, but failing. Every word carries more or less weight, depending on who utters it, and the fact that his interlocutors were Leonardo and Cecilia Gallerani could not leave him indifferent. The two people who were before him now had more brains than the rest of the residents in his castle put together, present company included.

"You will judge for yourself, Your Lordship."

"Very well." Ludovico turned to his councilors. "In that case, since I have to judge for myself, gentlemen, I ask you to withdraw."

* * *

"I understand," Ludovico said, hands joined together, knuckles over his lips and eyes closed, something which never happened in public.

"So, Ludovico . . . I mean, Your Lordship," Cecilia said, as though embarrassed at having addressed him by his first name. "Was I right? Is it or is it not a matter of capital importance?"

"Yes, Cecilia." Ludovico opened his eyes, seeming to real-ize only then, with a second's delay, that Leonardo was also in the room. "Yes, Countess. It is. In fact, it was important before, now it is even more so. But I must check. You can appreciate that what you say makes sense, resonates with me, and is consistent. Now I must see if it's true."

"But Your Lordship—"

"I have spoken with you. And I have also spoken with Accerrito Portinari this very day. I must compare your reports and see if they are true. Meanwhile, you, Leonardo, will remain at the castle. You still have an obligation toward me, and by staying here you will avoid distractions."

Leonardo bowed his head, slightly embittered. The first part was true, the second ambiguous. In this way, Ludovico was stopping Leonardo from going around making agreements with anyone or making anything disappear. It was obvious he still had his doubts about him.

"Good. There's one more person I need to speak to, and then I will make an informed decision."

And Ludovico headed for the door.

Yes, this was the right decision, Leonardo thought. There was indeed one person who absolutely had to be questioned about this matter.

"Castellan!" Ludovico called, knocking on the door.

The heavy door opened and the sallow, unhealthy face of Bernardino da Corte appeared.

"Send for Magistro Ambrogio da Rosate. I need him to consult the stars."

But it wasn't him he was thinking of.

To Ercole d'Este, Duke of Ferrara, ferre cito! cito!! cito!!!

My Most Illustrious, Most Respected Lord,
I send Your Excellency news of the events of today and last night, so that you may be aware of the developments and provide your counsel.

Last night, Messer Leonardo da Vinci was assaulted as he was coming out of the Castello Sforzesco on the side of the new Broletto, at the end of the Maino district. Two men with covered faces stopped him and attempted to do him violence.

As the aforesaid Leonardo was making an effort to escape, a young man arrived, screaming like a demon, and lashed out cum *the flat and the sharp of his sword.* Item *there arrived two other men from the Cusani district,* et *two more men armed with sword and hammer coming from another direction and* in specie *from the Nirone district, and all four leaped into the fray with such clamor and commotion that shouts, swearing, bad language, and I will not tell you what else came from the house of Giovanni del Maino.*

Members of the del Maino family joined in the confusion, attempting to put a stop to this disorderly merry-go-round in which everybody dealt random blows while Messer Leonardo made a great struggle to extricate himself from this tangle, reminiscent of Laocoön and his sons.

*Asked to calm down, the screaming young man was rec-
ognized by Leonardo as Jacomo Caprotti also known as
Salaíno, his apprentice. Two of the armed men said their
names were Graziano and Ottolino, in the service of the Most
Illustrious Bernardino da Corte, the Duke's castellan, who
confirmed their claim. The other two were identified as
Frenchmen, Gaspard Robinot and Geoffroy Mattenet, attendants to the Duke of Commynes. Finally, and this is the ulti-
mate reason for my most expedient letter, the last two men
said they were Veniero del Balzo and Coriolano Ferrari,
envoys of Your Most Illustrious Lordship, the Duke of
Ferrara.*

*The three pairs of armed men began insulting one
another, blaming one another for the assault on the aforesaid
Messer Leonardo, while the aforementioned Salaíno insisted
cum* force *et anco cum* coarse *words that his master and
teacher had been assaulted by the Frenchmen and, when
asked how he had recognized them, replied that it was by
their horrible stench. This unleashed another brawl, which
was immediately calmed by His Illustrious Lordship
Ludovico's nine guards, who had arrived* in itinere. *All these
men are currently confined in the prison of the Castello
Sforzesco, except for Leonardo and Salaíno, who are in the
house of the aforesaid Leonardo.*

*I am writing because His Lordship Ludovico summoned
me this morning at an early hour to put an end to the quarrel
and request the presence at court of Your Most Illustrious
Lordship for the trial of the two men claiming to be your
envoys, and so I am imploring Your Most Illustrious
Lordship's counsel.*

In other words, to put it in a nutshell, you sent soldiers
to Milan without telling me, and now, as usual, it's up to me

to get you out of this shit. So you'd better turn up in Milan
pretty damn quickly, my dear Ercole, Duke of Ferrara,

to whose benevolence I commend myself as ever.
Mediolano, XXIII octubris 1493
Servus Jacomo Trotti

TWELVE

"Signor Giacomo Trotti, ambassador of His Most Illustrious Lordship Ercole, Duke of Ferrara."

"Show him in," Ludovico said, without much ceremony.

And, without further ado, Giacomo Trotti came in, with his hat in his hand and a not-very-clear plan of action in his head.

Ludovico was waiting for him, apparently calm, sitting on the high-backed chair in the center of the Room of the Chevrons.

As Leonardo liked to say, speaking about painting, the artist must depict the appearance of a man and his mind's intention through the posture and movement of his body. In this case, all one would have to do to portray Ludovico and fully relate his intent would be to pay attention to how he was sitting.

His body firmly propped against the back of the chair, his chin high, his jaw clenched, his hands resting with palms down, relaxed, on the armrests. This is my place, Ludovico was saying. The chair, the room, the entire city around us. I am lord here, and that is not up for discussion. Now we are going to speak and explain ourselves, and it won't be easy, but don't forget that fact while we're talking. Or else? There is no "or else," I won't even deign to consider an "or else" option. I'm the one in charge here. Don't forget it. Period.

"I offer my respects to Your Lordship," Giacomo Trotti said as he walked in.

"A pity," Ludovico said.

"I beg your pardon?"

"It's a pity," Ludovico repeated, without any sign of getting to his feet. "I had hoped you would be offering me an apology from my father-in-law Ercole for sending undisciplined soldiery to a city I lead and govern without even asking my permission."

Giacomo Trotti rubbed his hands behind his back. This wasn't a particularly pleasant situation. Ercole on one side, Ludovico on the other, and, in the middle, specific orders to report. What one needed to do here was to be a kind of glue—to become fluid, adhere to both sides of the vise constricting him, then to dry, remaining firmly in his position, forcing the two parties to acknowledge that it was the only possibility.

"Your Lordship is entirely in the right. In family relations, especially when the individuals are powerful, mutual trust should be paramount. In justification of my Most Illustrious Lord's actions, I can only suggest that he meant well and took the same measures as Your Most Illustrious Lordship."

"I don't understand. What measures am I supposed to have taken?"

"You assigned two men to protect Messer Leonardo da Vinci, just as my Lord did."

"You're mistaken, Messer Giacomo. The two guards intervened after their sentry duty at the castle, when they heard a clamor and commotion coming from the Maino district."

"In that case may I be so bold as to suggest that when the war begins, Your Lordship might take these gentlemen into battle and appoint them couriers and messengers? They must be fast runners indeed to have arrived in the district all the way from the depths of the castle before Ercole's men."

"What do you mean?"

Giacomo Trotti took a deep breath. Showing a powerful man that he is wrong beyond any reasonable doubt was never easy, nor in the least useful.

"I presume, Your Lordship, that the men my Lord sent had

been instructed to watch over Messer Leonardo's safety, and so were following him discreetly, a few steps behind him, trying to pass unnoticed. Despite which, your soldiers arrived at the scene of the assault before the men from Ferrara."

"You presume?"

Trotti looked up. The moment had come to play *all-in*, as Texas Hold'em poker players would have said, had they witnessed the scene—highly improbable, given that America had been discovered barely a year earlier and during those months the *conquistadores* had had other things on their minds, like wiping out the natives, rather than inventing card games.

"Your Lordship, I am sure that Ercole intended to protect Messer Leonardo after I myself informed him of the secret project on which you are working."

"Secret project?"

"Call it what you will. The reason for Leonardo's leaving his house at night, every night, and coming to the castle in secret. The reason he's been in danger, so much so that the young man he calls Salaí has been following him, armed. So much so that you yourself have decided to keep him under protection. So much so that even Ercole, as a result of my letters to him, decided to keep him under protection."

Ludovico looked at Trotti, stony-faced. "I had my reasons for keeping Messer Leonardo under surveillance, and as you've seen, they were not unsound. Messer Leonardo was assaulted last night, and the work he is doing for me is something between him and me and has nothing to do with it."

"How do you know that?"

"Because it is a matter that cannot be of importance to anybody outside the castle."

Trotti tried to restrain himself, but didn't like being taken for an idiot. "Forgive me, Your Lordship, but actually, it's a matter of the greatest importance. I can understand your desire to keep it a secret, but it certainly wouldn't remain so for long. People would soon realize. They would realize and act accordingly. As you can appreciate, I cannot keep such a discovery secret from my Lord. In Ferrara, as well as in the rest of Europe, the reaction would be pandemonium."

It was now Ludovico's turn to look at Trotti as though he had turned into an idiot. "In Ferrara, Ambassador, yes, of course. But I honestly don't see what it has to do with the rest of Europe."

"Are you trying, then, to deny that Leonardo da Vinci has discovered the means to transmute base metal into gold?"

Ludovico was silent for a moment. His face turned scarlet.

Then he burst out laughing.

A belly laugh, like a boy who sees a man slipping and falling on the ice or a woman making twenty-six maneuvers to park her old clunker in a spot big enough for two.

The Duke of Bari and Lord of Milan was laughing so hard, he began to cry.

And all the while, Trotti stood there motionless, silent, and even somewhat shocked.

"Forgive me, Messer Giacomo, but these have been, and still are, trying days and I must have accumulated so much tension, like a loaded crossbow. And you pressed the trigger."

Ludovico took a deep breath, wiped away a tear, and was once again serious.

"No, Messer Ambassador, you're right, and I owe you an explanation. It's true that Leonardo is working for me. Can you keep a secret?"

"I'm an ambassador, Your Lordship. It's my job to keep secrets."

"You may not find it easy, but it's essential that you do. The thing is, as I once confided in you, pregnant women don't appeal to me."

"'I find pregnant women repulsive,' that's what Your Lordship told me."

"Oh, yes." Ludovico looked at Trotti with a conspiratorial air. "So, when my most excellent and beloved wife, your lord's daughter, was pregnant, I looked for enjoyment and distraction with one of her ladies in waiting. Men need to let off steam, you know."

"I understand," Trotti replied. He was seventy, and for him it was more a matter of vaguely remembering than understanding. "And, if I may, this lady is . . ."

"Lucrezia. Lucrezia Crivelli."

"That dark-haired young lady who looks a little vulgar?"

Il Moro smiled. The grapes are out of your reach, aren't they, you old fox? "It's you who are a little vulgar, Ambassador. I find Lucrezia very attractive. And Messer Leonardo agrees with me, so much so that he has agreed to paint her portrait."

"Oh."

"Precisely. That's why Leonardo has been coming to the castle at night. I could hardly ask Madamigella Lucrezia to pose during the day, when she might be in conversation with my wife, could I?" Getting up out of his high-backed chair, Ludovico displayed to Trotti his full one meter ninety, just to make it clear, once again, which of the two men was His Highness. "Can I rely on your discretion, Ambassador?"

"No fucking way, you lousy creep!"

Ludovico froze in surprise.

Not because Trotti had uttered these words, of course, since it wasn't him at all—he would never, ever have allowed himself to do so. No, Ludovico was disconcerted by the fact that these words had been preceded by a hollow crash and a sudden light, as though someone outside had thrown a brazier at the cloth that shielded the window from the wind, tearing it off with a bronze-like sound.

Which was, indeed, what had happened.

In the luminous frame of the window, now deprived of its

opaque protection, stood the haughty and very much pissed-off noble figure of Beatrice d'Este.

* * *

"My darling wife—"

"Darling wife my ass! I was hiding here so I could listen to you, because I was convinced you were going to tell the ambassador my father had been appointed commander-in-chief. Instead of which, I discover I'm being cheated on! And you're actually telling that to my father's ambassador, you piece of sh—"

"Look, Beatrice, I don't think it's appropriate to make a scene like this in front of everybody."

Ludovico had tried to assume an air of lordly detachment, rather like a cat that falls off a table while chasing a bird then gets back on its feet, as though nothing has happened, mustering all its recent but significant airs and graces. Unfortunately, although nobility and upbringing may prevent the man who possesses them from yelling his head off, it is nevertheless true that they cannot gag anyone else.

"Oh, really? So it's not appropriate for me to scream in front of everybody, but you're quite happy to fuck the servant girl and then shout it from the rooftops? For me to raise my voice is embarrassing, but it's all right for you to knock up the kitchen maid, is it? What kind of fucking morality is that?"

"Listen, Beatrice, you're the Duchess of Bari, you can't—"

Once again, Beatrice responded to nobility with decibels. "I've heard enough. Wasn't my sister noble enough for your Messer Leonardo da Vinci to paint her portrait? Isabella, daughter of Ercole d'Este, isn't an interesting enough subject, whereas he runs for his brushes as soon as he sees one of your common whores, is that it?" Beatrice took a deep, hard breath.

"As for what I can do, I'll do it right now by going back to Ferrara."

"If I may advise Your Ladyship," Trotti ventured, in a smooth tone, "it might not be appropriate to go to Ferrara at this stage."

Beatrice turned to Trotti as though seeing him for the first time. "For once, Messer Giacomo, I could advise you exactly where to go."

"Thank you, my Lady, I would rather stay here."

Beatrice turned, in a whirl of skirts and drapery, and walked out.

Ludovico watched for a few seconds as his wife left, walking slowly and, a few seconds later, hiding her face in her hands, like someone looking down at a precious object lying broken on the floor. Then he slowly turned his face from the window and returned to his high-backed chair, apparently calm and detached, but with his eyes downcast.

"Well, Ambassador," he said, sitting down. "My day began at terce with an assault on my most important engineer and artist, continued with a diplomatic misunderstanding, and proceeded to my getting insulted by my wife in front of my father-in-law's ambassador. Now let's see if we can get it back on track."

"The worst should be over, Your Lordship."

"I know from experience that when the first German mercenary dies of the plague, we have plague. I need someone who can counsel me. And to think that Magistro Ambrogio had foretold a day filled with success."

"The day is not over yet, Your Lordship," Trotti said with a knowing air.

"You're right, Messer Giacomo . . . Yes, what is it?"

"The Duke of Commynes and Signor Perron de Basche," Bernardino da Corte announced in a trembling voice. "They're asking to see you, Your Lordship."

"Now's not the time," Ludovico said curtly.

"If I may be so bold, Your Lordship, I think it might be a good idea to receive them," the castellan said, looking to his left with an alarmed and apparently slightly disgusted expression.

"Very well, show them in."

The Duke of Commynes's form was revealed in the doorway, lingering on the threshold.

"Duke, my respects. Please come in. I wanted to speak with you."

"And I wanted to speak with you, Your Lordship," the Duke said, reaching out with his left hand for something behind the door. "I wanted to speak with you about this."

And, having taken the object in question, the duke came into the room, dragging it along the ground behind him, while Bernardino da Corte watched the scene with a look that was decidedly more disgusted than frightened.

Giacomo Trotti was right. The day wasn't over yet.

I hope my readers will now forgive me, but the duty of a chronicler is to be specific, even if the scene to be described may seem utterly incredible as well as vaguely repulsive.

The object the Duke of Commynes was dragging was actually a dwarf covered in shit.

* * *

"I'd like you to explain this to me," the Duke of Commynes went on, literally dragging the dwarf toward il Moro. The dwarf glided across the floor, leaving skid marks on it.

Ludovico followed the dwarf's arrival with his eyes. This was not some random dwarf, but an old acquaintance of ours, good old Catrozzo, who had performed for Charles VIII's ambassadors on the first evening.

A dwarf who spoke French, as Ludovico had asked

Galeazzo Sanseverino. Both essential characteristics for lodging in the wide, square-based leg that held up the table in the ambassadors' room, the one with HERCULES DUX FERRARIÆ ETCETERA ETCETERA written on it, and listening, undisturbed, to the conversations of the two French legates and their henchmen. It was something Ludovico usually did with the diplomatic envoys of various Italian cities, placing a dwarf inside the wooden cavity then letting him out surreptitiously to relate private—or supposedly private—conversations and recompensing him in some way.

The day before, having heard an account of the Frenchmen's conversations from this analogue equivalent of a wiretap, Ludovico had rewarded him by sending him into the kitchens and giving him *carte blanche* with the cooks; good old Catrozzo had filled his belly with prunes in syrup, dried figs, dates, and other delicacies intent on waging war on the large intestine. Consequently, that morning, after taking up his position inside the table leg, the dwarf had felt a slight discomfort in his stomach, which had gradually turned into an unbearable pain, and what had first seemed like no more than harmless flatulence had been transmuted into a genuine disaster.

Alerted by the unequivocal smell, the two ambassadors had looked at each other with mutual suspicion; but once they had ascertained that neither of them had a problem, it hadn't been difficult to locate the origin of the warning signal. And so it was that, having established the presence of a human being by inserting a sword into a joint in the wood and hearing screams, the two men had pulled poor Catrozzo out of the leg, although not without a long and filthy struggle.

"I'll explain it to you immediately, Duke," Ludovico replied, pointing to Catrozzo, who was lying on the floor motionless but trembling. "It seems obvious that I didn't trust the two of you."

Ludovico got up from his chair, once again revealing himself at his full height.

"I didn't trust you, and I was right not to, judging by the fact that someone was planning to rob Leonardo da Vinci, an engineer in my service, of his private writings."

"Nobody ever imagined doing such a thing," Perron de Basche said boastfully. "The dwarf misunderstood."

"Then tell me, where are your two attendants?"

The two Frenchmen, the real one and the adopted one, looked at each other. It's never a good sign, Trotti thought, when it's not clear which of the two has to speak.

"Who, Robinot and Mattenet?" the Duke of Commynes said. "They're not back yet. They must have been making merry last night. In fact, I hope they haven't gotten themselves into any trouble."

"Indeed not. They're safe underground, in a warm, comfortable cell."

Perron de Basche and Commynes looked straight into Ludovico's face.

"They're under arrest," il Moro continued calmly, "given that last night they assaulted Leonardo, in my city, not far from my castle, and tried to snatch something he had on him. His notebook, I imagine. It was only the intervention of Leonardo's personal bodyguard and two of my specially appointed guards . . ."

Trotti gave a little cough to conceal a laugh.

". . . that prevented Leonardo from falling victim to his assailants."

Now the two Frenchmen were avoiding each other's eyes. There was a few seconds' silence, a heavy silence—a smelly one too, since Catrozzo was still where he'd been put.

"Your Lordship, as you can understand, I must confer with my legate," the Duke of Commynes said, looking as noble and respectful as he could.

"I'm in complete agreement with you," il Moro said gravely. "I think it might be best for all of us if you did so outside the walls of this castle."

* * *

"Just outside the castle walls, can you imagine, Caterina? But they hardly had time to touch him, the scoundrels. I was ten paces away, and I got there right away. There were two of them, but they weren't expecting it. I gave the first one a blow with the sword handle right here"—Salaí, having first mimicked holding an imaginary weapon in his hands, indicated the nape of his neck—"but the second one grabbed the handle and pulled the sword away from me. He was bigger than me, and stronger, but I did like the goat in my surname and busted him with my head, right in the stomach—"

"*Butted*. You butted him in the stomach," Caterina said, removing the wet cloth from Leonardo's head and replacing it with another, soaked in icy water.

Leonardo was lying in bed, silent, with his eyes shut. It hadn't been an easy day, the one that had just passed. And now he was at home, in his own bed, so the only thing he would have wished for was some peace and quiet.

"It's the same thing, what matters is that he got it in the stomach. He must have thrown up everything he had in him, even his mother's milk from when he was a child. Then—"

"Giacomo, please," Leonardo implored, in a tired but authoritative voice. "I was there too, last night. You may have dealt the blows, but I took them. Let's not talk about it anymore, I beg you."

"Anyway, when the guards arrived, you should have seen the commotion! Everybody punching everybody, screaming, shouting, *attansión!* stop right there! *sacré, merde!* But if I hadn't been there—"

"Truly, young Giacomo," Caterina said, putting a hand on her son's forehead, "if you hadn't been there, it would have been awful."

"If it had been light, young Giacomo," Zanino said, "you'd have taken so many blows, you'd have had to ask your mother for help to count them in Roman numerals. You're a boy, the others were soldiers."

Zanino da Ferrara was one of the many apprentices of Leonardo who, on hearing of his misadventure, had left the studio and the workshop and rushed to the house to make sure of their master's condition.

"And alzo, master," Giulio the German, the last to arrive in Leonardo's house, said, "if you hadn't come back from ze castle zo late, maybe nobody vould have attacked you."

A large, bearded man, who had turned up one day at the master's house saying that he had come to serve and to learn. And what can you do? Leonardo had asked him. I verk iron vith fire, the man had replied, hammering the air with blackened hands. And Leonardo needed blacksmiths, or people who knew even the slightest thing about working metals, like he needed air. So all right, then, come, Giulio the German, nobody is indispensable but everybody is useful.

"The master was working, not having fun," Zanino replied with bad grace. He hadn't liked the coarse bearded fellow ever since he'd arrived. Besides, Leonardo already had an expert on metal in the house. Him. And then there was Master Antonio, and, when needed, Sangallo . . . What could the master possibly want with this barbarian?

"Working is for daytime, nighttime is for sleeper," Giulio stated, Teutonic even in the content of his speech.

"*Sleeping*, actually," Salaí said, happy to be able to correct someone too. "And anyway, you know the master sleeps and works in his own time. He goes to bed for an hour when he feels like it, then works for four."

"Nobody knows better than you when the master goes to bed, right, young Giacomo?"

"Listen, metal expert my ass, if you want to see how hard the iron in my sword is, just keep it up and—"

"Enough!"

Leonardo bounced up so quickly that the wet compress flew out through the window. It was such a strange scene that at any other time it would have been comical; right now, though, there was nothing to laugh about.

"Enough, for Christ's sake!" Leonardo said, getting out of bed, while everybody else in the room quieted down instantly.

Everyone knows that Leonardo was sweet-natured. And, like all sweet-natured people, he seldom got angry. But when he did get angry, he was scary.

Downstairs, somebody knocked at the door, and Caterina took the opportunity to go see who it was. Meanwhile, Leonardo had launched into a rant.

"I've been accused, humiliated, attacked, and now I can't even rest in my own home! Out of here!"

"I'm sorry, master, if—"

"Out! For the love of God, out!"

Caterina's voice came up from downstairs. "Leonardo, you have visitors—"

"More?" Leonardo cried, out of control by now, heading for the door. "Who's come to break my balls now?"

And, with the menacing expression of a man unwilling to take it anymore, he leaned over the wooden banister and looked down.

And that is how, perhaps for the first time in his life, he had the opportunity to see Ludovico il Moro from above.

* * *

"Your Lordship must forgive me, I would never dare address Your Lordship so crudely."

Ludovico closed the bedroom door behind him. His head was practically touching the ceiling. He looked around, took the only chair in the room, and sat down.

"Let's not look at the form, Leonardo, let's look at the substance. I've come here with a request."

Leonardo, who had sat back down on the bed, said nothing.

"It's a request I am making as regent of the Duchy of Milan, not as your patron. You may agree or refuse."

Leonardo smiled, but his breath rose from his belly to his chest. This was no hint, no kiss on the neck, rather it was soap on the rope of the hanged man.

"But if you refuse, you will give me reason to believe that my trust in you is misplaced. Last night, you were assaulted by henchmen of the French ambassador. Do you know why they tried to rob you?"

"Yes, Your Lordship, I think I do. They wanted my notebook."

"They wanted your notebook?"

"Yes, Your Lordship. They'd already made one rather clumsy attempt in the past few days, and maybe, now that I think about it, even a second one."

"And why do they want this notebook? How come this damned notebook is so important? What's written in it?"

"Nothing that matters to anybody else but me."

"Then why do other people want to get their hands on it?"

"Your Lordship is asking too much of me. I can't possibly know what other people think."

"You're right, Leonardo. In that case I'll tell you. The French ambassadors, urged on by Louis, Duke of Orléans, believe that what you conceal in your notebook are the plans for a secret weapon. A warlike automaton to defend the city boundaries."

Leonardo smiled and shook his head.

"The ambassador of Ferrara, Giacomo Trotti, thinks it contains the secret of transmuting base metals into gold, and that's the reason the Duchy is so wealthy."

This time, Leonardo laughed heartily. "Your Lordship, this business of transmuting base metal into gold is something I've never dreamed of wasting my time on. I understood a long time ago that perpetual motion and the dream of King Midas are fairy stories, and I don't concern myself with them." Leonardo made himself more comfortable on the bed, trying to alleviate his unease. "But what concerns me more is what Your Lordship thinks. What, in Your Lordship's opinion, could possibly be in my very private notebook?"

"That's why I'm here, Leonardo. If what I think is false, then it does me no honor, but if it's true, then it would do great dishonor to you. I don't want to tell you. But I would like you to show it to me."

"I will show it to Your Lordship, and only to you, if Your Lordship agrees to tell me what he expects to find in it, or hopes not to find."

Ludovico looked toward the window and spoke in a subdued tone, almost a murmur. "I hope not to find one or more letters of credit signed by Bencio Serristori or other Florentine bankers, to be used by you or other members of your workshop in the manufacture of fake letters of credit."

Leonardo was quite still for a moment. Then he slowly pulled on the leather strap of his tunic and loosened the buckle. Then, still slowly, he slipped his hand between his shirt and his body and took out a small, thick notebook filled with sheets of paper, some more yellowed than others.

"As you wish, Your Lordship."

Ludovico put out his hand and took the notebook.

Before he could open it, however, Leonardo spoke again.

"You have asked me for this notebook as Lord of Milan, Your Lordship, and not as my patron. You made an important distinction, and I mean to make one of my own before you start reading."

Leonardo touched the notebook in Ludovico's hand, delicately and with care, the way a mother adjusts the blanket around her newborn baby in the arms of an old-maid aunt.

"As Lord of Milan, you welcomed me. As a patron, after reading my letter of introduction, you gave me your trust. You gave me your trust after reading the things I wrote you. Now you mistrust me before reading things I have written for myself."

Leonardo pushed his hands down on the bed and got to his feet in front of il Moro.

"As a citizen, Your Lordship, I am confident that you will be fair in administering justice and in recognizing that everybody has an equal measure of merits and faults. As an artist, Ludovico, I trust you will be able to understand that I am a free man, and that I am bound to a patron of mine not only if he recognizes my abilities but also if he recognizes my work in its true measure."

And, delicately lifting the cover of the notebook in Ludovico's hand, he opened it.

There was something strange in it.

Letters.

Not letters of credit, but actual letters. With the date at the beginning and a signature at the end. Filled with drawings, as Leonardo's letters were.

But . . .

"But they're written from right to left."

"That's the way I always write."

"So these are your letters? The drafts of your letters?"

"I'll explain while you read, Your Lordship. Here, look in this mirror. If you need a light, I'll have one brought to you right away."

* * *

"How long have they been up there?"

"Nearly two hours."

Caterina swallowed enough saliva to reach the second liter of the morning. Having the Lord of Milan in her home was not an everyday event to start with. But realizing that the Lord of Milan had come for her son, and that he might leave with her son, and that the four armed guards waiting in her kitchen might be there for that reason, did nothing to reassure her.

At last, the door opened.

Ludovico il Moro was the first to come out, with an expression on his face that was truly scary. He was clearly disappointed, but more than disappointed, he was angry.

Behind him, Leonardo. Clearly worried and contrite, but more worried than contrite.

Ludovico came down the stairs, slowly. He waited for Leonardo to reach the ground floor too before he spoke.

"You've disappointed me, Leonardo. Once again, you've disappointed me. Are you aware of that?"

"I realize that, Your Lordship."

"Good. Then let's go. I'd like to conclude this business quickly."

And, having made a sign to the guards, he set off. The guards closed in around Leonardo.

"What's happening, Your Lordship?"

"Your son must come with me, Madonna Caterina."

"So you're arresting him?"

Ludovico turned. For the first time that day, he smiled.

"Absolutely not, Madonna Caterina. I need your son as a witness. He's vital to me in a legal case. He'll be back home this evening, if not sooner."

Twelve Plus One
(THE MASTER OF THE HOUSE IS VERY SUPERSTITIOUS)

T he Room of the Chevrons was never an inviting or welcoming place, which was quite deliberate. It was
gloomy, dark, cold, and menacing, so that anyone who
was admitted to implore a favor or ask for justice would not
waste time chatting, and anyone called to account before the
Secret Council chaired by Ludovico il Moro would be intimidated just enough to provide a nice confession, which, during
the Renaissance, was the kind of evidence preferred by courts
everywhere. Whatever the reason for being admitted, entering
that room was not pleasant.

What made the situation even worse for those who now
found themselves there was the fact that the reason was
unclear. In fact, various people had come before the Council
today, and for various reasons.

Accerrito Portinari, director of the Medici Bank's Milanese
branch, who, as a petitioner, had brought before the Council
the bearers of a number of letters of credit he considered to be
fake.

Clemente Vulzio, Candido Bertone, Riccetto Nannipieri,
and Ademaro Costante, the bearers of these letters, whom
Accerrito was bringing to the Council as defendants, but who
claimed to be accusers eager for justice, in so far as Portinari
was refusing to pay them the sums stipulated by the letters
each of them had presented—a total of five thousand ducats,
not exactly a trifle.

Father Diodato da Siena, together with his fellow friar

Eligio da Varramista. In fact, it was the latter who had been summoned, on the advice of Bergonzio Botta, as an expert in promissory notes and letters of credit, being a former banker converted to faith on the road to Milan, a case that was not so much rare as unique of a person moving to Milan in order to stop devoting himself to high finance. Father Diodato was there simply as a companion, because letting one of his fellow friars go out into the big wide world on his own and letting him speak without himself being present just didn't seem right.

And, finally, the councilors. Seven rather than the usual six, since among them sat Leonardo da Vinci. Seemingly, the person most out of place in that room.

* * *

"So, Messer Accerrito, you claim that the letters brought by these gentlemen are fake and you have stated your reasons." Ludovico turned to his left. "While you, gentlemen, claim that these letters are authentic, signed by Bencio Serristori in his own hand on the stated dates. Do you confirm your statements?"

"I confirm," said Vulzio, a small red-headed man with a face ravaged by smallpox.

"I confirm," echoed Bertone, a tall, muscular young man with a strong Sienese accent.

"I confirm, as God is my witness," Nannipieri, a stout fellow, hunched over from too many hours spent at the loom, added his voice to the chorus.

"I confirm," came the final repetition, from Ademaro Costante, an extremely thin forty-year-old whose main source of protein was probably the fingernails of his right hand, which he hadn't stopped chewing for a second since he had entered.

"Friar Eligio, what is your opinion?"

Friar Eligio was a totally bald little man, except for a tuft of hair the color of a dead rat bursting out of his forehead and reaching for infinity. After nodding a few times, as though to remind himself that he was sure of his own opinion, he produced a voice as thin as the thread of a spider web.

"The letters are written on extremely fine Florentine paper, the same kind I used to employ when I dealt with exchange at the Medici Bank," he began, while everybody in the room listened hard. "The letter is drafted according to the rules of the bank, with date, sum, estimate of the exchange at destination, and specification of the banker of destination. I have no reason to suspect that it's false."

"Then why are we here? Why won't you give us our money? Who suspects these letters are false and why?"

"You're right, Messer Riccetto," Ludovico said, with a compliant air. "Galeazzo, would you care to explain?"

"A few days ago the body of a man who had died a violent death was found here, in the castle courtyard. His name was Rambaldo Chiti, a painter and artist, born in Milan."

"Peace be with him," Nannipieri said curtly. "And what's that to us?"

"In the house of the aforementioned Rambaldo Chiti, the captain of justice and I personally found equipment for minting fake coins, as well as a letter of credit signed by Bencio Serristori, which was also, beyond any doubt, a fake."

"Forgive me, Your Excellency," Friar Eligio cut in, "I should like to know, out of curiosity if nothing else, how you can be so certain. It's not easy to prove that a letter of credit is fake. I know that from experience. Many times, in my secular life, I had to hand over pure gold florins in exchange for a suspect letter."

"This letter was allegedly written in Florence by Bencio Serristori, but was dated June twenty-fourth."

"Ah," Friar Eligio said, relieved. "In that case there's no doubt whatsoever. Nobody works on the Feast of Saint John.

Therefore, the forger is definitely not from Florence. Although if I may be so bold . . ."

"Do go on, Friar Eligio."

"This Rambaldo Chiti whom you say was murdered was allegedly also the forger, is that it?"

"We believe so, yes. Messer Leonardo?"

Sitting with his hands on his lap, Leonardo slowly nodded. "I had Rambaldo Chiti in my workshop for a couple of years and had personal experience both of his great talent for painting and of his fraudulent, iniquitous nature. He paid a friend and customer of mine in fake money after getting real money from me, and the fake letter was found in his hiding place, where he kept a pipe for melting and equipment for minting fake ducats. There is no doubt about this."

"Thank you, Messer Leonardo."

"Very well," Vulzio said with an air of defiance. "Very well, Your Lordship. Chiti was a forger. But that has nothing to do with the letter in my possession, which is dated June sixteenth. I can assure you that on that day Bencio Serristori was still alive and capable of writing."

"Correct, Messer Clemente. On June sixteenth, Bencio Serristori was, indeed, still alive. This detail is relevant since Messer Bencio died at the beginning of July."

"Then what reason could there be to doubt the authenticity of our letters?"

"So you guarantee that your letters are true and authentic?"

"I guarantee that mine is, obviously, since I personally saw it being drafted," Vulzio grumbled. "I don't know about the others, but I see no motive for suspicion."

"Is that so? Your letters are authentic? Very well, gentlemen, our beautiful city is founded on its credit system, and if the letters are authentic, I myself can rule that Messer Accerrito pay them in ready cash. If Messer Portinari does not intend to pay them, not only will I put him in jail, but I will pay them myself. Messer Portinari, do you intend to pay these letters?"

"Not one penny."

"Well, in that case, gentlemen, if you agree, the situation becomes my responsibility. Messer Accerrito, kindly come here."

Accerrito Portinari went and stood before il Moro, who began writing a note on a snow-white sheet of paper. Once he had written it, Ludovico turned the sheet toward Portinari and said solemnly:

"I hereby take upon myself your debts toward the gentlemen present here today, in accordance with the conditions stated."

Accerrito looked at the piece of paper and felt his blood rush to his face, then drain away.

"But Your Lordship can't—"

"You had better sign it, Messer Accerrito, for your own good."

The four men looked at one another with glistening eyes as Accerrito Portinari signed, silently, the quill shaking in his hand. Once he had signed, Ludovico called the castellan and handed him the paper. With a bow, Bernardino da Corte took the document, walked out the door, and disappeared.

"Well, now, Your Lordship, when will we have our dough?"

"Dough, Messer Riccetto?"

"The lettuce, come on, the money. You just said you'd be paying, being such a gentleman."

"All in good time, Messer Riccetto," Ludovico said calmly, "all in good time. You see, as Accerrito Portinari explained to me yesterday in great detail, and as was just confirmed by Friar Eligio, it's often better for the bank to pay a fake letter rather than spend money and risk the life of a courier in order to verify the authenticity of the document."

Ludovico opened his hands wide.

"But what the banks can't do, I, on the other hand, intend to do and must do. I cannot pay Duchy money, which is tax-payers' money, for fake letters of credit. Just a moment ago, as you saw, I gave Messer Bernardino a paper countersigned by Accerrito Portinari."

"The paper with which you pledge to pay his debt," Clemente Vulzio said.

"No, Messer Clemente. That's not exactly what is written on the paper."

Clemente Vulzio turned to Portinari, who lowered his eyes, then back to Ludovico.

"What I actually wrote was a request to inspect the registers of accounts. The signature was necessary in order to obtain authorization to take delivery of Bencio Serristori's registers of accounts at the Medici Bank in Florence, on behalf of the Regent of the Duchy of Milan, Ludovico Maria Sforza, and with the permission and approval of the Medici Bank's representative in Milan."

Ludovico indicated the door through which the castellan had left.

"Having read the note, Messer Bernardino is, as we speak, instructing a courier to leave for Florence with the signed permit. The courier will be back within a week at the most. In the meantime, you will be my guests."

And Ludovico made a sign to Galeazzo Sanseverino.

The latter made another to the captain of the guard.

And the guards left their posts beside Ludovico's chair and went and took up position around the supplicants, turning them into defendants.

* * *

"As Messer Leonardo explained earlier, he knew Rambaldo

Chiti well, and on that there can be no shadow of a doubt."
Ludovico's tone had altered slightly after his men had taken
their positions. "But others here knew him and had the opportunity to become acquainted with his skills and talent. Isn't
that so, Father Diodato?"

Father Diodato looked at Ludovico with an untroubled
expression. "I?"

"You, Father Diodato, you."

"I think you're making a mistake," Father Diodato replied
serenely. "I've never been even remotely acquainted with the
gentleman you mentioned earlier."

"Really? Do you agree, Messer Leonardo?"

"I cannot, Your Lordship," Leonardo said in a level tone.
"There is tangible evidence, quite visible evidence, in fact, that
Father Diodato knew Rambaldo Chiti, even though he claimed
the opposite in my presence."

"Indeed? And where would this evidence be?"

"On the walls of your refectory, most excellent Father. It
was Rambaldo Chiti who provided the frescoes for the niches.
I recognized his hand." Leonardo stood up as he spoke. Not to
display his height, as Ludovico so often did, but to relieve the
tension. "I've had dozens of apprentices in my studio, and I
could recognize each and every one's stroke, the weight of his
brush, the tendency toward a particular color combination,
and the proportion between tension and looseness in his
hands. Especially in the talented ones like Rambaldo Chiti. So
I wonder why you claim not to know him, when he worked for
you."

"Is that what you're relying on, Your Lordship? On the
artistic judgment of a painter who claims he can carve giant
horses of which we still haven't seen a trace?"

When someone makes a specific accusation against us
and we respond with a personal insult, it usually means we
don't have any counter-arguments. This observation would

be formalized in a philosophical theory only a few centuries later by Arthur Schopenauer, but Ludovico il Moro had grasped it a long time ago.

"Yes, I do, Father Diodato. As far as I am concerned, Leonardo's word in matters of painting cannot be called into question. But I wouldn't wish to impose my opinion on you. Friar Eligio, I presume you have the financial registers of the monastery with you?"

"Yes, Your Lordship, I brought them with me, as requested."

Ludovico put his hand out and Friar Eligio passed him the large book. After placing it on his lap, Ludovico carefully opened it and began to run his finger down the pages.

The ostentatious opening of a register, in schools of every kind and level, has always caused a certain amount of unease among pupils. Now, Father Diodato was certainly no schoolboy, but it was very evident that, in consequence of Ludovico's action, the Jesuate had turned pale and his hands, folded over his white habit, had tightened around his leather belt.

"Here, Father Diodato. Could you explain to me how it is that on the twentieth of July this year, you instructed Friar Eligio to pay Rambaldo Chiti the sum of fifteen ducats for painting frescoes on the niches in your refectory?"

"I couldn't remember his name," Father Diodato said, trying to keep his voice as steady as possible, but not really succeeding. "You know, I see so many people."

"I know, I know. You know many people." As he spoke, Ludovico calmly continued leafing through the register. "Moreover, your monastery is a renowned producer of pigments and you yourself are a man of refined and cultivated tastes. A man like you is bound to know many people. For example, did you know a man named Giovanni Barraccio?"

"No . . . I don't think so . . ."

"Really? For a man of culture, Father Diodato, your memory

is truly unreliable." Ludovico put a finger on the register, on the back of the page he had reached a little earlier. "It says here that on the first of August you gave instructions to pay a thousand ducats to a certain 'Gio. Barraccio, wool trader.' Did you buy a thousand ducats' worth of woolen cloth, Father Diodato, or don't you remember?"

Father Diodato did not reply. Eyes downcast, hands tight and trembling on his leather belt, he kept silent, and it was clear that he would not reply.

Lifting his head from the register, Ludovico looked at Friar Eligio. "Friar Eligio, would *you* care to enlighten me?"

Friar Eligio was no fool. Having tried in vain to meet the prior's eyes, he spoke in an even fainter voice than before. "Your Lordship, it wasn't wool that was bought. Messer Giovanni Barraccio came to us with a letter of credit of the value of a thousand florins. He wasn't very familiar with such an instrument and had heard that the banker who had issued it was dead. He was worried that the death might invalidate the document. I explained to my prior that this was not the case, and that we could make a good deal by buying the letter from Barraccio at the mint rate rather than at the exchange rate, a thousand ducats for a thousand florins, and send the bearer of the letter to exchange it at Messer Accerrito's bank. So I paid Barraccio a thousand ducats, obtained the letter and gave it to my prior, who said he would deal with it himself."

"Messer Accerrito . . ."

"Never! I've never exchanged a letter from Giovanni Barraccio and then made it payable to Father Diodato at the monastery of Saint Jerome of the Jesuates."

"Are you sure?"

"Yes, I am, and I'm prepared to bring you my registers!"

"I believe you, Messer Accerrito. Bring the registers, so that we may conduct the investigation properly and look for some consistency in what happened, but I believe you. I believe you because I am entirely convinced that this letter was never taken or exchanged, but that it remained in the hands of Father Diodato da Siena, who then gave it to Rambaldo Chiti to be used as a template for producing fake letters of credit. Letters of credit given to you gentlemen here before me so that you could take them to Messer Portinari's bank and cash them." Slowly and majestically, Ludovico stood up from his chair. "I repeat, gentlemen, the offer I made you earlier. At this very moment, one of my couriers is on his way to Florence to fetch the records of Bencio Serristori. Within a week at most, he will be back with these records, which will be identified and examined by Messer Accerrito Portinari. The first of you to confess can leave this room immediately after providing a full explanation. For the others, the sentence for anyone circulating fake money is to have his hands cut off at the wrist."

* * *

The air in the room grew stifling. A few seconds of indescribable slowness went by before Riccetto Nannipieri raised his hand.

"Your Lordship . . ."

"Yes, Messer Riccetto?"

"The letter of credit I took to the bank was given me by Father Diodato da Siena, on the fifteenth of September last."

"How much did you pay for it?"

"Thirty ducats, Your Lordship."

"It sounds like a reasonable sum. Did Father Diodato tell you anything else after he gave you the letter?"

"He said I should use it on the last day of October, after Your Lordship had left."

"Then why did you use it today?"

"Because he's an idiot!" Father Diodato exploded.

* * *

"Because after Rambaldo Chiti died and an enquiry was launched into his death, I was afraid somebody would discover the fake letters. I myself had turned Chiti's lodgings upside down, looking for where he worked, but I didn't find anything."

Father Diodato was literally shaking with anger, a vein as thick as a vine swelling on the side of his neck.

"But then, at the Countess's house, I heard Leonardo say that a letter had been found that had been recognized as a fake, and my blood ran cold. The thing had gone belly-up, everything had gone belly-up. There was no way it would end well, it was too risky. But this cretin, these cretins, decided to make a profit. They decided to go all the same, and then hide out in Tuscany with their dirty money. You're cretins, all of you! Cretins!"

Father Diodato took a deep breath.

"Then, when Leonardo came to see me at the monastery, I saw him looking at the frescoes, and at one point he asked me if I knew Rambaldo Chiti. That's when I understood, I understood that he had understood."

All heads in the room turned to Leonardo, who now opened his hands and spoke in an apologetic tone.

"Every branch of a tree is connected to the trunk. I had two branches, Father Diodato. One branch was Giovanni Barraccio, who frequented Countess Cecilia Bergamini's house. The other was Rambaldo Chiti, who had manufactured the fake letters. Both men had died violent deaths. Where was the point of connection? The person they had in common, that they both knew? You, Father Diodato, who frequented Palazzo Carmagnola, and to whom the Countess sent the hapless Giovanni Barraccio when, because of his inexperience, he thought he might have problems with a large credit of his. And you, Prior of the Poor of Jesus in Saint Jerome, whose monastery was painted with frescoes by Rambaldo Chiti. When Messer Accerrito told me of the murder of Giovanni Barraccio, I worked out why you denied having known Chiti. And, after thinking over what you'd said to me, I realized what was going on."

"But Messer Leonardo . . ." Galeazzo Sanseverino's voice was hesitant, as few things were in his life.

"At your command, Captain."

"I'm not sure I've quite grasped what's going on. Why would Father Diodato have sold these letters for so little?"

"Oh, very simple. It was probably the price stipulated by Chiti for his work. If I know Father Diodato, that's the criterion, isn't it? He definitely didn't want to profit from it."

"So what would he have gained? What kind of forger doesn't want to profit from his work?"

"Ah, but we're not talking about forgers here, Captain. We're talking about *conspirators*."

* * *

"Conspirators?"

"Messer Accerrito, you once explained to me that a bank is like a juggler. You lend money with interest at fifteen percent, and borrow money at twelve percent. Is that correct?"

"Correct."

"What's your turnover? About three hundred thousand ducats, am I right?"

"Yes, you are."

"And what's your capital? How much do you have deposited, in ready cash? Fifty thousand ducats, am I right?"

Accerrito Portinari wiped his forehead, which was dripping with sweat. "Not exactly. About thirty thousand ducats at the moment. Almost."

"And what would happen if all your depositaries, all the people who have lent you money to be increased with interest, turned up at the bank on the same day and claimed their capital back?" Leonardo's voice was gentle, almost embarrassed.

"I couldn't give it to them. I wouldn't have it."

"So you would go bankrupt," Leonardo almost prompted.

"Yes, but not just me. As I told you, Leonardo, my bank is the most important in Milan. Besides His Lordship Ludovico, there are merchants, carders, metalworkers, weavers, wine growers. They wouldn't be able to buy the supplies they needed, or pay their workers. It would be a disaster. It would—"

"And tell me, how would one go about persuading all the depositaries to rush to the bank and withdraw their money?"

"That would happen if there were a rumor of a delay in settling bills, because everybody would then realize I don't have that much money in deposit."

"And what would happen then?"

"A crisis, Leonardo. A crisis. If money stops circulating, everything collapses. There would almost certainly be an uprising."

* * *

"Have we understood correctly, Father Diodato? Was that your intention?"

Father Diodato was no longer shaking. He was calm now, almost resigned. "You heard it too. Without money, everything would collapse. Without money, everything would go to rack and ruin. Because money is not a value! A value is eternal, immutable, while money is uncertain, it fluctuates, it inflates and deflates like a sail, and whoever boards a boat with a sail like that doesn't know where he's going, or where he'll end up. To go out to sea, to travel, to navigate correctly, one must look to the stars, which are eternal. And to find one's direction in life, one must look to the Almighty, to Him and Him alone."

Father Diodato looked at Leonardo as though he were solely responsible for what was happening.

"We've become convinced that man is the measure of all things. But in order to measure things, to know what they are worth, we must buy them with something. We need a true currency against which to measure them, so that we can assess their value, and the only valid currency against which to measure them is God!"

Father Diodato's voice, still low, had turned furious, like that of a man denouncing an injustice.

Not looking very convinced, Leonardo raised his eyebrows. "Father Diodato, you're saying that in order to assess the value of something we need a reference point, a yardstick to hold up to whatever it is we are valuing. But how can man refer to God—infinite by His very nature—to value finite things? If we're talking about length, infinite thumbs are no shorter than infinite palms, and infinite palms are no shorter than infinite arms. If we're talking about money, infinite lire are no less than infinite ducats. Man's intellect can assess value only by measuring something as being equal to, or smaller or larger than, his yardstick. But when it comes to the infinite extension of God, a man cannot measure himself against Him, but only surrender. With money, on the other hand, man can compare things because we all value it in the same way."

Leonardo indicated the sleeve of his own garment, lifting it delicately between the thumb and index of his left hand.

"What color is my clothing, Father? It's pink, right? How can we be certain that it's pink? Because we all see it as being the same color, and if we see an object of that color, we recognize it. Nobody has ever been known to see a pink garment as pink, but a pink paper as green. The same applies to money. Money is understood by all men on earth. We all agree that a ducat is worth a ducat. This makes it a value, just like the length of a palm."

Enraged, Father Diodato lifted his chin. "It's a mistaken value! Otherwise, why can I obtain money with a wicked action, like killing or stealing? Money rewards you for any action, whether it is good or bad. Money should be a means, not an end, and we can't look to the money we earn to understand where we should be going! But perhaps by being shown its true nature, its fallacious nature, people would have understood! They would have turned back to the true currency, the true value, the word of God!"

Leonardo looked at Father Diodato as only Leonardo could look at something. His eyes, his neck, his hands, his clothes, his pupils making rapid, almost imperceptible darting movements. After a few seconds, Leonardo looked at the friar gravely.

"There would be death and destruction. Have you thought of that?"

"God also destroyed Sodom and Gomorrah, so that His message might be heard."

"And are you God? If I look at you, Father Diodato, I see two legs, two arms, and one head. You're a man, like me. And you've acted like a man."

"Like a man, but guided by the word of God."

"Like a man and nothing else, and I'll prove it to you."

Leonardo turned and, with the palm of his hand facing upward, indicated his fellow-Florentine.

"Now, Messer Accerrito, you've won your battle. The letters have been declared fake, without a shadow of a doubt, through confession. Why are you so downhearted?"

All those present, who had followed the exchange between Leonardo and Father Diodato as though spellbound, now turned to the banker. His face was pasty, his forehead beaded with sweat, and there were two small white wedges of saliva at the corners of his mouth. Far from looking like a winner, Accerrito Portinari looked like someone who had been dealt a fatal blow.

"Because I . . ." Accerrito looked at il Moro, who sat there, silent and stern. "Your Lordship, I . . ."

"Among your indebted customers, among the people to whom you've lent money, are the most prestigious merchants and individuals in Milan. Is Father Diodato also one of them?"

"Yes, Messer Leonardo. Yes, of course he's one of them."

"How much money did you lend him?"

"Ten thousand ducats. Ten thousand ducats that . . ."

That if you sentence Father Diodato to death I will have lost forever: Accerrito Portinari completed the sentence with his eyes, which he turned to the Lord of Milan in supplication.

Ludovico shook his head, confirming Father Diodato's fate, as well as the closely connected fate of the aforementioned ten thousand ducats.

"I can't help thinking, Father Diodato, that in causing Accerrito Portinari's bankruptcy, you would have cancelled your debt." Ludovico's voice, firm and crisp, seemed to make the air vibrate. "Ten thousand of those ducats you claim to despise so much and yet did not hesitate to borrow. You have invoked God as a yardstick, Father Diodato, but let me tell you, you are small even beside a man."

Then, without changing the direction of his gaze, his voice changed.

"Master Leonardo, please accept my respects and my apologies."

Leonardo lifted his head toward Ludovico. His gaze was weary but serene. "I am glad to have complied with your requests, Your Lordship. With your permission, I should like to take my leave and go home."

"As you wish, Master Leonardo."

"Please excuse me . . ."

Standing among the others, Riccetto Nannipieri had raised his finger, trying to attract attention.

"Messer Riccetto, do you have a request?"

"Well, since I was the one to confess, and you did promise you'd let me get out of here as soon as I'd provided a full explanation, Your Lordship, and since Messer Leonardo is leaving, perhaps I could also go . . ."

Ludovico slapped himself on the forehead, emphatically. "Yes, of course, how absent-minded of me. Captain, take Messer Riccetto to the executioner right now. Have his hands cut off at the wrists, then throw him out of my castle immediately."

"But . . . but . . . Your Lordship promised—"

"To release you as soon as you confessed. I never said you'd get back home in one piece."

TWELVE PLUS ONE AND A HALF
(SEE ABOVE)

The group of men proceeding through the San Nazzario district was a curious one, to say the least.

Four armed men, with swords and chain mail, surrounding two other men who were talking calmly, one of them tall, dressed in dark cloth, the other of average height, with fair hair and a well-trimmed beard, wearing an impeccable pink outfit.

"So how did you get to the right person?" Galeazzo Sanseverino asked, looking around.

Fortunately, the street was semi-deserted.

After furtively leaving by the wooden bridge in back of the castle, the two men had walked through the Cusani district as far as the junction with the Rovello district, then taken the narrow street known as the district of San Nazzario alla Pietrasanta. To go where they were going, it would have been better to proceed through the Solata district, which was much wider and more brightly lit, as the name suggested, but they would have been even more visible, and that was something neither Leonardo nor Galeazzo wanted in the least.

"Well, Captain, I noticed a couple of times that conversations in the house where we are going had a specific connection to what happened the following day, or even the same day."

"I see. So whenever you said something about the death of Rambaldo Chiti . . ."

". . . something else would immediately happen that concerned the people involved in the matter. It happened every time it was discussed in Countess Cecilia's house."

* * *

"Not in your house, Countess. I couldn't have come to your home to tell you what I'm about to tell you. Or rather to ask you what I'm about to ask you."

"As far as I'm concerned, every wish of yours is an invitation, Your Lordship," Cecilia Gallerani said, her head down but her eyes open toward il Moro. Eyes that once caressed and now scrutinized.

"Don't even say it. You see, Countess—"

"There was a time when you called me by my name, Your Lordship."

"Cecilia, there was a time when I wasn't married. Now I am, and my wife, the mother of my son Ercole Massimiliano, is very jealous."

"I had occasion to notice that," Cecilia replied, turning her gaze to the outside courtyard, and it wasn't clear whether she was looking at the Rocchetta, where she had lived during the first few months of il Moro's marriage, or at the brand-new cloth over the east window. "I think you should treat her with the respect she has earned. We are talking about the future Duchess of Milan, after all."

"The same respect you owe your husband, His Excellency, Count Bergamini. Where is he at the moment?"

"In the country, at San Giovanni in Croce, Your Lordship."

"It might not be a bad idea to be with him over the next few months, don't you think?"

"Do you mean I should join him or call him back home?"

"The former, Countess. I'm sure a bit of country air could only do you and little Cesare good. By the way, Countess, there's something else I need to tell you. It's the second reason I asked to speak to you in the castle."

"About my husband?"

"About your house, Countess."

* * *

"Twice, while I was in the house, I happened to mention the unfortunate events in the Piazzale delle Armi and Chiti's death. The first time was when I recounted how the wretch had been killed, and said that he hadn't died from a divine bolt of lightning or a disease. But the second time was when I told the Countess that I knew the name of the dead man and had made a connection with the fake letter of credit fabricated by him. If you remember, I went to the castle that very day with Botta, to provide the names of a few people I knew had been in business with the hapless Bencio Serristori."

"I remember. And Botta told me you also mentioned this Giovanni Barraccio."

"I congratulate you on your memory, Captain. You see, I was struck by the fact that, having mentioned Giovanni Barraccio and Countess Gallerani having told me that she had referred Barraccio to Father Diodato herself, the wretched Barraccio was then murdered that same night. To prevent him from talking. He was the only eyewitness to the delivery of the letter, a letter which was then not cashed. Father Diodato could have easily said that he'd received no visit from Barraccio."

"And you're saying that the same hand killed Rambaldo Chiti?"

Leonardo shook his head gravely, despite the fast pace at which he was walking. "Not the same hand but the same head. There are two different murderers. It wasn't Father Diodato who killed Rambaldo."

As he walked, Leonardo tripped over a stone and lost his

balance for a moment. Then he resumed his previous rhythm and continued:

"At first, I thought Chiti had been forced into a corset of armor and squeezed until his soul was expelled together with the air. But then I realized it wouldn't have been easy to persuade a man to wear a suit of armor against his will, or to force it on him. No, there was an easier way of doing it. As easy as eavesdropping behind the door when the Countess is having a heart-to-heart with a man who knows many things."

Leonardo turned to Galeazzo, while continuing to walk briskly.

"If that man had been at your home for a romantic assignation, it would have been easy to persuade him to get into a clothes chest, with his legs bent, in a fetal position, then close the chest and press it down on the wretch like pincers."

"It takes a lot of strength to do that, Messer Leonardo," Galeazzo objected. "I don't know if a woman would be capable of it, especially with a man as strong and healthy as Chiti."

"Oh, she would be. All she needs is a chest with a device that multiplies your strength, following the principle of the lever and the pulley, so that every arm's length rotation, made with minimum force, corresponds to a movement of the thumb, but made with enormous force."

"And does such a mechanical chest exist, Messer Leonardo? Are you sure this person owns one?"

"I am sure of it, Captain Galeazzo. I engineered and built it myself. And it's located in the house we are about to enter."

Galeazzo and Leonardo stopped outside the door. The rear entrance of Palazzo Carmagnola, the home of Countess Cecilia Gallerani Bergamini. Leonardo stepped aside for his companion.

"I think you should be the one to knock, Captain."

Which Galeazzo did, with determination. A few seconds later, a pretty young woman opened the door, saw Galeazzo, saw Leonardo, saw the four armed men in particular, and turned white as a sheet.

"The Countess is not at home, gentlemen."

"That's of no matter, Madamigella Tersilla. It's you we've come to see."

FOURTEEN

Cecilia Gallerani stood motionless in the middle of the courtyard.

Around her, frescoes depicting the most important episodes of Milan's recent history, from the peace of Ferrara to the wedding of Francesco Sforza.

At her side, Leonard had just explained the ins and outs of how the two of them had also played an active part in the city's history, although it was unlikely anyone would put their words and arguments in a fresco. We know that for those who paint it, history is made up of battles or conquests; but painters, just like generals, forget that battles are won by historians, as someone would remark about four hundred and fifty years later, not too far from where our characters were standing now.

"I knew that Tersilla and Father Diodato had a soft spot for each other, but I would never have believed that he could have told her to do something like this."

"So you knew?"

"I knew, and didn't know."

Cecilia was holding her hands in front of her lap, one behind the other. Countess Cecilia Gallerani Bergamini was barely twenty, but seemed already to have lived more than one life, judging by the way she moved and spoke.

"Tersilla's family was ruined by Botta some years ago. Taxes are heavy on those who own extensive lands if those lands do not yield as they should. There was a flood, the crop was destroyed, the seeds rotted. But Botta and the Duchy still wanted their taxes and these were taken from her dowry. I took her in because in many ways I saw myself in her. We're both merchandise that has expired before its time."

Cecilia looked around, as though she did not deserve what she had, but didn't want it either.

"I loved il Moro and was loved by him in return when I was sixteen years old, Messer Leonardo, after a promise of marriage had been broken because I lacked a dowry and I was almost sent off to become a nun. A woman's life isn't easy, even when she's young. Then we grow old and invisible, or bothersome."

Leonardo nodded gravely, looking at the portico. "But il Moro wasn't to you what Father Diodato was to Tersilla. He made her kill a man. And he himself killed the wretched Barraccio, who trusted him because he thought he'd gotten him out of trouble."

"And how has il Moro been with you, Leonardo? How did you manage to regain his trust?"

Leonardo continued looking at the histories of Milan painted on the walls around them. "I don't like fresco," he said after a moment or two. "It doesn't allow you to correct, to amend errors. Because all of us commit errors. I could never paint a fresco. I've actually been asked but I don't know whether or not to accept."

"So you commit errors too?"

"Constantly, Countess. Constantly. But I hide them from everyone except myself. Only il Moro accidentally discovered one of my errors."

"What error, Leonardo?" Cecilia asked, slightly incredulous.

"The most serious of all, from his point of view. The equestrian statue."

"The horse?"

"The horse, Countess. I miscalculated the amount of bronze

needed to cast it. The way I'd planned it, that horse wouldn't stand up. And il Moro, as I said, discovered it by reading my own notes. By an irony of fate, now that the clay model is finished . . ." Leonardo sighed. "I'll have to start all over again."

* * *

"Please explain something to me," Cecilia said, in the tone of someone who changes the subject and is a past master at doing so. "You must forgive me, but Tersilla has been in my house for two years and I can't fathom how you suspected her. What made you think of her?"

"Actually, Countess, my original thought was that it had been a woman. You see, one question that troubled Messer Galeazzo was: *Why* abandon Chiti's body in the middle of the Piazzale delle Armi? What troubled me was: *How?* How could someone dump something like that without anyone noticing? It could have been done, I decided, if the body had been transported on a cart."

"But Ludovico's guards don't just let every cart into the castle—" Cecilia began, then broke off. She had understood.

"Precisely. Not every cart. A few. Yours, for instance. A cart like yours, driven by a pretty girl who, in the dark, even looks a little like you, is possibly something that encourages one to turn a blind eye. Countess Gallerani can come into the castle any time she pleases and His Lordship will always receive her, so it may be better to pretend not to have seen her come in, don't you think?"

Cecilia nodded, slowly, as the two of them continued to walk around the courtyard.

"That made me realize that it couldn't have been just any woman, but one woman in particular." Leonardo pointed his left index finger at the palm of his right hand. "Tersilla, who could use your cart. Tersilla, who had a chest I myself designed, which can be handled easily and which amplifies one's strength when opening and closing it. The images in my mind were consistent, they held together like stones forming an arch, not a heap. I then went on to the *why*, taking it for granted that the *how* was as I'd put it together in my head."

Leonardo stopped.

"The *why* was unclear to me until I understood the intention of Father Diodato, or of someone through him. To provoke a financial crisis, a crisis of money. More generally, to provoke a crisis and turn Milan against herself. Anything that scares people encourages a crisis. Like divine wrath, or the possibility of pestilence or, worse still, a disease we don't yet know." Leonardo opened his arms. "That's why Rambaldo Chiti was left in the castle. Given Magistro Ambrogio's uncertain grasp of medical science, the body of a man who had died for an unknown reason could not help but increase the fear. That's why, once Rambaldo was dead—"

"I'm sorry, Leonardo, I must ask you this too. Why kill him?"

"It was necessary for the safety of the conspirators, Countess. Rambaldo Chiti had requested an audience with il Moro the day before he was murdered. He was probably hoping to save his life by confessing. He was a skilled forger, but deluded and foolish about the ways of the world. If he had managed to speak with il Moro, not only would the conspiracy have failed but the conspirators would have been arrested, tortured, and killed."

Leonardo opened his arms slightly.

"Father Diodato somehow came to know of this. I think it was through Father Francesco Sansone, the General of the Franciscans. Jesuates and Franciscans speak to one another, are both poor in Christ, and their communities are driven by the same noble principles, in speech at least."

* * *

"Yes, yes, truly a fine speech," Caterina said, putting on the table a roast capon as large as any Christian, whether a Franciscan or a layman. "I'm very happy that His Lordship Ludovico has thanked you, paid homage to you, excused you, and so forth. But when is he going to start putting his hands in his pockets?"

"He's already started, Caterina," Salaì said, holding out his plate and receiving a hard rap on the knuckles. "Ouch!"

"The older ones first, young Giacomo. Leonardo, shall I cut you a tiny piece?"

"Mother, are you also an alchemist? Did you obtain this capon with the philosopher's stone, or by touching a pumpkin, or is it an animal, born then slaughtered?"

"Oh, Leonardo, how stubborn you are. What were you saying, young Giacomo? Who's started?"

"The friars of the Confraternity of the Immaculate, Caterina. They paid today. One thousand, two hundred lire to the master, and four hundred to Master Ambrogio."

"What's Master Ambrogio got to do with it? That pompous ham of an astronomer who confuses a fart with a south-westerly wind and only looks to the stars? What did he do?"

"Not Magistro Ambrogio Varese da Rosate, Caterina," Leonardo said. "Master Ambrogio de Predis, who was my worthy assistant and painted the angels in the work I did for the Confraternity."

"Oh, yes. Because, you know, according to Magistro Ambrogio Varese, the wretched Chiti died from sleeping. If you hadn't been there, son, to recognize not just the disease, but also the diseased . . ."

"I think that's why the conspiracy failed, Caterina." Helping himself to a large piece of roast capon, Zanino da Ferrara put it on his plate and began working on it with his knife. "There are three hundred thousand souls in Milan. Good old Father Diodato must have thought nobody would recognize the living man in the dead man, not if he was found far away from his own district. He didn't take into account our master, who used his hands and his eyes."

"And I was damn lucky not to land on my ass," Leonardo said, quite deadpan.

A full minute's laughter followed, the kind that explodes when both mind and belly are free of anxieties.

"You manage to joke even at the most terrible moments, master," Zanino said. "That's another thing I envy you."

"I wasn't joking at all. You said it yourself, Zanino, Milan has a population of three hundred thousand. I would never have expected to come across Rambaldo Chiti again."

"And did you recognize him right away, master?"

"No, not right away. One doesn't always recognize the living man in the stillness of death. But almost right away, yes."

"But you didn't tell il Moro right away."

"No, I didn't."

And Leonardo turned to Salaì, who was finally filling up his plate and acting as though this conversation didn't concern him.

Chiti hadn't been the only one to use fake money the previous year, and everyone knew that. But Chiti was an adult, and he'd been the brains. Salaì was practically a child, and had grown up considerably since then. He'd also been sufficiently punished, and had learned his lesson.

Leonardo remained silent for a moment, then shook his head.

Zanino misunderstood his silence. "So do you plan to stay in Milan, master, in il Moro's service?"

"You're the second person to ask me that question today, Zanino."

"Good, master." Zanino wiped his mouth with his napkin. "It means you've already thought of an answer."

"Yes, Zanino. I'll answer you as I answered this morning. If you remain alone, I began, you will always be your own."

* * *

"Are you alone, Your Lordship?"

Ludovico il Moro stood motionless at the window of his own room in the Rocchetta. At Galeazzo Sanseverino's slight but resolute touch, he barely turned his eyes, although his gaze remained elsewhere.

"Ah, Galeazzo. Come, dear friend. How are you?"

"I'm not sure, Your Lordship. I tried to put my head around the Most Illustrious Duchess of Bari's door, but all I got was a scream and a silver pitcher."

"I see. Do close the door, Galeazzo."

Which he did, gingerly.

"She'll soon get over it, Ludovico, trust me," Galeazzo said, moving to first name terms, as always. "It's just the way it happened that upset her. She'll soon get over it."

"You think so? I don't know, my friend, I don't know, Galeazzo. Trust is something you build up over a long period and can lose in a single toss of the dice. I may be able to regain my wife's respect, but never her trust."

Ludovico looked at Sanseverino as though not completely able to focus on him—not that he cared much.

"You asked me just now if I was alone and I didn't answer you. Yes, my friend, I'm alone. Messer Leonardo once said to me, 'If you're alone, you'll always be your own.' But you see, Galeazzo, even when I'm alone I'm not my own." With a movement of his chin, Ludovico indicated the city stretching outside the window. "Even when I'm alone, I'm here, and see everybody. I'm a man who can see farther than anybody else, and at the same time I'm an easy target."

Ludovico started walking around the room, moving into the middle.

"At times like this, I feel like one of those men sentenced to quartering, who are tied to four horses, one horse to each limb, and each horse moves forward, and the poor wretch can't indulge all of them and so is torn to pieces." Ludovico opened his right arm and indicated his left leg. "On the one hand, I have my duties as a husband and father, and on the other my passions as a man." Ludovico opened his left arm wide and stretched his right leg, forcing it. "On the one hand, there are the interests of the State, the wellbeing of Milan, and on the other the alliances with the league I have formed. With Venice, with Florence, with Ferrara. Especially with Ferrara. We have to trust one another, and yet each of us aims to expand his own power, and we all know it."

Ludovico relaxed his limbs and began walking around the room again.

"And I, my dear Galeazzo, can't trust anybody. I can't confide in anyone, either in here or out there, as you've seen. That's the reality, Galeazzo. I was wrong to trust Trotti, I was wrong to trust the dwarf, and I was wrong to confide in other people."

"Not everyone, Ludovico, not everyone. There's still somebody you can trust, in here, and you know it."

Ludovico stopped and looked steadily at his son-in-law. "Yes, Galeazzo, you're right. There is one person. And I think right now I need his advice before anything else." Ludovico put a hand on his son-in-law's shoulder, while Galeazzo almost imperceptibly straightened his back, which was already as straight as a marble pillar. "Thank you. Are you coming too?"

"Where?"

"To the astrologer's room."

"The astrologer's room?"

"I know, I know, I usually send for Magistro Ambrogio, but

I don't want to waste any time. I need to know what the stars say, and I need to know now." Ludovico stepped resolutely to the door and opened it. "It's best I go right away in person. So, are you coming too?"

"No, Your Lordship. I think it's best you go alone."

* * *

"If you're alone, you'll always be your own. That's what I used to say." Leonardo shook his head. "But in order to be alone the way I mean, you have to be among people. Of all the jails I can imagine, I think the desert is the worst."

"I don't understand you, Leonardo."

Leonardo looked at Cecilia then resumed speaking, his eyes on the ground. "It's true I've had offers. From various lords, and from various places. But for the time being, as far as I'm concerned, Milan is the best place to work because it's the best place to live."

Leonardo had now stopped and sat down on the low wall that enclosed the courtyard, between the pillars. Cecilia stood next to him, looking in the same direction and listening.

"I think I may say without false modesty, Countess, that I am a man of intellect and skills. And I think those skills came to me by birth and by upbringing. By birth because I am the fruit of a free love like that of my parents, a love devoid of obligations or interests of State. And by upbringing because I never needed to worry about my safety or my survival. Cared for by my mother, then by my father during my childhood, I had everything I needed. I suffered neither hunger, like the poor, nor solitude, like the nobility. I was able to grow up in peace, free but not just free."

Leonardo waited for a moment, almost wondering if he was talking too much. Then, seeing that Cecilia said nothing, he continued.

"In order to grow up well we need freedom and tranquillity. In a word, trust. But we also need rules and respect for rules, otherwise the strong overpower the weak, the cunning deceive the foolish, and there is no more freedom."

Cecilia smiled and gave Leonardo a sideways glance. "And do you mean to keep growing? You're over forty, Messer Leonardo."

"There's so much I don't know, so much I can't do, Countess, so much I don't just intend to do but must do. And Milan is the ideal place for me. You're here, with your salon and the lovely people who speak there. There are the people who work here, who encounter problems every day, and for me every single problem is the source of ten possible solutions."

"And there's Ludovico il Moro putting pressure on you."

"Stimulating me. Forcing me to finish my work. If it weren't for il Moro, I wouldn't finish any of it. I'm not like Bramante, who starts three projects, finishes six, and claims payment for ten." Leonardo also smiled, then turned serious again. "You need both things in my trade. Freedom and stimulation in good measure, depending on the size of the fire. As with fire, blowing on a candle extinguishes it but giving air to a hearth rekindles it, and the wind blowing on a building on fire fuels that fire, makes it grow and grow. In the same way, for the time being, Milan is the best place for me, and Ludovico my best patron."

* * *

"Excuse me, Leonardo . . ."

"Yes, Countess?"

"About patrons. You used the word and I was struck by it. And even earlier, you said 'Father Diodato, or someone through him.' Why? Whom do you suspect?"

Leonardo shook his head. "You've had Father Diodato in

your salon, Countess. I've spoken there only once. Did he seem to you such a refined intellect as to think up such a machination?"

Cecilia raised an eyebrow. Perhaps not, her face said.

Leonardo spread his hands. "That's one of the things that surprised me, as a matter of fact. Here too, I'm only constructing theories in my mind. But I fear Father Diodato was just a thick skull well trained by somebody else." He sighed. "Who that other person was, I neither know nor am able to find out. Nor do I know what fate awaits your Tersilla. Or perhaps you already know something more?"

As it happened, Cecilia had wrung her hands when Leonardo mentioned that name. But she shook her head.

"No, I don't know either. I can only hope."

THREE LETTERS, TO END WITH

To Ercole d'Este, Duke of Ferrara, ferre

My Most Illustrious and Respected Lord,
Today at lauds, Father Diodato da Siena was taken from
the prison at Porta Giovia et *led into an open field,* et ivi *his*
head was severed from his body. A prayer.

Fertur, *but these are palace rumors, that the whore*
Tersilla has been tonsured and sent to be a nun in a convent
outside the city. They also say that Ludovico did not send her
to her death at the express request of Cecilia Gallerani,
Countess Bergamini, who left Mediolano *two days ago for*
San Giovanni in Croce, to be with her husband, Count
Carminate.

The clay statue of the horse made by Messer Leonardo is
complete and I was able to see it yesterday in all its majesty
in the Corte de l'Arengo, from where it will be taken to the
square outside the castle. Imagine if you can, My Most
Illustrious Lord, the beauty and wonder this work inspires. It
seems to move and walk like a horse of flesh and blood, and
almost everyone who sees it flees the courtyard, afraid of
being kicked and trampled.

This horse will remain of clay. Leonardo will not cast it,
having discovered an error in his calculations, originating from
the fact that the hundred thousand pounds of bronze he has
estimated as sufficient would not hold up, and the animal's
joins would break. But it was a useful error. The mistake

yielded a good result, since in calculating the melting and cooling of the bronze, Leonardo learned the secret of the manufacturing of the contraptions the French call cannons.

Up until yesterday, it was the custom to cast the cannon cum *its mold placed so that its mouth was down and its rear was up, and in this way the casting is easier and the bronze hotter and runnier so that it fills the mold better in the part of the mouth, which is narrow and hard to fill. But if the bronze is poured into the cannon mold the other way around, that is, with the rear at the bottom and the mouth up, the bronze that flows to the bottom cools down much more quickly, and is richer in copper than tin, and the rear remains solid and does not melt or burst open like a flower at the first shot, as happens with our bombards.*

His Most Illustrious Lordship Ludovico has therefore decided to use for cannons the bronze he was saving for the horse, and Leonardo is now teaching the skill to our Master Zanino. When there is war, we will have cannons that function well.

Because war there will be. His Most Illustrious Lord has approved the loan to His Most Christian Majesty and sent Signor Belgioioso beyond the Alps to attend to the manufacturing of the contraptions and then bring them here. In the New Year, His Most Christian Majesty will go to Genoa and from there set sail for Naples. Ludovico states that it is his firm intention not to move any soldiers from Milan.

Giacomo Trotti put the quill down. This was how it would be. King Charles would head for Naples, and the alliance between Milan, Ferrara, Venice, and Florence would protect the rest of the peninsula, unless some new upheaval altered the alliances once again. And so King Charles would squander all his forces on conquering the Kingdom of Naples from the Aragons, while Milan and

Ferrara would remain undisturbed, the former under the will of Ludovico il Moro, and the latter, his homeland, in the strong and capable hands of its undisputed lord, Ercole Duke of Ferrara,

to whose benevolence I commend myself, as always.
Mediolano, XXX octubris 1493
Servus Jacomo Trotti

My Most Illustrious Lord,

I present my respects to you and to His Most Christian Majesty. In the end, despite the various accidents that occurred, Duke Ludovico has agreed to lend us the thirty thousand ducats we need to start the war. Signor Belgioioso has received specific instructions to ensure that they are spent judiciously.

There has recently been an extraordinary event in Milan, that is, the killing of a man in the Piazzale delle Armi, and Father Diodato da Siena, whom I introduced to you last year together with His Eminence Cardinal Giuliano della Rovere, was found guilty. They say he was at the head of a ring that forged fake letters of credit, and that the quantity of fake money it would have unleashed would have put the bank in a crisis. They are saying on the street that Messer Leonardo had a role in investigating the matter and resolved it.

At this point, the next thing is for Ludovico to be appointed Duke. The young Duke Gian Galeazzo is in very poor health, and many people are saying that he will soon die.

Your most humble servant, Perron de Basche

It was early November in Lyons, and the cold was damp and heavy. The only cheerful thing in the room was the crackling fire, near the desk.

The Duke of Orléans folded the letter, folded it again, and threw it into the flames.

Then, leaning back in his armchair, he sighed.

It had been a possibility, but it had gone up in smoke.

He remembered that Jesuate well. Giuliano della Rovere had introduced him the previous year and they had spoken for a long time. They had spoken of the way il Moro held the city in his fist with money that wasn't his, and of how little respect his government showed toward Christian values.

It was then that the Duke of Orléans had said that if the Medici Bank were to go bankrupt, there would be a great upheaval in the city. And how can one bankrupt a bank? the Jesuate had asked, laughing. You would just need to persuade all its customers to withdraw their money on the same day, the Duke had replied, laughing too.

But it was no laughing matter.

The fellow had tried it in earnest.

* * *

The Duke of Orléans started thinking about what could have happened.

* * *

The bank bankrupted, its credits uncollectible, money in short supply. Crisis. Just like in Florence a hundred and fifty years earlier, when Florentine bankers had faced the same situation. And they had gone bankrupt, dragging the city into a bottomless abyss.

In Florence, the Bardis had been replaced by the Medicis. In Milan, people worn down by taxes and enraged by the crisis would have invoked the only possible contender to the throne. That is, himself, the Duke of Orléans.

And he would have been nearby, on reconnaissance with Charles VIII's expedition, an expedition that would have set off as soon as news of the crisis arrived, while Ludovico would have had to be away, at the head of the procession taking the new bride to the Emperor.

* * *

The Duke shook himself out of his reverie.

It hadn't turned out that way. It would never turn out that way. Well, never mind.

As far as he was concerned, his entry into Milan had merely been postponed. One day, he would enter that city that had entered his heart, not as a warlord, but as Duke and ruler.

And when that day came, he would like to have at his side a man like Leonardo da Vinci.

My Most Excellent Lord, whom I alone may call mine,

There is no greater pain for a man than to strive at a task, see it almost reach completion and in the end crash to the ground, destroyed beyond remedy. This is what would happen to the horse, my horse, if I were to melt it and cast it in the form and in the proportions I have conceived so far. Look at the legs of a rat, so slight and thin in comparison to its body. They are much thinner, proportionately, than those of a rabbit or a cat, which have thicker supports, just like horses and dogs. Look at the elephant, whose legs are enormous and fat, almost like pillars in comparison with the architrave of the body, rather than, as in the case of the rat, like twigs beneath an onion.

The weight of the beast increases like the cube of its height. Take a ten-sided cube; the area of the sides of the cube is ten times ten, that is, one hundred, and its volume and therefore its weight is ten times ten, taken another ten times, that is, a thousand.

In this way, it becomes clear that if the animal is one pace tall, and its weight one pound, when it is two paces tall it weighs the cube of two, or two times two times two, that is, eight pounds. And the weight that must be borne by the legs of an animal that is twice as tall as one of its companions equal to it in all its proportions is not two times but eight times.

If you maintain these proportions, you will have a leg that is four times as thick or that has four times the surface of the section, but the weight that it must bear is eight times.

This is why nature gives the rat slender legs, the cat and the rabbit plump legs, and the elephant large, pillar-like legs. An animal as tall as an elephant, and with the shape and proportion of a rat, would collapse to the ground. The same would happen to my horse.

So that it may bear the weight of a small specimen, one pace tall, the bronze must be one finger thick; but if you make the horse ten paces tall, the bronze can no longer be ten fingers thick but will have to be much larger, or the weight of the bronze on top of it will overwhelm it, like an elephant that has the shape of a rat.

The specimen horse I made from clay cannot be used as a model for casting the bronze horse. And that was my first error.

I estimated that one hundred thousand pounds of bronze would be enough to cover the horse, using simple proportion, but as I have said, that is not sufficient. Much more than that would be needed, but I do not feel in the right state of mind to make the calculation now. And that is my second mistake.

These pounds of bronze that Ludovico has already accumulated will be used for making bombards, the way I taught Zanino the Ferrarese, according to the system you learned while making casts for your horse.

Never in these papers have I written two errors on the same paper. But that is the purpose of these letters, which I send to you, Leonardo di ser Piero da Vinci, so that you may remember two things.

The first is that no thing or creature is without error, and that the taller you become, the farther you may fall. Only he who does nothing never errs.

The second is that without error, and without the knowledge of his error, man can never learn from his experience. In the same way as an infant learns to crawl, then pulls himself up, and only when he falls on his backside does he learn the art of standing on his own two feet, in just that way, every time you err and acknowledge the fact, you will immediately amend it, and you will remember it.

You will immediately amend it, unlike Rambaldo, who did not realize the seriousness of what he was doing until it was too late, although he thought he could remedy it by asking forgiveness. And you will remember it because man tends to commit the very same errors over and over again, that is his nature.

Respect every man for the way he deals with his every error. Because we are born small and defenseless, and a two-year-old child is weaker and less complete than a dog, a horse, or even an elephant of the same age. But as we grow we overtake and dominate every animal in the world and that is why it is in growing and learning, and not in his birth, that we see the measure of a man.

It is only by observing nature, and other men, that man learns. But without comparing what we do with what we believe, what we expect with what happens, man cannot grow to be healthy in his intellect and judgment. And the only way to have knowledge of one's error is to measure oneself against nature itself, since, unlike man, she never lies.

I bid you farewell until we meet again, yours and ever yours

Leonardo

A Book Full of Errors

For a historian to attempt to write a book about Leonardo da Vinci that contained no errors would be presumptuous. For a novelist to believe he can do so, especially a novelist with a chemistry degree, would have been madness. So I have no doubt that there are many errors, both historical and artistic, in this book, and that sooner or later they will be spotted. On the other hand, some aspects that might seem curious or far-fetched are historically verified.

* * *

It is true, for example, that one of the things making Milanese life at that time particularly stressful was traffic congestion, caused by carts driven exclusively by women; equally true is the story of Pesserer and Crancz, the two men arrested for forgery who were released after being recognized as alchemists.

It is plausible that Leonardo, during the period covered by this book, lived with his mother: starting with a note he makes on a sheet of paper dated 1493, in which he writes *Caterina came on 16 July 1493*, and finishing with a sheet from 1494 concerning the expenses of the burial of Caterina amounting to 123 soldi, that is, six imperial lire, or if you prefer, about a ducat—a not inconsiderable sum for a funeral at the time, and one that would have been hard to justify for a domestic servant. It is also interesting that the note about Caterina's arrival does not contain the formula *to stay with me* which is used for the arrivals of his apprentices, from Salaì to Giulio the German. A number of scholars, among them Luca Beltrami, agree with this hypothesis.

The use of the term *do* to indicate the first note of the musical scale is inaccurate, but only just: such a term is not known to have been used until the beginning of the sixteenth century.

The title of duke attributed to Philippe de Commynes is undeserved. The fact is, as I have noted, there are so many dukes in this story that I couldn't help myself.

It is plausible, though, that Salaì was something halfway between a favorite pupil and an adopted son. He would follow Leonardo practically everywhere, and even though there would be plenty of quarrels and disagreements, it seems that the relationship between the two was never thrown into question.

It is possible, although unlikely, that Leonardo received the payment for *The Virgin of the Rocks* as I have indicated. The whole "you owe me money for this painting" question dragged on for about twenty years. The other thing that went on for a long time was the matter of the Sforza horse, which in the end Leonardo never completed, due to both technical and financial problems.

For a detailed account of the problems posed by the casting of the horse, and the huge effort involved, the best source, without any doubt, is *Leonardo e il monumento equestre a Francesco Sforza*, by Andrea Bernardoni (Giunti). Which leads me to mention some of the books that might be of interest to those who, even if only for their own pleasure, would like to learn more on the subject of "Leonardo the Renaissance man" from sources much more serious than this novel.

* * *

As suggested above, a lifetime would not be long enough to learn all there is to learn about the genius of Da Vinci. A good starting point is Walter Isaacson's fine book, *Leonardo da Vinci* (Simon and Schuster). An agreeable read, although prone to a perhaps excessive lyricism, is Dmitry Merezhkovsky's novel, *Leonardo da Vinci: The Resurrection of the Gods* (Alma Classics), among other things the first work of fiction to feature the hypothesis that Leonardo lived with his mother during his time in Milan. (By the way, there are many—perhaps too many—fictional works in which Leonardo appears as either the protagonist or as a supporting character. My favorite imaginary Leonardo is the one who appears in the animated film, *Mr. Peabody & Sherman*, along with the absent-minded genius who struggles to understand the workings of a toilet flusher in the Roberto Benigni-Massimo Troisi film *Nothing Left to Do but Cry*.)

* * *

It is impossible to talk about Leonardo without talking about the Florence the Medicis, where he trained, in Verrocchio's workshop and elsewhere, or without talking about the importance of money. Florentine society is probably one of the first societies for which money becomes a fundamental, abstract value, and not just an ancillary object, giving rise to the kind of finance we still use today.

On the academic level, Raymond De Roover's book *Rise and Decline of the Medici Bank 1397-1494* (W. W. Norton) is still, I think, the benchmark work for anyone interested in the history of the Florentine bank. It is a difficult book, far from easy to read, and requires time and patience, as well as an economic and financial expertise that not everyone has; I, for example, don't have it, and some concepts only became clear to me after reading the livelier and much more enjoyable *Medici Money*, by Tim Parks (W. W. Norton), and *1345. La bancarotta di Firenze*, by Lorenzo Tanzini (Salerno). This aspect is also explained in a very engaging way in Eric Weiner's fine book *The Geography of Genius* (Simon & Schuster).

* * *

The other protagonist of this book is Ludovico il Moro, and therefore, indirectly, Milan itself. If Florence was the city where the Renaissance was born, Milan is the city where it developed most completely, in all its artistic, scientific, and social aspects.

The court of Ludovico il Moro was a focal point of this development, and it is worth trying to find out more about it.

A perhaps somewhat dated but highly enjoyable account is provided by the four volumes of Francesco Malaguzzi Valeri's *La corte di Lodovico il Moro* (Hoepli). For anyone wishing to take a look at court life, not superficially but in depth, as revealed in the correspondence between ambassadors and rulers, the two books by Guido Lopez (*Leonardo e Ludovico il Moro. La roba e la libertà* and *Festa di nozze per Ludovico il Moro*, both Mursia) are definitely pleasant reads, as well as solidly documented. Just as pleasant, but I don't know how easy to find, is *Beatrice d'Este* by Silvia Alberti de Mazzeri (my edition is Fabbri), a fictionalized but well managed account of the short but intense life of Beatrice d'Este.

* * *

To approach a figure like Leonardo, and claim the right to describe his thoughts, requires a certain amount of nerve. I wouldn't have done it on my own initiative, but now I can't help but be pleased. I therefore thank my publishers, Giunti, for thinking of me for this project, and Giulia Ichino, a friend first and an editor second, for following this book every step of the way and putting me in touch with genuine experts on the subject whenever my ignorance made it necessary (in other words, often). The number of things I learned in this year and a half of studying the Renaissance man *par excellence* far exceeded my expectations. I thought I knew a lot about Leonardo, and I discovered that I had barely scraped the surface.

I would, of course, never have managed to learn all these things alone. *In primis*, my thanks go to Dario Dondi for introducing me to the world of Leonardo's autograph manuscripts and for his skill in grasping exactly what I needed to know. I also thank, in no particular order, Edoardo Rossetti for his matchless expertise in the history and urban development of the Milan of the Sforzas, Gabriele Baldassari for helping me with tenacity and a sense of humor to write in the Ferrarese idiom of the fifteenth (almost sixteenth) century, Luca Scarlini for his advice on the history of fashion and armor at the time, and Maristella Botticini for reassuring me on certain aspects of the history of finance with which I was unfamiliar—not that I know all that much now, but at least I know how to write about it . . .

* * *

Which leads me, in concluding this note, to caution the reader against using this as a history book. It is a novel, and even though many historical events depicted in it are verified, the same cannot be said of the relationship between these events. It is true that Leonardo never completed the equestrian monument to Francesco Sforza, just as it is true that Leonardo recognized the inconsistencies of scale in the proportions of animals; that the two things are connected is, I fear, pure imagination. But I also believe that, in writing a book with the genius of Da Vinci as protagonist, not using my imagination would have been not just mistaken but disrespectful toward him.

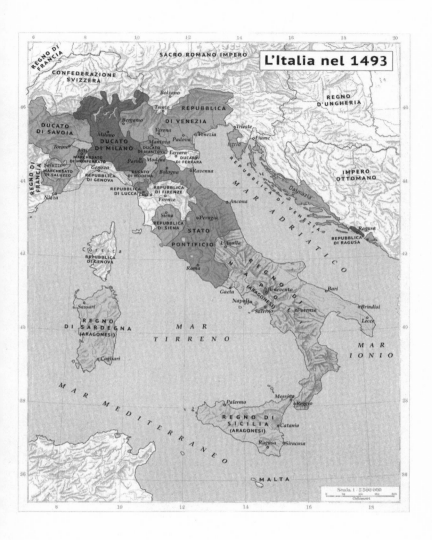

Italy in 1493.

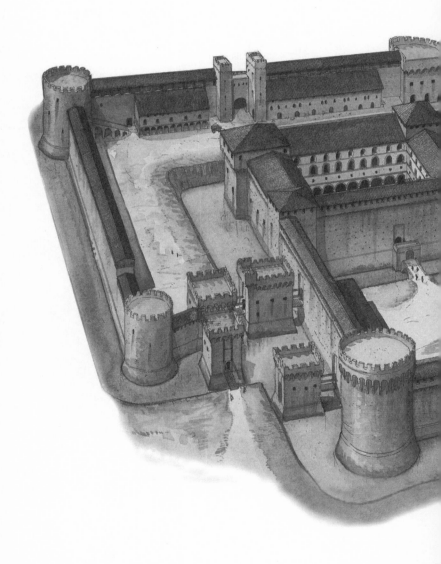

The Castello Sforzesco at the time of Leonardo.

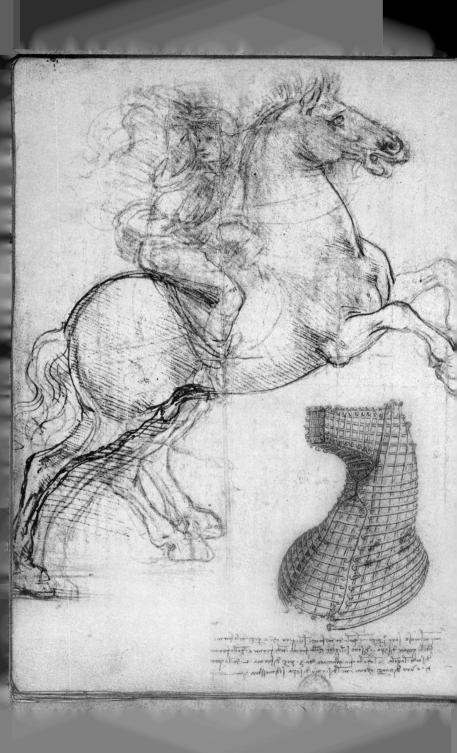